THE
DOME

"je refuse!"

THE DOME

Suzanne Craig-Whytock

A. Craig-Whytock

BookLand
press

Published by BookLand Press Inc.
15 Allstate Parkway
Suite 600
Markham, Ontario L3R 5B4
www.booklandpress.com

Printed in Canada

Front cover image by Pamela Fazio

Library and Archives Canada Cataloguing in Publication

Title: The dome / Suzanne Craig-Whytock.
Names: Craig-Whytock, Suzanne, author.
Identifiers: Canadiana (print) 20190130377 | Canadiana (ebook) 20190130407 | ISBN 9781772311013 (softcover) | ISBN 9781772311020 (EPUB) | ISBN 9781772311037 (PDF)
Classification: LCC PS8605.R3467 D66 2019 | DDC C813/.6 – dc23

We acknowledge the support of the Government of Canada through the Canada Book Fund and the support of the Ontario Arts Council, an agency of the Government of Ontario. We also acknowledge the support of the Canada Council for the Arts, which last year invested $153 million to bring the arts to Canadians throughout the country.

For my family.

1

Dee

Heart pounding, feet pounding.

"Pick up the pace, Dee!"

"Just dump them, Rogan—it's not worth the risk!"

"No!" he gasped. "We can eat for a week on this. Keep going!"

My lungs had started to burn as soon as we'd hit the third set of stairs in the abandoned apartment building, but with a Lobot on our tails, I couldn't afford to slow down. Rogan showed no signs of giving up the search for a hiding spot, despite the fact that so far, the doors to every floor were locked. Fourth floor—no luck. Fifth floor—the same. Sixth floor—the whirring noise was getting closer. Seventh floor—finally! The lock was broken, and we pushed through, looking wildly behind us as we raced down the hallway. The apartments were mostly empty as we passed them but the second-last place, despite half the exterior wall being blown out, had some furniture in it—better yet it had an old stovetop with an oven. We could stash the baubles in there, hide in the closet and either wait for the Lobot to give up or make a run for it while it was distracted. I slammed the apartment door shut behind us as Rogan threw the baubles into the oven, then we dove into a closet with louvered doors and pulled them closed. I pushed back up against the wall, while Rogan knelt down to look through the slats.

"*Shhh!*" he whispered sharply to me. "Listen." I tried to control my breathing so that I could hear what was happening. There was a faint hiss — the Lobot was using one of its lasers to cut a hole through the apartment door. Then there was a thud, as part of the door fell onto the floor, and a low whirring sound. I inhaled and held my breath as the small, mechanical creature flew slowly by the closet, tracking the microchip signal coming from the baubles. Suddenly it stopped and hovered in mid-air, rotating its antennae toward the old appliance. Then I could hear banging, and Rogan smothered a giggle. He moved back and motioned at me to look for myself. I knelt down and I slapped my hand over my mouth so I wouldn't laugh out loud. The Lobot was slamming itself into the glass door of the oven; it was able to sense the microchip signal and see the baubles, but it couldn't figure out how to get to them.

I turned to Rogan, and in the dim light, I noticed an old blanket on the shelf above us. I pointed to it and Rogan nodded. This would be tricky and dangerous, but we didn't have a lot of choice at this point — we needed to act before it started using its laser on the glass. Rogan took the blanket down and quietly opened the closet door. I just hoped that the Lobot was so preoccupied with the baubles that it wouldn't notice much else. Rogan began creeping towards it — it was still unaware of him. Finally, at about three feet away, he took a deep breath and threw the blanket over the Lobot, knocking it to the ground. Before it had a chance to squirm or struggle, he jumped on the blanket with all his strength, over and over, until the Lobot was still and silent. He smiled triumphantly at me.

I hesitated. "We should make sure," I whispered. I tiptoed over to where Rogan was waiting and gingerly lifted up a corner of the blanket. Sure enough, the Lobot was dead — its lights were out and it looked pretty crushed. We both stared at it in distaste — the tranquilizer darts and locator cuffs it carried were spilling out of it like guts. Suddenly I was filled with fury, and I turned on Rogan.

"That was really stupid, Rogan! Do you realize how close we came to being caught?! Which body part are you willing to lose for a couple of coins?!"

He looked taken aback and his brow furrowed defensively. "Neither of us is losing anything, and that stash is worth more than a 'couple' of coins. Otherwise, we wouldn't have been chased by a Lobot for so long, you know that. I had everything under control — it's all good, Dee. Now come on." He opened the oven door and took out the baubles — a necklace and two rings — which glittered in the light. "That stupid Fancy won't miss them — she probably has plenty more where these came from, anyway. Serves her right for wandering so close to Divinity without any Blues nearby to protect her."

I sighed in frustration. "Well, it was still awfully close, and I happen to like my hands and feet just as they are, thank you very much."

Rogan leered at me. "I like your hands and feet too, my lovely!"

"EWW! You sound like a Fancy!" I slapped him on the shoulder in mock-anger.

He slapped back at me then peered around the corner of the apartment door. "All clear. Anyway," he continued cavalierly, "you could always choose an eye, although I hear it's pretty painful. Come on. We need to get out of here before some ambitious Blue tracks her Lobot and shows up."

My stomach flipped at the thought of having an eye removed, and then I was overcome by a wave of emotion — a sense of questioning and worry. It was my twin brother, Cee. I focused inward and sent feelings of calm

and reassurance back to him. Not only did we look exactly the same—green eyes, and hair that was called straw-
berry blond when strawberries used to grow, but we were
on the same wavelength, so to speak. We couldn't read
each other's minds exactly, but we could project feelings
to each other. Right now, he was sensing that I was scared
and mad, and I was telling him that everything was okay.
He hated it when I went out thieving, especially with Rogan, who was a real risk-taker. It was one thing running a
scam or getting a Fancy to cough up a little spare change,
but outright robbery in broad daylight wasn't for the faint
of heart. Not that I had much of a choice. Cee and I used
to be workhouse kids, and like all provincial wards, once
you hit 15, you were sent to the agri-complexes up north
as farm labour. The alternative was to run away and fend
for yourselves as Freeworlders. And after spending most of
our lives as workhouse kids, neither of us wanted to finish
out our days as agri-slaves in the Upper Belt, so we made
our way to Divinity, a tent city in Metro.

Cee and I had been left at Happy Valley, one of the
workhouses up North, when we were about three months
old. After the Frag riots in 2087 and the Water Wars that
followed, babies were being abandoned on a regular basis
by parents who couldn't afford to take care of them, sometimes as many as twenty a day, so The Consortium, a super-
group of countries across the water, set up the workhouse
system. All the kids were given letters of the alphabet instead of names, and he and I were the third and fourth
babies dumped there that day, so they called us "C" and
"D". Our actual designations are a lot longer and include
the date as well. By the time most ward kids were 4 or 5,
they'd been given nicknames or picked out new names for
themselves, but we were fine with Cee and Dee. The workhouses weren't great, but if you kept your nose clean and
did what you were told by the Protectors, the adults who
ran the place, you could survive. And you were told a *lot*.

By the time you were a One, you were expected to stay with an older kid, a Guardian, who either worked in the dorms or the kitchen—like an apprentice. Depending on who your Guardian was, you either got slapped regularly or ignored most of the time. When you got to be a Five, you were responsible for making beds or washing dishes, or garden work. At Ten, you worked in the nursery with the babies, in the kitchen doing meal prep, or in the schoolhouse, teaching other kids about soil and plants from a textbook. At Twelve, you started working the fields full-time, in preparation for a life-time of servitude in the Breadbasket, which was the area of the Upper Belt where farms could still exist. All the fruits and vegetables from up North were planted and harvested by agri-slaves, mostly the workhouse kids who had chosen farm labour and three meals a day over freedom and starvation. But it was a hard life too—from what I heard, most agri-slaves didn't make it into their thirties— too much exposure to chemicals. I was pretty sure that Cee and I stood a better chance on our own—if we didn't end up in The Dome, that is.

Cee and I ran away from Happy Valley right before our 15th Drop-Off Day. That wasn't like a birthday exactly—none of us really knew when we were born, but the workhouse had a record of the dates that all of us had been left there, and if you'd been a good little "agri-slave in the making", you got a piece of candy on your Drop-off Day each year. Kind of a twisted thing to celebrate, but we didn't have much else. Anyway, Cee and I had no intention of going to the Breadbasket so we took off and headed for Divinity, the biggest tent city in Trillium Province, where we've been for over a year now. Scraping together a living hasn't been easy. Cee brings in a little money at the Hidden Market, where he sells his handmade "pretties" to the Fancies, the rich people who come into Divinity on Sundays with their Blue bodyguards, looking for unique objects to impress their friends with. He's an amazing woodcarver—

he can take an old scrap of anything and turn it into an elephant or a parrot, things that sell really well because they're extinct now. I don't know how he knows what they all look like, but they're beautiful, and the Fancies will pay a lot for them. The problem is that we can't both be out at the same time. It's a cutthroat world, and your tent and everything inside it is fair game for squatters if you leave it empty. Someone has to be there at all times to protect it, so Cee can't come thieving with me, and I can't go to the Market with him. Not that either of us minds. His hands are his most important asset—if he got caught by a Lobot, he'd get sent to The Dome, and more than likely the crowd would choose hand over foot—they usually do for thieves unless, like Rogan said, you want to give them a real thrill and choose your own eye. As for me, I hate the Hidden Market. Well, I don't hate the Market, I just hate the Fancies. They come in their finery and jewels, with their servants and bodyguards, sometimes with Lobots hovering around them for extra protection, and then they want to barter for lower prices. It's sickening really, when I think how long Cee works on his pieces and how little he has to sell them for sometimes.

I felt his wave of worry start to subside, and I sent a projection of the idea of home to him, so that he'd know we were on our way. Rogan once asked me what the "idea" of home was, since I couldn't actually send a picture of the tent to Cee—the only way I could describe it was to say it was like the emotion you felt when someone you loved squeezed your hand. I know it sounds stupid, but home to me was always just Cee, never a place. Whenever I was scared or sad, I could always count on him to take my hand and hold it tight, to let me know that, no matter what, we were together and that nothing could separate us. That was home. Then, just for fun, I sent him the feeling of being well-fed—we were going to eat well as soon as we pawned our hard-won treasures.

2

Cee

Heart pounding, head pounding.

I'd been pacing around outside the tent for what seemed like hours, picking up the streams of emotion that Dee was sending out. As always, I was terrified that she and Rogan had gone and done something really reckless — I hoped I was wrong, but her fear at one point made me dizzy. She was sending me "calm" now, but I still couldn't concentrate on carving, even though the Hidden Market was in two days, and I needed some goods to sell. I couldn't stay inside anymore — the sensations from Dee were driving me crazy. I paced back and forth in front of the tent, being watched all the while by a family of squatters who were waiting to see what I was going to do. They had lean, hungry looks and never took their eyes off me, hoping that at some point I would have to leave, and they could race in and claim the tent for their own. Well, that was definitely *not* going to happen — Dee and I had worked too hard to make this a home to let some scrummy squatters steal it. I did feel a little sorry — the woman was holding a baby, wrapped in rags, crying and wailing non-stop. I knew it must be hungry, but I had nothing extra to offer. Besides, if I did, Dee would be furious. She said squatters were like stray cats—if you fed them, they'd just keep hanging around.

Beyond the squatters, I could see Old Kensington, and in the other direction, the harbour, its waters murky and slow-moving, the container ships from Chin sluggishly converging on the docks, ready to unload everything from spatulas to solar cars. Adanac imported everything—and I mean *everything*—from The Consortium. We had no choice, apparently. I didn't get much knowledge from the work-house about history, but I learned a lot about the past by listening to Old Mac, the Divinity historyteller. Every tent city had its own historyteller, an elder Freeworlder who, for a coin or a piece of bread, would tell you anything you wanted to know. Most people didn't care, but I was always interested in how things got to be the way they are, with the great divide between the Fancies and the rest of us, so I would make him little carvings from the scraps I had, beads and such that he could trade for a bowl of soup at Blaw-blaw's, and then I'd sit and listen for as long as I could.

The way Old Mac told it, as the desert began creeping closer to the border, the Fragmented States of America started getting desperate for water—their economy had hit rock bottom and they couldn't afford to run their desalinators anymore—and soon the riots, raids, and border skirmishes turned into all-out war, with the Frags launching attacks on our water depots and landing their troops further North. Adanac had always been known as a peaceful nation, but had become fiercely protective of its natural resources in the wake of what Old Mac called "global environmental catastrophe". Without a standing army, or much in the way of a military machine, things were looking pretty bleak in old Adanac. But just when it seemed like we were done for, our leader, who used to be called the "Prime Minister", announced that we had formed an alliance with The Consortium. Next thing you know, hundreds of Chin battalions and thousands of Russe gen-modded soldiers with sonic destroyers, laser cannons, and echo bombs were garrisoned around the water depots, and their trace bombers and EMP tanks were beating the Frags back down from the North. Everyone was so overjoyed and relieved at the time that nobody thought to ask what they wanted in return.

As it turned out, the price was pretty steep — a complete economic stranglehold on Adanac. It wasn't really surprising, considering that The Consortium, or what was once Chin, Jan, Russe, and EastInd, had banded together, becoming a military superpower. The treaty that had been signed bringing The Consortium to our rescue also brought all export and manufacturing to a shuddering halt, just as it had in the other countries which had allied themselves. Now, everything people bought, ate, wore, and used were all made exclusively in Consortium nations and imported here. And let's not forget about Fujian — it's the part of Adanac's west coast that was handed over to ease the intense overpopulation on mainland Chin. Of course, if you weren't a Fancy, aligned somehow with The Consortium, you lived in a tent city like Divinity and did what you could to survive.

It might have been worse, I suppose — we could have ended up like the Frags, instead of a country with no source of income. It wasn't so bad for people like me, who had some sort of skill or talent. The Fancies would gobble up anything handmade because it was such a novelty. Of course, it was black market — the Fancies all worked for Consortium companies, and there were huge fines for anyone caught buying or selling non-Con goods. Repeat offenders were sometimes sent to The Dome, a giant stadium in the middle of Metro, to be publicly punished by the Dome Master — not the Fancies, of course, just the people like me. And the people like me couldn't be any more different from the Fancies if we tried. The Fancies came here originally from Consortium countries, bringing their strange habits and behaviour with them. They prize having the palest of skin, wear light, airy clothes treated with special solprotectants, and spend most of their time under hoverbrellas to guard against the harsh sunlight and hot rain. And to keep their faces as untouched by the sun as possible, they wear what we call "sim-masks", special silicone masks that fit over their faces but are identical to their own features. It's strange to see them walking around the Hidden Market, talking and gesturing, their faces immobile like dolls.

So much for history though—the present was much more in my mind as I continued pacing, waiting for Dee to make an appearance. I could sense her in my mind always, sometimes even when I was sleeping, and I couldn't remember a time when it hadn't been that way. When we were just kids at the workhouse, I knew when she was being mistreated. She would appear, eyes red, walking stiffly sometimes, and vehemently deny that anything was wrong, but she couldn't fool me—I'd felt her fear, and her anger. Things were easier for me—I kept quiet, did what I was told, and tried to stay out of the way of the Protectors. Not Dee though. She has a natural obstinate streak that got her into trouble every time, and the way she would mouth back to her Guardian, and the Protectors—which was the worst possible thing to do—made sure she never got any special favours, or even a break from working on holidays. Instead, it was beatings, and sometimes a few days in the Shed. And of course, that meant I never got a break either— we were in this life together and I wouldn't abandon her for a lousy piece of Drop-off Day candy or an extra fifteen minutes in the hard cots they called beds. But once we left the workhouse, I began to really appreciate Dee's personality—her confidence and cockiness had saved us on more than one occasion from having our belongings stolen by the homeless gangs, and she refused to let the Fancies barter me down to pennies on a pretty that I'd spent days making. I needed her here *now*—I had work to do if we were going to eat this week, and the worrying was sapping my energy. She was sending thoughts of well-being and full stomachs, but that wasn't going to happen unless I could carve something special. Most of my carvings are animals that I've never seen in my life, but I dream about them, and after a few dreams, I feel like I know them well enough to recreate them. Elephants, tigers, dolphins, creatures that haven't existed for decades except in my mind. Lately, I've been having dreams about a strange-looking beast with an incredibly long neck, tall spindly legs, and a kind face. I'm not sure what it is yet, but once I carve it into life, someone, a Fancy most likely, will tell me what it's called.

Just as my frustration was reaching its breaking point, I heard laughing, and saw Dee and that thief Rogan beyond the last tent in our row. At the sight of them, the squatter family began to look nervous and hopeless, and then shuffled away. The mother looked back over her shoulder wistfully, and I had to suppress a wave of pity.

"Don't you dare!" Dee called to me from a few tents away. "What do I always tell you? If you feed them once — "

"They'll keep hanging around," I finished with a sigh, suddenly feeling exhausted in my bones. "What have you been up to? You've had me worried sick."

Dee looked at Rogan, one eyebrow arched. He looked sheepishly back at her, then pretended to find the sky above our tent immensely interesting.

"It was an adventure, no doubt," she said. "*Someone*, not mentioning any names, thought it would be a wonderful idea to 'borrow' some baubles from a Fancy with a Lobot."

"A Lobot!!" I exclaimed, horrified, looking at Rogan. "What the hell were you thinking, you scrappy-ass thief?!"

He looked at me defensively. "It's fine; stop your hen-clucking. We got what we wanted and smashed the Lobot in the bargain."

"You destroyed a—are you kidding me?!" I was beyond angry. A Lobot could transmit images—what if it had seen their faces and a troop of Blues was descending on us as we spoke?

Dee, sensing my fear, interjected. "It didn't see us, Cee, I promise. Rogan snuck up behind it while it was trying to break through an oven door." She and Rogan looked at each other and snickered. "Calm down, come into the tent, and see what we have. I've really earned my keep today—you can give your hands a rest tonight and we'll celebrate with a real feast once we pass these baubles along. One of them looks like it might be a diamond!"

I felt calmer now, knowing they were safe, and was getting more interested in their story. "Oven door, huh? Sounds intriguing," I conceded. "But Dee, you *have* to be more careful—"

"I know, I know. What would you do without me, huh?" We all laughed, but deep down, I knew it was true. If anything ever happened to Dee, I'd be well and truly lost.

3

Dee

Now that Cee was feeling calm and reassured, my next priority was pawning off the baubles. I was determined to get a good price to prove to Cee that today's close call had been worth it, and the best way to do that was to fund an amazing feast. We'd been barely scraping by these last few weeks and were down to our last cans of stew. "Stew" was the generic name for a can without a label, traded or sold cheap at Blawblaw's, Divinity's underground food store. You never knew what was in the can until you opened it — it might be something mouth-watering, like pressed ham (although whether it was really ham, no one wanted to know), or it might be something disappointing, like wax beans. Cee and I made a game of it — we played "Guess What's Inside" every afternoon before dinner to take our minds off how hungry we were. We only ate once a day most of the time, and had our meal mid-afternoon to carry us through the night. When I'd looked in our little cooler yesterday, there were only three cans left, and one very tiny head of lettuce. It had been bigger last week, but Cee and I had been eating a leaf a day each, savouring the luxury. Now, it was starting to look shrunken and limp. I'd stolen it right out of the shopping bag of a Fancy who'd been skirting the edge of Divinity, looking for some black market spices maybe. She'd been coming from The Farm, an exclusive chain of very pricey grocery stores that got fresh produce from the Breadbasket, fruits and vegetables that Freeworlders like us would normally never see. She was probably thinking she was safe, escorted by a couple of Blues, when I popped out of an alley behind them, snatched the lettuce off the top of the groceries in her bag, and ran! She started bawling, her sim-mask crinkling and peeling away. The Blues gave a half-hearted chase, but we all knew that they wouldn't bother to go far for a head of lettuce. It served her right for flaunting her goods so close to the edge of the tent city.

I opened up the little cooler again now, just to double-check what we had. The lettuce looked even worse today. I turned to Cee.

"We're getting low." I raised my eyebrows at him. He knew right away what I was thinking and groaned. Rogan supressed a smile.

"Dee, you're killing me. Can't you just take them to Blawblaw's? You can trade them for some stew," Cee pleaded. He ran his fingers through his reddish-blond hair in dismay.

"Stew!" Rogan exclaimed, throwing his hands up in the air. "They're worth way more than a couple of cans of cat food!"

"It's NOT cat food!" Cee was adamant. "It's pressed —

"Enough!" I laughed. "Come on, Cee, you know as well as I do that we won't get anywhere near what these things are worth at Blawblaw's. We have to go to Trick."

Rogan nodded. "It's the only way we'll get even half the value. Trick's the man — well, boy."

Trick was a thirteen-year-old fence, small for his age, but the toughest kid in The Belt. He'd run away from the workhouse when he was a 6, so the stories go, and survived on the streets on his own. By the time he was eight, he was the leader of his own gang and had developed a network of "associates" who would pay top coin for merchandise of value. But Trick was more than just your average bauble dealer. While Blawblaw's dealt with the ordinary run-of-the-mill stuff, Trick could find a buyer for the special, even the priceless, so it was rumoured. On top of being tough, he was shrewd in business, incredibly knowledgeable about precious metals and gemstones, but also extremely fair and honest to those he liked and trusted. To anyone else, he was dangerous. I'd never met him—only ever seen him from a distance—but Rogan had a contact named S-Sam who acted as a messenger for Trick and could hopefully get us a meeting.

Cee looked gloomy. "I suppose this means you have to go and see S-Sam. I can tell from the way your mind is working right now that I can't talk you out of this. Fine. Just be careful."

Rogan laughed. "Careful of what? S-Sam is a harmless fool."

"Don't be ignorant, Rogan," I snapped back. "There's nothing wrong with S-Sam. He just has trouble speaking. He's as smart as you—probably smarter!"

Rogan snorted. "Whatever," he said dismissively. "Fool or genius, he's the only way to get to Trick. Let's go." He walked out of the tent, squinting against the strong sunlight, and waited with his back to us.

"Great," I whispered to Cee. "Now he's upset."

"Well, you insulted him. He really likes you, and you hurt his feelings."

"Likes me?! Don't be ridiculous!" I hissed. "We're friends, that's all."

Cee smirked. "Whatever you say, Sis." Then his expression turned serious. "I meant it about being careful. I've heard terrible stories about Trick and the Baby Gang."

"You worry too much. Rogan will take care of me, since he *likes* me so much, and you take care of the tent. Get some work done—it'll take your mind off things." I kissed his cheek and walked out of the tent. Rogan looked at me out of the corner of his eye, and I punched him on the shoulder lightly.

"Ready to go? Promise you'll be nice to S-Sam. "

"Fine, whatever." He rolled his eyes, but his voice was softer now. He punched me back on the shoulder and smiled down at me. I had a sudden, weird feeling that maybe Cee was right about Rogan liking me, but I pushed it aside. There was business to be done.

4

Cee

I waited at the doorway until Dee and Rogan disappeared down a row of tents and I couldn't see them anymore, then I went back inside. Work, she said. Right. I knew I had to do *something*, but it was going to be hard to concentrate. I went over to the small table where I kept my carving tools. I'd made the table, and the box that contained the tools, from pieces of scrap wood and pallets from the docks that Dee had stolen. The table was a little scruffy, but I had carved designs into it to make it seem more like "real" furniture. The box was my pride and joy. I'd run out of nails from the pallets, so I'd put it together with interlocking joints called dovetails, just like furniture from hundreds of years ago. The dovetail joints were something I'd seen in a dream, as was the looping, intricate knotwork pattern I'd carved all over the box. Just like my animals, I had no idea where the images came from.

I opened the box and touched each one of the carving tools fondly. They were my treasure of treasures, and meant almost as much to me as Dee. We'd found them not long after we came here from the workhouse, in one of the darker stalls in the Hidden Market. I knew the second I looked at them that they were meant to be mine, and when I touched them, a hundred images flashed through my head in an instant. Dee looked at me then wonderingly, sensing my rush of emotion, and nodded.

The owner of the stall was a shrivelled, tough old woman named Auntie May. She laughed at first when we made our proposal — that she let me borrow the tools until I could sell enough carvings to pay for them. But after giving us a long, hard look — young, skinny, dirty, but determined to earn our keep — she agreed to see me work and gave me a piece of scrap wood that she found in a bucket of odds and ends under a shelf. I carved my first piece for her on the spot — a horse. I'd never seen a horse, but she must have known what they looked like, because she gave me the tools in exchange for the carving right then and there. When Dee asked her how much she would charge for it, she looked at it wistfully and said she thought she might keep it for a while. Then I carved some beads for her to sell later. I kept one for myself as a souvenir, and it's still in my pocket today, something I reach for whenever I'm worried or uncertain. Lately, I've been taking it out a lot, so much so that it's become highly polished and smooth from rolling it around between my fingers. After our introduction to Auntie May, Dee started going down to the docks every day and scavenging for pieces of scrap wood, driftwood, anything that could be turned into something useful. Within the week, I had carved enough animals to sell at the Hidden Market myself. Auntie May let us borrow a table and we set up outside her stall, on the condition that we would send any of my customers back to her with the promise of "exotic and rare objects which could be found inside". She had nothing as far as we could see that would qualify as either exotic or rare, but it seemed like a great deal. By the end of the afternoon, we had sold every carving I'd made that week, and she had made a few coins too. The deal became permanent — we benefitted from not having to pay for our own stall, and she benefitted from the business I brought to her. She wouldn't be too pleased though, if I had nothing to offer this week, so I decided to get down to work, or at least make an effort until Dee came back.

As I lifted out my carving tools, my hand brushed another object which lay beneath them, hidden. It wasn't a treasure exactly, but it was the thing that drove me on, that secretly helped me survive the worst despair. Dee didn't know I still had it; she had thrown it at me one day in a fit of anger. I'd kept it, and she had forgotten about it. It was a note, given to her one day when we were Eights, by her Guardian, a spiteful girl named Zed55, but who called herself Anishka. It wasn't a gift, given in the spirit of love or even affection. Dee had done something to make Anishka furious, and then made matters worse by screaming at her, "One day my mother and father will come to get me, and then you'll be sorry!" Anishka stopped beating her, stormed off, and came back with the note that she claimed she'd stolen out of our file. It said, *Take care of them. I can't.* She showed it to Dee, and told her mockingly that it had been pinned to the carrier that we were found in on the stairs of the workhouse when we were babies.

"Hah!" Anishka had smirked, giving Dee one last hard slap. "No one's coming for you, you stupid little bitch, so stop acting like you're better than anyone else." I found all this out later, when Dee stomped into the Boys' sleeping ward and threw it on my cot. That's when we first started talking about leaving the workhouse and making our own way in the world instead of going to the Breadbasket. But Dee never realized that my reason was different from hers — I knew that the person who wrote the note was heartbroken. Don't ask me how; I just knew it, just like I knew that the person who wrote it had a waterfall of hair the colour of a golden sunset, hair exactly the same colour as Dee and me. And I was determined to find that person one day. As for Dee, I don't think she ever thought of the note again.

At least I was pretty certain she'd never thought of it again. I would have known if it was on her mind, of course. That was the strange thing. As we got older, I seemed to be more attuned to her thoughts than she was to mine. I knew that she never wondered about our mother anymore—that to her, our mother hadn't really loved us, and didn't care about what had happened to us—but I don't think Dee realized that I thought about our mother all the time, and hoped that one day, we'd be together again.

I found a block of wood the right shape in the bin that Dee kept stocked for me, and pondered it for a while. The afternoon was quiet, with most people inside to escape the midday heat; the hum of the cooling unit in the corner was the only sound I could hear and it was soothing in its own way. I relaxed and let the wood dictate what it would become in my hands. An image slowly took shape in my mind—a bird, a tall, graceful one with long legs, a long arched neck, and an enormous wingspan. I began carving it as I saw it, standing in a pool of cool, fresh water. As I carved, a word formed on my lips—"Heron". Was that what it was called? I didn't know, of course. The only birds I'd ever seen were the little, grey, anonymous things that pecked the ground looking for worms and grubs, and fluttered in the puddles after a rain storm. I'd heard them called "sparrows", so that wasn't what I was carving right now. In the workhouse, we were taught to read and write, of course, but all the books were focused on agriculture. Even the earliest alphabet books—"A" is for Agriforming, "B" is for Beans, "C" is for Consortium—none of them had animals or stories in them. It was all about teaching us to become obedient agri-slaves.

As I became more focused on my work, I began to relax a little, and found myself enjoying how the wood slipped away and the heron, if that was what it really was, revealed itself to me. Finally, the bird was finished. I looked it over with pride—this would fetch some good coin at the

Hidden Market. I put it in my pocket, waiting for Dee to arrive so that I could go out. Then I realized that the sun was starting to go down—I must have been working for over three hours, and Dee and Rogan weren't back yet. I stifled the panic that started bubbling in my chest, and reached out to her. Slowly, as though from a great distance, a sound began to well up in my mind, and built into a crescendo of screaming! At the same time, the opening to the tent was flung wide, but I was blinded by the sound in my head and the fear and panic that it was creating. I didn't know what was happening or who was yelling—the screaming was too loud. The ground began to shake and I fell to my knees, holding my head in agony and terror. I don't know how much time passed—the blur of fear and pain was relentless, and I was immobilized by it, until finally a voice penetrated the fog, and I could hear my name being called.

"CEE!! CEE!!" I looked up. Standing in front of me was Little Jimmy, another "graduate" of the workhouse, who lived three rows over with a woman called Nonny.

"Jimmy," I gasped. "What...?"

He looked at me down on the ground, confused, and bent to put a hand on my shoulder. "Cee, have you already heard?!"

"Heard what?! Tell me what's going on!!" I shouted at him over the screaming in my mind, but I already knew what he was going to say. "What's happened to Dee?!" I demanded, struggling to my feet.

"It was an ambush! The Blues—she's been hurt! I can take you to her!"

He held open the tent flap, and I staggered through. "Where? Where is she?"

Little Jimmy grabbed my arm and started to pull. I pulled back, looking wildly around, suddenly not knowing what to do. Little Jimmy understood immediately and pointed to a sturdy, brown-haired girl about my age standing by the tent, holding a heavy-looking stick. "This is

Nonny's little sister Sarah. She'll guard your tent for you until you get back. Don't worry."

Sarah slapped the stick into her open hand. "I can take care of things," she said. "Go!" I had no choice but to trust her. I let Jimmy lead me on to Dee, not knowing what I would find, and terrified of the possibilities.

5

Dee

I screamed only once, when the laser rifle cut through my skin, but it reverberated through my head and through the space between me and Cee. I knew he would hear it, and that made things worse.

Everything was chaos. It had started out so well — it seemed unreal that things would have ended like this. Rogan and I had gone to see S-Sam, hoping that he could connect us with Trick. S-Sam lived on the other side of Divinity with his mother in a scruffy, run-down tent that looked like it could barely keep out the rain. We had to wait a while — if anyone saw Rogan and me talking to S-Sam it could spell trouble for all of us, so we loitered a few tents away, a signal for the Baby Gang to take action. They were called the Baby Gang because they were all under the age of ten, tough little kids, both boys and girls, who had heard about Trick somehow, and had run from the workhouses to Divinity. They'd traded one hard life for another, but there was more dignity in thieving than slaving. There was a system in place, involving members of the Baby Gang who would wander the rows of tents until they spotted someone who looked like they needed a hook-up. At some point, one of the kids would casually saunter past S-Sam's tent and run his fingers across the fabric as he passed by. That was the signal for S-Sam to appear.

When he finally came out of the ramshackle tent, he squinted into the distance, stretched and yawned, then nonchalantly hitched up his pants. He was almost as wide as he was tall, round-faced, with greasy hair plastered down onto his forehead. He stood there for a moment staring straight ahead, hands in pockets, then slowly began strolling down the row. At this, the Baby who'd signalled him at the tent moved towards us. As he went past, he very subtly indicated with a nod of the head that we should follow S-Sam.

We kept our distance so we wouldn't attract attention. It was a long walk, meandering through Divinity, skirting the North edge of the boundary of Old Kensington. Old K, or the haunted city as it was equally known, had once been a thriving borough of Metro, until the Frag wars, when it had been sonic bombed until it was uninhabitable. The majority of the scrapers were standing but walls were missing, and sometimes floors would suddenly give way under your feet. It wasn't an area that the Fancies frequented, but it was a great place for illicit activity. Just when Rogan and I were thinking that S-Sam would never stop walking, he suddenly stepped into the shadow of a building and disappeared.

"What?!" exclaimed Rogan. "Where did he go? I didn't think he could move that fast."

"We have no choice but to follow him," I answered. "He couldn't have gone far."

Rogan and I slipped into the shadows together. The temperature immediately dropped once we were out of the sunlight, and the sounds of Divinity seemed to fade into the distance in the silence of Old K's towering scrapers. No wonder people called it the haunted city — it was like being in a cemetery, surrounded by gigantic tombstones. I felt tiny and frightened by the overwhelming silence, and instinctively reached out to Rogan.

He took my hand, enveloping it with warmth, then whispered, "Do you see him anywhere?"

"Not yet—my eyes haven't adjusted." I peered into the gloom. "I'm not seeing anything moving." With that, a sound rang out, like a metal pipe against concrete. Once, twice.

"It's coming from in there!" Rogan pointed to a doorway half a block away.

The door was cloaked in shadows. My stomach flipped at the thought of what might be inside. I'd heard stories at the workhouse about creatures who inhabited the dead cities, gruesome spirits who waited in the dark and reached out to grab you as you passed by. When we got to Divinity, Old Mac, the historyteller there, used to talk about the Frags. How they were dying of thirst, and had filed their teeth down into points so that they could rip open your throat and drink your blood. Despite having some first-hand knowledge of the dangers the Frags posed, Cee loved hearing Old Mac's stories. Me, on the other hand—I didn't care much for the past. History was a mistake made by someone else, and I couldn't fix it. I shivered. Rogan was already moving towards the doorway, carefully picking his way over the rubble that littered the streets. Considering the slow pace that Rogan was keeping on his way to the door, I couldn't for the life of me understand how S-Sam had gotten in there so quickly. I followed along behind Rogan. When he reached the doorway, he waited for me to catch up. We both stood facing the door, hesitating. The sound rang out again, definitely coming somewhere inside the building. I took a deep breath and looked at Rogan. "Let's do this."

Stepping inside the building was like entering another world. Dust motes danced in the faint light from a blown-out window in one of the upper stories. Broken furniture was overturned and some old tech lay in parts on the floor. The sonic bombs had hit their targets over three decades ago, and it looked like nothing had been touched since. As Rogan and I looked around, I realized that a large figure sat on a chair in a shadowy corner of the room. I nudged Rogan and nodded towards the corner.

Rogan cleared his throat. "S-Sam?"

The figure nodded and moved into the faint light. It was definitely S-Sam. He looked at us questioningly. I'd heard that S-Sam didn't say much—he had a terrible stutter that some said started when he saw his father killed in front of him in The Dome. Prisoners weren't supposed to fight to the death unless they'd committed a terrible crime like murder, but sneaking in a blade was a sure-fire way to guarantee victory. He continued staring at us, and I nudged Rogan again to let him know that I was putting him in charge of all the talking.

"We were hoping to get in touch with Trick. We have some baubles..." Rogan quickly reached into his pocket and pulled out the necklace and rings. He held up the diamond and it glinted in the dark room like a star in the night sky. S-Sam looked interested.

"W-w-w-wait." With that, he hitched up his pants again and walked past us, out of the building.

Rogan and I moved into the far corner of the room and sat together on the floor in the dark where we had a good view of the street outside the doorway, but where no one could see us. Time passed—we didn't know how long, but it seemed like at least an hour. We amused ourselves by whispering about what we were going to buy with the coins that Trick would surely give us for the baubles. Rogan had his eye on a new laser blade to replace the rusting metal knife that he carried in his sock for protection. It probably couldn't do much damage, aside from giving someone tetanus, but it made him feel secure. As for me, I was planning the feast that Cee and I were going to enjoy—spicy fried potatoes and meat at the Hidden Market. No one knew what kind of meat it was, but who cared? It was a treat that we'd never been able to afford, and even the less wealthy Fancies who frequented the place didn't seem bothered by where it came from. All I know was that it smelled delicious, and I couldn't wait for the look on Cee's face when he took his first bite.

My mouth was still watering when we heard noises from the street. We both tensed, then relaxed as S-Sam's large frame filled the doorway. He came into the room, followed by a much smaller figure with dark eyes almost obscured by a thick shock of black hair that hung over them. Although I'd only ever seen him from a distance, I knew right away it was Trick from the way he carried himself, confident and self-assured. He looked around and saw us on the floor. We both jumped up at the same time, Rogan fumbling in his pocket for our treasures.

"S-Sam tells me you have some nice baubles you're hoping to give away," Trick said in a voice that was surprisingly low and deep. "Give away" was slang for "sell", but it helped people like Trick avoid the law. He continued, "If they're really nice, I might let you give them to me. Then I might be able to loan you some money." "Loan" was yet more slang. If a fence "loaned" you money after you "gave" him something, then technically he wasn't buying anything.

"Y-yes," Rogan stammered, holding up the baubles that he had pulled from his pocket.

Trick came closer and took one of the rings, the diamond, from Rogan. He pulled a small magnifying glass from his jacket pocket and examined the ring closely. "This one is very nice. I'll let you give it to me, and I'll let you throw in the other two pieces as well as a gesture of good will." He spoke with a mature, business-like air which seemed to run counter to his youthful appearance.

"We would like to give them to you very much," Rogan answered in the proper fashion, and then looked at me nervously. I nodded back quickly.

Trick put the baubles into a small drawstring bag that looked like it was made out of animal hide, then tucked it away out of sight inside his jacket. Very few people could afford *anything* made from animal hide, since there were so few animals left in the world. I was wondering what kind of animal it might be, as Trick was saying, "All right, now let's discuss how much money you'd like me to loan you —" when suddenly the room was filled with a brilliant light. A flash bomb! We all started shouting and holding our eyes, groping for each other as heavy footsteps came charging into the room. I was clinging to Rogan for dear life when a booming voice called out, "Don't move! Stay where you are!" Rough hands grabbed me and pulled me away from him and I heard Trick shouting, "Leave us alone! We haven't done anything!"

The blinding light started to fade and I realized at once what was going on. It was a Blue squad, led by a Lieutenant-Commander with a hard face. One had Trick, who was struggling against the metal restraints they already had on him. Two more were trying to subdue S-Sam, and Rogan, red-faced and furious, was held by a fourth in a chokehold.

The Lieutenant-Commander smirked. "Well, Thaddeus, how does it feel to finally be caught? You thought you could skirt around the law forever?"

Trick stopped struggling and his eyes narrowed. "Nice try, Durand. I didn't 'buy' anything. You have NOTHING on me!"

"That's where you're wrong, you tent city moron. Try reading official notices more often — or can't you read? The Governor-General just changed the law to make sure scum like you couldn't get away with stealing anymore. You accepted thieved items from these two workhouse dogs, and now you're all guilty. I hope you enjoy public appearances, you traitor."

Trick began swearing and shouting. The Lieutenant-

Commander walked over, stared at him for a moment, then suddenly punched him hard in the face. Trick collapsed in a heap, and the other Blues started laughing riotously.

The Blue who was holding me tight with my arms against my back stopped laughing and leaned over me. "Does this one really have to go to The Dome? She'd be perfect for the Sex House." He rubbed against me and licked my ear. I felt a scream rising in my throat and I tried to pull away, but they all started laughing harder. Rogan grunted against the chokehold and looked at me through the dark hair that was hanging in his eyes. He was almost doubled over by the Blue who had him. Suddenly I knew what he was going to do—he reached down quickly and grabbed the rusty old knife out of his sock. Before the Blue realized what was happening, Rogan slammed the knife back into the Blue's leg. The blade might have been old and worn, but in that moment, it did its job. The Blue screamed and let go of Rogan. At the same time, I twisted and kneed the Blue who'd licked me as hard as I could in the groin. He grabbed himself and started gagging, while I ran for the door, Rogan at my heels. The last thing I saw was S-Sam gathering all the strength he possessed and breaking free of his captors. In a second, he had disappeared into the shadows, leaving the Blues scrambling. I was almost out the door when a sudden arc of red light hit me—a laser rifle, fired by the Blue I'd attacked. I screamed in shock as the laser tore into me, and I started to fall forward in mid-flight. Strong hands scooped me up and, stumbling and blinded by pain, I ran. All I remember hearing was the hard voice of the one Trick had called Durand. "Let them go for now—we have what we came for...."

6

Cee

"They've taken her to The Doc's," Little Jimmy panted, as I followed him through the maze of tents. The Doc was Divinity's equivalent of a medic — part doctor, part dentist, part veterinarian. People said that his great-grandfather had been something called a "surgeon" and had actually cut into people with knives instead of lasers, and that everything he knew about healing had been passed down to him. All the tent cities had someone like The Doc. After the Frag Wars, The Consortium had closed down the public hospitals — treating people who couldn't pay wasn't worth their while, and anyone with medical knowledge scattered into the vast population of the poor. Now, there were "Healing Centres" that only the Fancies could afford — state-of-the-art lasers and Medibots instead of real doctors. We Freeworlders were lucky, though, to have someone like The Doc. If you were an agri-slave and you got sick or injured, you were left on your own to either get better or die.

"What happened?! How did she get hurt?! Is Rogan with her?!" The flurry of questions flew out of my mouth. The fear and panic I'd sensed was starting to numb down now, and I wondered if The Doc had given Dee something to knock her out. Or worse, but I couldn't think about that yet.

"All I know is this," Little Jimmy wheezed as we ran. "Rogan came tearing out of Old K like a Frag was on his tail, carrying Dee in his arms. She was bleeding really bad, right out of it, and he made a beeline for The Doc's."

Rogan! I knew it! That no-good thief was the reason Dee was hurt, dying maybe. I clenched my fists as we veered around a corner towards The Doc's tent. There was a small crowd gathered outside, murmuring anxiously. The murmuring grew louder as someone saw me and shouted, "Her brother! Make way!" I shouldered roughly through them towards the entrance to the tent and flung the flap back. Then I stopped in horror, and my heart dropped.

Dee was lying on a makeshift cot, face down with one arm flung lifelessly over the edge. Her back was a mess of burns and flayed skin around a long, bleeding open wound. The Doc was kneeling beside her, towels soaked the colour of crimson in his hands. Rogan was covered in blood—his own or hers, I couldn't tell. He looked like he was in shock. As we stared at each other, I suddenly had the sickening realization that I couldn't hear her in my head anymore, not even faintly, and I didn't know if she was just unconscious or if she was dead.

There was only one other time in our lives that she was lost to me like this. It was right before our Fifteenth Drop-Off Day. I was assigned to the fields and Dee was part of the kitchen crew. She hated it, hated having to make something decent out of the soy bars and the leftovers that we got. The good stuff, the best fruits and vegetables, got shipped into the high-class food chains that the Fancies frequented, and Dee despised having to pick through rotting tomatoes, peppers, and beans, cutting away the bad from the still edible so that the workhouse kids wouldn't starve.

One night, when I was coming back from the fields, I heard a scream in my head. Then nothing. It was like a vacuum of silence roaring at me, like nothing I'd ever experienced before. She just wasn't there. I was terrified and took off running towards the compound. I looked everywhere, but I couldn't find her. I felt like I was drowning in emptiness, like I was completely alone. I saw two other Fourteens, Micah and Florin, and asked them if they knew where she was. They both said "No" right away, but they looked uncomfortable. When they started to walk away, I grabbed Florin by the arm.

"Tell me where she is! Please!"

Florin swivelled his head to make sure we weren't being seen together, then he gave Micah the nod.

"Check the Shed," Micah whispered, and they hurried off, looking over their shoulders.

As soon as Micah said the Shed, I knew something terrible had happened. The Shed was a small, windowless concrete bunker with a dirt floor and nothing else. It was the worst form of punishment at the workhouse — you could get sent there for days, depending on what you'd done, sitting alone in the dark, no food and only a bottle of water. Dee had been in there before for a variety of reasons, but never like this. I could always hear her fuming in my head, furious with the Protectors, the Guardian who had her thrown in there, and the unfairness of the world in general. But this time — this time was different, and I couldn't even go to her. I would have to wait until it got dark, try to bribe someone to unlock the door for me, to look the other way. When the sun finally went down, I was beside myself. Sitting at the long workhouse dinner table earlier, I could see people trying not to look at me, whispering too low for me to hear. When the Protectors dismissed us, I sought out one of the older Guardians, Melissa, to see if she would help me. When she saw me coming, she started walking away more quickly, but I caught up and grabbed her arm.

"Stop it, Cee. I can't." She sounded angry, but I knew that she was as lazy as the day was long, and I could trump her anger with bribery.

"You know where she is, Melissa. Please, help me see her. I'll do anything!"

Melissa smiled triumphantly. "Anything? Agree to clean Protector Jerome's quarters at the crack of dawn for a month and I might open the door for you."

"I'll do it. I promise." Little did she know, I would have done it for a year, five years, anything to get that door open.

She took me to the Shed, sneaking along the side of the compound under cover of darkness. When we got there, she took out a small key and unlocked the padlock on the door. My legs were shaking, and I felt faint at the sight of it.

"There you are," she smirked, swinging the door open. "The crack of dawn, remember?" With that, she disappeared into the shadows.

I peered into the gloom. It was almost impossible to see anything in the dark, so I started to feel my way around the edges of the room, calling out "Dee" very softly. Then I almost tripped as my foot hit something solid lying on the ground. It was her. I fell to my knees, crying and stroking her hair. My hand came away feeling sticky and wet. Panicked, I reached out again in my head to her, and a faint sense of confusion and pain came back to me. She was alive! I started to shake her and call her name, louder than before. I could feel her stirring in my mind, her body moving slightly. She groaned.

"Dee, it's me. Wake up. I need to get you out of here." I wasn't sure how I was going to do it, but she wasn't staying in the Shed a minute longer. I half picked her up — she was like a dead weight at first, then she braced her knees and sagged against me. "You have to try to move your feet, Dee. I'll hold you up."

She groaned again, but shuffled forward, leaning on me, until we made our way back to the compound. When we got inside, Melissa was waiting. I felt a wave of fear, but she said, "I figured if you were willing to clean Jerome's toilet for a month just to get the door open, what would you do for me if I helped patch her up?"

"Anything you want," I grunted under Dee's weight. "Do you know what happened to her?"

"It was Songe," she replied with distaste. "I don't know all the details, but I hear Dee was pretty stupid. Still, she didn't deserve to have this done to her. Songe is an asshole at the best of times, but this is too much. Everybody thinks so." Songe was an older Guardian, half Chin, rumoured to be the son of a Chin official who had taken a liking to an agri-slave girl on a tour of the Breadbasket. When Songe's mother died giving birth to him, he was brought here. He was handsome, a favourite with the Protectors, but he hated everyone and everything, and never missed a chance to make someone else's life miserable.

Dee muttered, "Asshole is right," under her breath, and sagged down again. I looked at her closely now that we were in the light. Her golden hair was matted with blood, and she had a black eye and a swollen, cut lip. In that moment, I felt rage for the first time and I knew I was capable of terrible violence. Melissa and I took her into the Girls' sleeping ward. I could feel everyone's eyes on us as we lay her in her cot. No one said anything, but I knew what they were thinking: "This could be me." Suddenly it hit me how our lives were so tenuous, at the whim of other, more powerful people, and there was nothing we could do about it except run away into a life that might not be much better. Melissa went to get warm water and towels, and I sat down on the edge of Dee's cot. I held her hand and squeezed it, and thankfully, she squeezed back.

"Can you talk, Dee? What happened?"

She opened the eye that wasn't swollen shut and whispered, "I stole some candy out of the Reward cupboard in the kitchen. Songe caught me. He told me to turn out my pockets. When I refused, he hit me and turned them out *for* me. When he saw the candy, he lost it. He dragged me by the hair to the Shed, threw me inside, and—and I think I hit my head on the concrete wall. I don't remember anything else."

"Why?! Why would you steal candy from the kitchen?! It's insane!"

She sniffled and turned her head away from me. "It was supposed to be a surprise for our Drop-off Day. It's so unfair that you never get any treats because I'm always getting us in trouble."

I wanted to cry—she had done this for me, out of love, and here was the result. I felt sick. Her mind was in mine, full of anger and pain, but as I reached out to her, suddenly there was something else too, something darker and more awful. When I tried to reach it, she slapped me away. But I knew. I knew what it was that she didn't want me to know, and the rage began to build again.

Melissa helped me clean her up as best we could, and she gave Dee something from the apothecary cupboard to help with the pain. Then, when Dee finally fell asleep, I kissed her on the cheek, and turned to Melissa.

"I have something I need to do. Can you stay with her until I get back?"

Melissa looked scared. "Cee, leave it. Songe is 3 years older than you and much bigger. It'll only make things worse. For you *and* her."

"Just stay with her." My voice was hard. She nodded slightly and I left. I went down to the equipment warehouse, where we kept the machinery and tools for farming, and found what I needed. Then I made my way to the male Guardians' recreation room.

When I got there, the lights were still on. The older Guardians got to stay up as late as they wanted, dicing for coins, drinking Al Cool, a harsh moonshine that they made out behind the Shed, and bragging about the latest kid they'd beaten. They looked up as I threw the door open—

there were six of them, some looking amused at the sight of me, others looking worried like they might be involved in something over their heads. Songe was the first to his feet.

"Who the hell are you?" he demanded. He was big, with powerful looking hands. He had a sneer on his face. "Wait a minute...I recognize you." He laughed and came closer, leaning down towards me menacingly. "You're the brother of that little bitch I caught stealing candy." He leered at me. "Mmm. She was — "

He didn't get a chance to finish. I whipped the laser pruner out of my pocket and slashed him diagonally across the face. He fell to the ground screaming, holding his eye to stop it from coming out of its socket. The other Guardians started towards me, yelling and knocking over their chairs. I stood immobile, incensed, and barely controlling the desire to attack them all. My head felt like it was about to burst with fury. Then the ground began to shake under our feet, and they hesitated, looking around wildly.

I waved the laser pruner at them. "You *all* know what he did. Just try me." They stopped in their tracks and the quaking of the ground beneath them began to subside. Songe was still screaming, but, ignoring him, they went back to the dicing table, righted their chairs, and sat down.

"Six coins on the double," one of them, dark-haired with broad shoulders, said shakily, and the game continued as if nothing had happened, Songe still writhing on the floor as I left. After that, Songe was sent to the agri-camps, scarred and one-eyed. Dee never asked me, and I never told her. We all have our secrets, our burdens to carry. Not long after that, Dee and I decided to run away to try and find a better life, and I made a vow to never use my hands for violence again.

But now, things were different. It was a laser rifle, and blood everywhere, and I couldn't hear her no matter how much I tried. I started to shake uncontrollably. The Doc looked up at me from what he was doing.

"She's not dead," he said. "At least not yet, so calm yourself down. I gave her some TastiRum and Lullybies for the pain." The Doc wasn't known for his bedside manner, but his offhandedness actually made me feel as if there was some hope—if *he* wasn't panicked, then maybe she was going to be okay, even if things looked pretty bleak. I stopped shaking, but then I looked at Rogan and felt the old rage rising in me again like a phoenix from the ashes.

"You stupid piece of shit," I said slowly and quietly. "If she does die, the first thing I'll do is kill you myself, Dome or no Dome."

He blinked and swallowed hard, knowing that I was serious. I'd only ever felt this way once before, and in that moment, I knew that if he was the reason I would have to live the rest of my life without Dee, I could rip his throat out and smile while doing it, despite the vow I'd made to myself.

He put out his hands towards me in a gesture of mollification and started stammering. "Cee, it—it was an ambush—the Blues—they were waiting for Trick—I didn't know—"

"Save it, Rogan. I don't want to hear it from you. You knew how dangerous this could be and—"

"Either quit your posturing or take it outside!" The Doc interrupted. "I've got delicate work to do and I need to focus!"

We both immediately turned our attention to him, and Dee's limp form. He was holding a large, threaded needle in one hand. He rolled his eyes and sighed when he saw our expressions of horror.

"My laser-grafter went on the fritz last week, so I'm doing this the old-fashioned way, and it requires a lot of concentration to not screw it up. It's probably better if you both leave until it's over." Then, as we went through the doorway towards the growing crowd outside, he said, "She might make some noise. It can't be helped, so prepare yourself for it."

I shuddered, and Rogan looked like he was going to be sick. Good, I thought. Now he's getting a small taste of how I feel. Then the crowd surrounded us, and voices of concern overwhelmed us. A slight figure pushed towards me — Auntie May. She put a hand on my arm and pulled me down to her level with surprising strength for her age.

"What happened, boy?" she demanded.

"Not sure, Auntie May. She went into Old K to sell some baubles. With *him*." I nodded towards Rogan, who was standing off to the side, one hand over his eyes. "There was an ambush, and she got lasered. *He* seems to be just fine," I finished angrily.

"Don't put too much of the blame on Rogan." Her voice softened. "You know how stubborn your sister can be. You could have told her 'No' twenty times over, and she still would have gone if that's what she wanted to do."

"She wouldn't have wanted to if he hadn't suggested it!" I countered. "He—" I stopped as a sharp stab of pain filled my head. The Doc was at work. I could feel Dee's confusion and panic, so I stifled my own fear, and sent out waves of calm. Nothing. Then suddenly a sense of relief and the feeling of my hand being squeezed. She knew I was here, even in her barely conscious state.

Auntie May looked at me curiously. "What?" she asked.

"Nothing," I smiled. "I trust The Doc. She's going to be all right."

7

Dee

It was dark. Something bad had happened, but I couldn't remember what. I opened my eyes and saw a woman with pale golden-red hair — she was leaning over me, whispering to me quietly. I couldn't hear exactly what she was saying, and as I strained towards her, she smiled, but I could see tears in her eyes. I tried to speak to her, but she stroked my forehead and said, "Hush now, love, hush," her tears falling onto my face as she kissed me. Then she started to move away, and I struggled towards her, but she faded back into the dark. I howled in anguish, and a voice broke through.

"Dee! Dee! It's all right — I'm here! Stop thrashing around or you'll pull out the stitching!" It was Cee's voice. I opened my eyes, for real this time, but all I could see was the floor. Why was that? Then I turned my head and he was sitting in a chair next to me. He went to the table and turned on the solar lamp. I could see in its weak light that his face was etched with worry.

"Cee." My voice sounded weak and raspy. I struggled to get up, but searing pain slapped me back down. I settled for lying partly on my side so that I could see him. "What happened? What did I do?!"

"*You* didn't do anything, aside from being caught in the Blue ambush of a known criminal, then getting shot with a laser rifle. You're lucky to be alive." Cee sounded angry, and I reached out to him with my mind. He *was* angry. But relieved too. I held out my hand, and he took it, squeezing it reassuringly like he always did. Then suddenly it all came flooding back to me, the flash bomb, then Blues, Trick on the floor, and Rogan — where was Rogan?! The last thing I remembered was being hit by the laser blast — what if they'd gotten him too?

"Cee, I need to see Rogan! Now! Where is he? Is he okay?"

Cee pulled his hand away from mine. "Don't talk to me about Rogan. Yes, *he's* fine. And you almost died, thanks to him."

"Not true and you know it," I said stiffly. "It was just as much my idea as his. I'm not some baby who does whatever other people tell her."

"Well, I wish you *would* once in a while. If you'd listened to me, then maybe you wouldn't be lying there with thread holding your torn-up back together, making me sick with worry!"

I was suddenly overcome with pain and exhaustion. Cee was right — this was unfair to him. I shouldn't have been so cavalier, thinking that I could waltz into Old K with diamonds, deal with someone as notorious as Trick, and come out unscathed. Cee sensed my remorse, and my pain, and stood up.

"I'll get The Doc." He paused. "And Rogan."

While he was gone, I thought about my dream again. Who was the woman? She seemed familiar somehow. And it felt familiar too — sometimes, when I was just on the verge of waking up from a sound sleep, I would feel someone stroking my forehead, or tears on my face. Then I would open my eyes and no one would be there. I never told Cee any of this — I think he sensed it but I didn't know exactly how to explain it to him. Now, of course, I had a face to go along with the feeling, but who was she? Then the tent flap was thrown back, Rogan rushed in, Cee and The Doc close behind him, and I put the dream out of my mind.

"Dee!" Rogan looked ecstatic. "You're awake! How do you feel?"

"How do you think I feel?" I laughed weakly. "Like someone chewed me up, spat me out, then put me back together with fishing line."

"Not far from the truth," said The Doc. He turned his attention to Cee and Rogan. "It's time for another dose of Lullybies. She needs to rest. You can stay for a minute, but none of that nonsense from before, do you hear me?"

I raised an eyebrow at Cee and Rogan. They shuffled their feet and looked sheepish as The Doc handed me a tablet and a glass of water with a metal straw in it. I put the tablet in my mouth and started sucking the straw to wash it down. "Yuck!" I gagged and coughed. "You didn't say this was TastiRum. Gross!"

"Drink it all," The Doc commanded. "I need you out for a while so I can check your dressings, maybe do a little more repair work, depending."

I groaned. "Not that I'm not grateful, but how long do I have to stay here?"

"At least a couple of days. You lost some blood — need to get your strength back. Now go to sleep."

I *was* feeling sleepy already. I looked at Cee and Rogan. "Stay with me? And when I wake up, I want to hear more regarding the 'nonsense' Doc was talking about."

"It was nothing," Cee said, looking pointedly at Rogan. Rogan nodded, and pulled a chair over to sit next to me. As everything started to go fuzzy from the TastiRum cocktail, I felt someone take my hand. At first I thought it was Cee, but it felt different. I smiled to myself as I sank down into the blackness again.

The next time I opened my eyes, the tent was enveloped in darkness, the only light coming from the moon, its beams spilling in through the cracks in the tent flap. I was slightly disappointed; I'd hoped to see the woman again, but my sleep was dreamless this time. I could hear breathing, and as my eyes adjusted to the dimness, I could make out Rogan and Cee, both asleep in their chairs, Rogan with his head thrown back, and Cee leaning his head on one hand. My mouth felt like it was stuffed with cotton, and I was suddenly incredibly thirsty for something other than TastiRum. I tentatively tried to turn on my side again to see if there was anything available before I had to wake up Cee and ask him to get me a drink. I was in luck; there was a small pitcher of water and a glass on the table next to my cot that The Doc must have put there while I was out. I turned a little further—it still felt like my back had gone through a meat grinder, but the pain was bearable. I was reaching for the pitcher when I realized that a shadow in the corner of the tent had just moved. I froze, my hand in mid-air, paralyzed with fear. What if it was a Blue, come back to finish the job and kill Cee and Rogan in the process? But as I stared, it became obvious that the shadow was wide and round, and somehow familiar.

"S-Sam?" I whispered.

He emerged from the shadowy corner and came closer to my cot. He picked up the pitcher, poured me a glass of water, and handed it to me silently. As I drank the water down, I watched him in the dim light. He looked worse for wear, grim and more pasty than usual. His clothes were dirty and torn, and the hand that had passed me the glass was cut and bleeding.

"Where have you been?" I asked him quietly. I had a flurry of questions swirling around in my mind, but there was no use asking S-Sam more than one at a time.

He swallowed hard and said, "F-f-f-f-following...." He sounded like he was choking on his own voice. The events of the last day seemed to have affected him to the point that he could barely talk—not that he was a chatterbox before.

"Following the Blues and Trick?" I finished for him. He nodded. "Where did they go?" I asked, trying to sound calm. I had a pretty good idea where they were taking Trick, and the thought of it filled me with dread.

"D-d-d-d-d…" He groaned, and his face screwed up like he was trying not to cry.

"The Dome?" S-Sam nodded, and my heart sank. I didn't know Trick that well, but The Dome was the worst thing that could happen to anyone. It was a cruel joke played on us all by a government that was more concerned with profits than people. You could murder someone in Adanac, but you wouldn't go to The Dome unless it was something really sensational, like killing a famous or powerful Fancy or something equally scandalous. Otherwise, you'd just disappear. Same thing with people who protested against the government. There was no point in taking *them* to The Dome — it would just create more protests. No, The Dome was reserved almost exclusively for thievery and other minor crimes. The Fancies were rich and the rest of us were poor; as far as the government was concerned, that was the natural order of things, and it needed to stay that way. So they had a special place in their lousy hearts for Freeworlder thieves and blackmarketeers. Of course, Freeworlders never stole things from each other — no one had enough "things" to make it worthwhile, and there was an unwritten code against it that very few people would ever violate. Squatting, of course, was another matter. Leaving your tent unguarded was just as stupid as leaving a coin in the middle of the road and walking away from it. It was fair game, everyone agreed. The only Freeworlders who were exempt from squatting were people like The Doc, who performed a necessary service, or elders like Old Mac and Auntie May who everyone respected. But thieving from the Fancies? That meant The Dome for certain.

S-Sam put his face in his hands and let out a cry. Cee and Rogan began to stir, then Cee jumped out of his chair.

"What's going on? What are you doing in here?!" He charged towards S-Sam, who stepped back, wielding the water pitcher like a weapon.

"Cee, wait!" I yelled, then groaned as the pain in my shoulder and back sprang to life again. "It's only S-Sam. He has information about Trick." I sank into the cot, as Cee stopped in his tracks. S-Sam put the pitcher back on the table, and went back to the chair in the corner, breathing heavily. Rogan stood up, switched on the lamp and went over to S-Sam anxiously.

"What happened? How long did you follow Trick for? What's the Baby Gang saying?" Rogan peppered him with questions while S-Sam just stared wildly at all of us and struggled to speak.

"Who cares about Trick? If it wasn't for him, my sister wouldn't be lying here half-dead!" Cee exclaimed angrily.

"I'm not half-dead," I laughed weakly. "Don't be so dramatic. One of you give S-Sam some of that TastiRum — it might loosen his tongue up a bit."

S-Sam nodded eagerly, and Rogan poured him a tall glass which he gulped down. When he'd drained the glass, he sighed deeply, leaned back in the chair and closed his eyes. We waited, watching him and not saying anything, until finally, he spoke:

"Th-thank you," he said, his eyes still closed.

"Can you tell us now what's going on?" Rogan asked, as Cee retreated to his own chair, still looking furious. "Did they take Trick to The Dome?"

S-Sam nodded. "Y-yes. They have him in The T-Tower. Josee from the S-Sex H-House told C-Ceridwen th-that some B-Blues c-came in c-celebrating. They s-said, 'We f-finally c-caught the little m-m-maggot — it's g-gonna be a f-fight to-to-to —'"

" — the death?! For thieving?! He's only a kid! That's insane!" Rogan was outraged and started pacing the tent, punching his fist in the air.

S-Sam just swallowed hard and stared at him. He looked absolutely exhausted from the sheer effort of speaking.

"S-Sam, why don't you get Ceridwen to come by?" I asked quietly. "Then she can tell us what she knows."

S-Sam nodded and eased himself up from the chair. He was starting to look a little wobbly from the TastiRum, but it was better than the petrified way he looked when I first saw him. He slipped out of the tent, less quietly than he had come in, and disappeared into the night.

8

Cee

"Ceridwen! The White Witch?! As if we don't have enough problems!" I exclaimed after S-Sam was out of earshot.

Dee waved a limp hand at me from the cot. "She's not so bad...once you get used to her. Besides, if she knows what happened to Trick—"

"What difference does it make what happened to Trick?! It has nothing to do with us anymore. Just be grateful you're alive and leave it at that!" I shouted.

"Cee, calm down. It's important that we hear what Ceridwen has to say." Rogan put a hand on my arm and I shoved it off roughly.

"No, I—" I stopped short as a wave of pain filled my mind. Dee was struggling to sit up and wincing with the effort.

"Rogan's right, Cee. It's important," she said. "First, we need to know if the Blues are coming after us too. Second, we need to know how we can help Trick."

"Help Trick? Are you insane or have the TastiRum and Lullybies completely addled your brain?"

We stared at each other in silence, her pain filling my head and my anger filling hers. Things were getting more and more complicated, and I needed to think, away from here, away from the distractions of Dee suffering, Rogan pacing the tent, and the imminent arrival of Ceridwen.

"All right," I said finally, breaking the silence. "I have to go back to our tent for a bit. Nonny's sister has been watching it for hours, and she needs a break." I moved towards the tent flap.

"Wait!" Dee called. I turned around—she looked frightened. "You're coming back, aren't you?"

My anger faded and my voice softened. "Of course I'm coming back. It'll be a while before Ceridwen shows up, and I want to get my carving tools. I might as well be doing something useful while I wait for you to heal." I sent her a wave of reassurance, and her eyes started to well up.

She swatted at the tears and said bitterly, "No more feast. I screwed everything up again."

I went back over and knelt down next to her. "No, you didn't. It's not your fault." I looked up pointedly at Rogan, but stopped myself from saying anything else. I smiled at Dee. "We'll have our feast. I'm pretty sure I saw a can of stew at the bottom of the cooler—"

"Get out, you with your cat food!" she laughed weakly, and then sank back into the cot with a small groan.

I stepped out into the night, took a deep breath, and started making my way up the row of tents. Everything was dark and still, the moon hiding behind the clouds now. In the far distance, I heard a wild dog bark. They say a long time ago, people used to keep dogs as pets, for company and to love. Everyone, not just the Fancies. Now, the Fancies are the only ones who can afford to waste food on an animal, but they favour tiny hairballs that they can carry in their bags, nasty little things that look like fluffy rats and eat delicate morsels of meat from their owner's hands, meat that Freeworlders like us will never taste. Me, I prefer the wild dogs that scavenge at the edges of Divinity, big and bold. I'd like to have a dog like that, a proper dog, but they're not tameable, not anymore, and I barely have enough for Dee and me to eat as it is. Still, I could carve a dog…

My thoughts were suddenly interrupted by a sound, much closer than the wild dog, a rustling sound. I froze, the stories of Frag monsters prowling the dark in search of blood whirling in my head. I was poised to run in panic back to Dee when figures emerged from between two tents. It was the squatter family from earlier today, slowly making their way through Divinity, still looking for shelter. The baby was whimpering quietly, too tired and hungry to cry, and the mother looked at me with sad eyes as they shuffled past. I wished that I had something to give them, despite Dee's warnings. Suddenly, I remembered the heron, the carving that I'd finished right before Dee had been hurt. I fumbled in my pocket and my fingers closed on it. It felt smooth and powerful, and I knew that I was giving up a lot of coin. I went over to the man and held it out to him. He looked at me fearfully, and the woman huddled behind him, the baby pressed against her.

"Here," I said. "Take this. You can trade it at Blaw-blaw's for some food."

"Why?" the man whispered.

"Why not?" I answered. His hand shook as he took the heron from me, then he shoved it inside his coat anxiously as if afraid I would change my mind.

"Thank you," he said, his voice catching. I watched them walk away, more quickly now, with purpose. Before they went out of sight, I saw him take the woman's hand, then lean over and kiss the baby's head. At least they would eat tonight.

I knew I could never tell Dee—she wouldn't understand. But I could always carve another heron, now that I knew what they looked like. In fact, I could probably do it tonight, before Ceridwen arrived.

Then dread came flooding back. They didn't call her The White Witch for nothing, and the thought of her in the same tent as me and Dee made me shiver. Ceridwen. Some people said her father was a Frag. Some people said her mother was a Frag. Either way, she was...well, intimidating. Old Mac said she was something called an "Al-bino", which meant she had white hair and white skin, and her eyes were a translucent blue. She always wore a black cloak with a hood pulled up around her face, because unlike most Freeworlders, whose skin came in varying shades of tan to dark brown either naturally or thanks to the relentless sun, hers was so unusually pale that it burned very easily. But it wasn't the way she looked that was so disturbing; in fact, she was beautiful in a kind of wild way. She spoke in riddles, in the old language, and people said she was Fey. I asked Old Mac once what "Fey" meant, and he said the Fey were from the old land, that they knew things and had strange powers. When I told him that people said Ceridwen was Fey, he laughed and said, "No, boy. That girl is just plain Frag mad." But he looked uncomfortable and changed the subject.

With The White Witch weighing on my mind, I reached our tent. It was illuminated from within by a faint light. I called out quietly, "Sarah, it's me, Cee." After a moment, the flap opened slightly and Sarah peeked out, blinking sleepily, her dark hair tousled.

"Oh," she breathed. "You're back. How's Dee?"

"The Doc thinks she'll survive, but she was hurt pretty badly. I just wanted to see if you were all right, and pick up a few things."

"I'm fine," she answered, opening the flap wider and letting me in. "This is a pretty nice tent. I—um, I ate your lettuce. I hope you don't mind. I've never had lettuce before."

"No," I laughed, "it's fine. It's the least I can offer you for staying here. It was better when it was fresh though, sorry."

She laughed, her brown eyes crinkling at the corners in a kind way. "I wouldn't know the difference. Anyway, I'm glad Dee is going to be all right. I like her. She has...spirit."

"That's what they're calling it these days, huh? Her 'spirit' almost got her killed."

We both sat down in silence, then she offered, "I can stay for as long as you need me to. It's nice to have somewhere quiet to be. I love Nonny, but she and Little Jimmy need their space too."

I smiled. "Well, it'll be at least another couple of days before Dee can walk, so you're welcome here." I got up and went to my workbench. "I just came to get my carving tools. I have to go back now. Ceridwen is coming."

Sarah's eyes widened. "The White Witch? Why?"

"S-Sam told us that she has some knowledge of what happened to Trick. Dee thinks we should help him, and she's convinced that Ceridwen will know how." I laughed derisively. "Me, I have my doubts."

"Don't dismiss it so lightly," Sarah warned me. "Once, she passed me at the Hidden Market, then suddenly she turned and called out to me, "Neither a borrower nor a lender be!" Later that day, Little Jimmy came to me—he said there was a rich game happening at Caseeno and that if I'd only give him the two coins I'd been saving for months, he'd make it back and then some. I'd put what she'd said out of my mind, but I should have listened. He lost everything, including my two coins. Nonny was furious with him."

I snickered. "If she'd really wanted to help, she could have told Little Jimmy 'You're no good at cards. Don't waste your time and money' instead. Only she would have said it in some weird way that Jimmy wouldn't have understood, so..."

Sarah rolled her eyes and nodded in agreement. "He's a good man, I know, but he doesn't always think right. Anyway, if I were you, I'd listen to what The White Witch says. She's Fey."

"That's just a story. And what if she says we have to go to The Tower and help Trick escape? You know that Dee would want to do it. She feels like it's her fault he got caught. She'll rush in headfirst without thinking, and probably get us all killed."

"Don't worry, Cee. Your sister isn't a maniac. She'll be careful — besides, she's in no condition to go rushing off to rescue anyone." She came closer and then, impulsively, she put her arms around me. Surprised, I hugged her back and we stood for a moment like that in the glow of the lamp. Then she broke away, laughing and looking a little embarrassed. "Go on now. Get back to your sister. And let me know what Ceridwen says."

I gathered up my tools, smiled and nodded, then ducked out of the tent. It was the second time in less than an hour that I'd stood in the quiet dark, breathing in the night air. Only this time, the sweet smell of a girl's brown hair lingered in my mind.

I started to make my way back to The Doc's. The moon was out from behind the clouds again, and in the far distance, I could see The Dome, its white, curved roof gleaming in the moonlight. Looming over it was The Tower, standing like a horrible beacon. The Tower is a dizzyingly tall structure and can be seen as far away as the Lake District. It's a constant reminder of the power of The Consortium — their forces had defended it ferociously against the Frag incursion, and while the war had taken its toll on the rest of the city, levelling huge sections, The Tower had held. It was barely damaged, and it's been used ever since as the main communications hub and command centre for The Consortium in Trillium Province, connected to at least seven other Towers across Adanac. It's also used to house prisoners before they're taken to The Dome. "House" is a poor word to describe it, though. Most of the regular prisoners are kept inside, but the special prisoners, the ones who are slated to fight to the death, are kept on an open-air platform outside the main pod of The Tower, almost half a click above the city. Sometimes they're out there for a short period of time, freezing or dying of heat for only a few days before they're taken to The Dome. Sometimes though, and especially if it takes a long time to find an opponent, they're out there for weeks, months even. There's no escape, no respite from the terror of falling to your death in your sleep. All you can do is pray to the old god that a strong wind doesn't blow you over the edge. I've heard stories of people who were brought to The Dome, Tower-mad and raving. Suddenly, my mind conjured up an image of Trick on the platform, small and shivering in the night air, younger than me, and I understood what Dee was saying.

I arrived at the tent, and quietly pulled back the flap in case Dee was sleeping. She wasn't. And sitting by her cot was a figure dressed in a black hooded cloak. Ceridwen was here.

9

Dee

After Cee left, I dozed a little, his words echoing through my mind. How could he not want to help Trick? Cee was always the cautious one, the careful one, never wanting to get noticed, always wanting us to keep to ourselves. He hated taking chances and was content with the pitiful life that we had. Even at the workhouse, he was always pulling me back, telling people "Oh, she didn't mean that" or making excuses for each new injustice. I know he was just trying to protect me, but there comes a point when people have to stand up for something. Trick might be a fence and a gang leader, but he was only thirteen—hardly a hardened criminal or a murderer. He didn't deserve to die because of a few baubles. How could I make Cee understand that what happened to Trick was my responsibility?

Suddenly, I heard a noise, like the whisper of fabric being blown by the wind, and the light from the solar lamp flickered. Rogan heard it too—he started up from his chair as the tent flap was pulled back. A tall figure was silhouetted against the doorway.

"Who are you?" Rogan demanded.

The figure stepped into the tent and a voice spoke from within a black hood, lyrical and low. "Friends to this ground. The honourable lady of the house, which is she?"

Rogan and I looked at each other. "Um, I suppose that would be me," I answered. "Ceridwen?"

"None other," she replied. "My lord, we were sent for."

"Uh, yes," I said, trying to decide if she was speaking to Rogan or me. "S-Sam said that you had information about what happened to Trick."

"My purpose is indeed a horse of that colour. My lord, I have news to tell you. Such news, my lord, as grieves me to unfold."

I decided that she was referring to both of us in her strange way, so I said, "Do you know what's happened to Trick? S-Sam said he was being held at The Tower."

She nodded. "Stay, yet look back with me unto the Tower. Pity, you ancient stones, those tender babes whom envy hath immured within your walls! He that dies pays all debts." Her uncanny blue eyes met mine as she sat down in the chair next to my cot.

"I don't understand," I said. "Why would the Lieutenant-Governor sentence Trick to a fight to the death?! He was only caught with stolen goods — *our* stolen goods!"

Before she could answer, I heard a sharp gasp and swivelled my head. Cee was standing in the doorway, staring at Ceridwen's robed and hooded figure. She followed my gaze and, seeing Cee there, slowly removed the hood of the cloak from her head, revealing a fall of snow-white hair and an elven face. Her lips and those crystalline blue eyes were the only colours we could see — her skin, her eyebrows, and even her eyelashes were white. Cee stepped into the tent. Ceridwen watched him silently for a moment, then turned back to me.

"If this were played upon a stage now, I could condemn it as an improbable fiction," she answered.

Rogan looked confused. "I don't understand…"

"I think she means that she can't believe it," said Cee.

Ceridwen smiled at him and nodded her head. "The youth bears in his visage no great presage of cruelty. Why, this is very midsummer madness."

"His crime wasn't serious enough to warrant a death sentence — he's not a bad kid and this is all just crazy," Cee translated. Ceridwen's smile widened and she held out her hand. Cee hesitated for a minute, then took it.

When they touched, she raised her pale eyebrows slightly in surprise and said quietly to him, "We know what we are, but know not what we may be." She released his hand. Cee looked at her wonderingly as she turned back to me again and frowned. "There is something in this more than natural, if philosophy could find it out."

"There's more to this than meets the eye," Cee agreed. "But what? Why would the Lieutenant-Governor be concerned with someone like Trick?"

Ceridwen thought for a minute, then said to me, "What is it between you? Give me up the truth."

"You mean, what happened? Well, Rogan and I stole some baubles from a Fancy. We wanted to sell them and S-Sam took us into Old K to see Trick. Just as we were about to finish the deal, the Blues attacked. One of them had Trick, called him a tent city moron and a traitor. Then Rogan stabbed one in the leg, and we managed to escape. But we left Trick behind. I don't know how they knew we'd be there. It was like an ambush."

Cee said, "Why would they call Trick a traitor just for fencing jewelry?"

Ceridwen's brow furrowed. "Yet your mistrust cannot make me a traitor. Honour is the subject of my story. Let us be beaten if we cannot fight — take me in his dominion."

We all looked at each other in shock. "Honour? Fighting? Dominion? You mean Trick is... part of the Dominion?!" Rogan exclaimed.

The Dominion was a legend, a myth. They were a
rebel group so far underground that no one knew if they
actually existed. There were rumours of uprisings in other
tent cities, echo bombs going off in the Bread Basket, an in-
surgence in The Dome in Mont Royal. But those were only
rumours. We knew of no one who was even aligned with
the Dominion, let alone a member. It wasn't something
people were willing to talk about or admit to.

Ceridwen looked at us steadily and nodded. "By
innocence I swear, and by my youth, I have one heart, one
bosom and one truth."

"We believe you," I assured her. "But how do we
help? Who's his contact?"

"I have a widow aunt, a dowager of great revenue,
and she hath no child," Ceridwen said solemnly.

"Who on earth can that be?" Rogan looked at Cee,
who shrugged.

"I'm not sure. An older woman, a widow, who has
some money and no family — what about Auntie May? I
don't know about her having a lot of money, but she makes
enough at her stall to get by — and her husband was killed
in the Frag Wars. As far as I know, she doesn't have any
children either," Cee suggested.

Ceridwen smiled and nodded, then her face became
serious again. "But you'll be secret? Never make known
what you have seen to-night."

"Of course," I said. "We won't say anything. But
this is really important. Now we can at least find a way to
help Trick —" I looked at Cee, worried. "I know you don't
think it's a good idea, Cee, but I need to do this."

"I'll talk to Auntie May in the morning," he answered. "I can't promise anything else. Don't get your
hopes up, though — you're in no condition to take up arms
and lead a rebellion. You need to rest and get better."

I *was* getting sleepy again, and the pain was re-
turning in larger and larger waves. "Maybe you're right.
For now." I looked at him pointedly, letting him know that

I wasn't planning on letting this go, then lay my head down on the cot wearily.

Ceridwen stood up, robe swirling, and drew her hood back around her face. "For this night, to bed, and dream on the event. Farewell." With that, she slipped out of the tent and vanished into the night.

We all looked at each other in stunned silence for a moment. "Well. That was…interesting," Rogan said.

"I've never really had a conversation with her before," I added. "She's different, but I like her. What about you, Cee?"

Cee was staring down at his hand, the one that Ceridwen had taken in her own. "What?" he answered, looking back up at me.

"Ceridwen," I said. "What do you think she meant by "We know what we are…whatever she said?"

Cee still looked lost in thought. "It's been a long night. You should get some rest now." He came closer to my cot and poured me a small glass of TastiRum.

"Ugh, no more of that firewater, please! I'll be fine. But back to what Ceridwen said — do you really think that Trick is part of the Dominion? I mean it makes sense when you think about how much effort the Blues put into capturing him. And calling him a traitor…"

Rogan nodded slowly. "I've been hearing some talk, very quiet talk, in the last couple of months about rebels. You know there was an uprising in King's Town about six weeks ago — the Blues tried to suppress it and the rebels hit back with an EMP that completely disabled the government there for two days. I doubt if it's anything so organized as the mythical Dominion, but do you think Trick was involved in something like that?"

"How could he be?" Cee asked. "He's just a kid."

"I wouldn't put it past him," I said. "He might be just a kid, but he's pretty tough, and he has a lot of contacts — not just here, but in other tent cities as well. Where else could he sell the baubles that he fences? He must know Fancies, as well as Blues, from other areas."

"I just can't picture Auntie May as some kind of rebel freedom fighter," Rogan stated emphatically, but then wavered. "Although who knows—maybe Ceridwen is right."

"Auntie May is pretty tough," I answered. "I remember once, when we first came to Divinity, that a couple of the Caseeno Boys came by to shake her down for 'protection money', you know, like if she paid them, they wouldn't destroy her stall. She was all shy, told them sweetly, 'Just let me find my cashbox'. Then she went in the back and came out with a billy club. She cracked the one Caseeno Boy hard on the head and told the other he'd be in for the same if he didn't piss off. They both ran away in a panic, her shaking the club at them. I was scared stiff, but she just laughed and said, 'Some people never learn.' But I guess they did because the Caseeno Boys never came back."

"Well," said Cee, "I just hope she doesn't do the same thing to me tomorrow morning when I ask her about the Dominion. Now, it's been a long night, and I don't want to have to tell you again. You're never going to get better if you keep squirming around, wanting to be a part of everything that's going on. TastiRum or no TastiRum, you are going to sleep now."

I knew that Cee meant business by the tone of his voice. "All right," I said, mock-seriously. "Are you staying here or are you going to vanish into the vapours to seek out your White Witch?"

Cee threw me a strange look. "No, I have some carving to do, if we want to eat for the rest of the week. Wait—no, I'm not blaming—"

"It's OK," I said, smiling. "I know you aren't. Carve me something I've never seen before."

Cee smiled back, and I yawned, then before I knew it, I was asleep.

10

Cee

Well, since Dee hadn't seen the heron yet, I got out my carving tools and the piece of wood I'd saved, and started trying to carve it again. Normally, I could feel the wood come to life in my hands, the curves and lines taking shape almost by themselves, but I was so distracted that my small V-tool kept skipping over the surface.

Dee was breathing quietly and deeply on her cot, and Rogan had gone out to find some food for us. This should have been the perfect time to create, but instead, my mind was swirling with doubt, fear, and wonder. Doubt, because I couldn't quite believe that Trick, a thirteen-year-old fence, was a member of a mythical, secret underground rebel movement. Fear, because what if he was? I knew that Dee would want to go forging ahead with a rescue plan, and what would become of us then? Leave Divinity? Join the underground ourselves? Frankly, I couldn't see the point — the government and the Blues were too powerful, and we would only end up getting hurt, or worse, killed. And wonder? I kept going back to Ceridwen. She wasn't at all what I'd expected. Instead of being intimidated by her, there was an immediate connection, as though we understood each other. When she took my hand, I definitely felt something, a spark in my mind that was almost like the way Dee and I communicated.

The first time I realized that Dee and I were able to sense each other's feelings, that we were in each other's heads was when we were Threes. My Guardian was a Sixteen who called himself Dosto—he ignored me most of the time, just made sure I had enough food to survive and that I didn't wander off into the fields and get attacked by a coywolf. Like a lot of the older Guardians, he was able to stay at the workhouse rather than go north to the agri-stations or leave and fend for himself because he had a certain something. That's what people would say—"a certain something", which I found out when I was much older meant that he was a willing partner to the Protectors. Young, old, male, female—it made no difference to Dosto. He wasn't particularly good-looking, but he *was* enthusiastic. Protectors would suddenly appear at any time of the day or night, and Dosto never turned them down. If it was during the day, he would find another Guardian to watch me, but if it was at night, he would tie me to my cot with a long woven leash to make sure I couldn't sneak out of the sleeping ward to find Dee while he was otherwise occupied.

It was on one of those nights when I first realized that Dee and I could "hear" each other. Up until the previous year, Dee and I had been in the Nursery, sharing a crib and sleeping side by side, but once we were Threes, we had to be separated, her to the Girls' Ward and me to the Boys'. It had taken me a long time to get used to it, not hearing the sound of her breathing and feeling her warmth beside me, and any chance I got, I would tiptoe out and make my way to the Girls' Ward, hence Dosto's leash. It must have been after midnight—Dosto had already done his entertaining for the evening, and I'd been sleeping, when suddenly I woke up. There was a ghostly figure dressed in a hooded white robe floating past my cot. I was frozen with fear — Dosto loved scaring me with stories about the Frags, blood-thirsty monsters from beyond the southern border who came up to Adanac looking for fresh victims. Was this one of them?! Was it going to tear out my throat?! Fear filled my mind and I was breathless with it. But then the figure moved past my cot and stopped further down where the Guardians slept, next to Dosto's bed. The figure shook his shoulder roughly, and Dosto sat up quickly, looking confused and frightened. I silently pulled my covers up around my neck, and I felt a shameful twinge of joy that, after all the horrible stories he'd told me about how the Frags would rip my skin and drink my blood, *he* would be the victim while I could sneak out unnoticed. Then my joy turned to terror as I looked at my wrist and remembered the leash — I wouldn't be able to escape! Then the figure pulled out a knife and held it up to Dosto.

"What are you doing?!" Dosto half-whispered, half-hissed.

The figure's hood fell back, and I realized it was one of the Protectors, an older woman I only knew as "Protector Marta". She looked terrible in the moonlight, her face drawn and thin, her hair dishevelled and her eyes wild. I was even more afraid — she'd obviously been bitten by a Frag and now she was one of them! As I strained to see if her teeth were sharpened to points, I heard her whisper, "How could you do this? I told you. You're mine, not his." His?! Was there another Frag coming?! Were they going to kill us all? In that moment, I felt a rush of warmth between my legs and realized that I'd wet the bed. As I lay there shivering, filled with terror and shame, three things happened. The ground began to rumble ominously, which distracted Protector Marta. Dosto used the opportunity to grab her arm, forcing her to drop the knife, then he gathered her in his arms and began whispering to her as she started to sob. At the same time, the door to the sleeping ward flew open and there was Dee, a tiny whirlwind of a figure flying into the room, with her Guardian, a tall, dark-haired Fourteen named Jenna, frantically chasing her.

Dee ran over to my cot as fast as her little legs could take her, Jenna right on her heels. "Cee!! Cee!!" Dee cried. "Why you scared?!"

I sat up, trying to hold back the tears in my eyes. My head was throbbing, a sharp pain that made breathing hard. Then I felt a strange sensation, like the feeling you get when someone squeezes your hand. Dee and I stared at each other for a long minute. The rumbling stopped and the ground was still again. In the meantime, Jenna had come to a sudden halt. She looked back and saw Dosto with his arms around the heaving shoulders of Protector Marta, the knife on the floor, and yelled, "What the bloody hell is going on here?!"

"I peed the bed," I whispered to Dee, and then I couldn't hold back the tears any longer. Dee just stared at me, and I felt that squeezing sensation in my mind again as she hugged me and said, "'S okay, Cee."

After that, Dosto took Protector Marta out of the sleeping ward, and Jenna, as much as she complained and snapped at the other kids to go back to sleep, got fresh pajamas and clean sheets for my cot while Dee and I huddled close to each other. As Jenna made the bed, grumbling about "daft jealousy" and "you'd think she'd know better at her age," Dee and I sat on the floor solemnly. At least we looked solemn. In our heads, we were sending each other the giggles, mostly over Jenna, and trying not to laugh out loud. Then I sent embarrassment because of the bedwetting, and she sent back something that felt like a shrug of the shoulders, as if she was saying, "Big deal. It happens." I felt my fear and shame melt away, sitting there with her on the cold tile.

I found out later that, at the same time I thought Protector Marta was a Frag come to eat me, Dee had woken up like a shot, ran across the room, and practically dragged Jenna out of bed. I overheard Jenna telling some of the other Fourteens, "That little girl is wild! She pulled me out of a deep sleep, yelling something about Frags, then ran off to the Boys' Sleeping Ward. I go after her, and what do you think? Marta's got a knife, the stupid old bitch, holding it to Dosto's throat, you know, like if she can't have him, no one else can. And there's the brother, scared to death, his bed full of piss, and some kind of earthquake happening. How did she know? She must have seen Marta, or felt the ground moving, or had a bad dream herself."

From that moment on, Dee and I practiced until we were in each other's heads whenever we wanted, or whenever we needed. We got so that we could "hear" each other from as far away as the fields. But having someone in your head all the time can be overwhelming, especially when there are things you don't want them to know. That's why after the incident with Songe, I taught myself how to put up a mental wall, so that I could control how I reacted to what Dee was feeling as well as what she could sense from me. It was different with Ceridwen though. Not as intense as feeling, but more like an intuition, like when you smell the air and you know a storm is coming.

A glimmer of light had appeared on the horizon. It was early yet, but I still couldn't focus on carving. Might as well see if Auntie May was up. I quietly packed up my carving tools and stowed them safely under Dee's cot. If anyone tried to take them, even in her wounded state, she'd protect them with her life.

I slipped out of the tent and stood, looking out over Divinity towards the horizon, where the sky was beginning to glow red. The heat of the day was already starting to build, and I was glad for the slight breeze that was stirring the tents in their rows. Auntie May lived closer to The Square, and it was a good 15 minute walk, so I headed off down the main thoroughfare. Everyone called it the

Queen's Street—the reason why was lost a long time ago. I liked to imagine that once, before the world began to burn, a beautiful queen lived in the castle on the hill, and every day, she would ride down the street in a carriage pulled by four white horses. Of course, there were no horses anymore, except in my imagination, and the castle on the hill was a ruin, laser-cannoned by the Frags a long time ago. In my mind, the queen had golden-red hair, bright green eyes, and a sad face, just like the image I'd pieced together of our mother. But just like our mother, she was long gone.

I'd reached the outskirts of The Square by this point, and I could see Auntie May's tent. It was a patchwork of bright colours, fabric scraps pieced together like an old quilt. Even at this early hour, Auntie May herself was sitting on a stool by the tent door, smoking scrubweed in a pipe. She was fiddling with a small plastic box of some kind. She had it in two parts, its intricate circuits visible. She looked up as I approached and gave me a broad grin from behind a haze of scrubweed smoke.

"Do you know what this is?" she asked. I shook my head. "It's an em-queue-nine. A long time ago, there were places that sent out signals of music or people talking, and you could listen to it all with this—you could even store your own music on it. Much better than those government streaming implants for "propatainment" that the Fancy folk have, talking in their ears all day long. I keep hoping that if I can put it back together properly, music might still come out of it. Pull up a stool."

I dragged a stool from around the corner of her tent and sat down. "I need to talk to you about—"

"I know," she interrupted. "Ceridwen has already been here. Strange girl. I never know the half of what she's saying, although I've gotten much better over the years at piecing it together. I did come to understand that there was a plot afoot to help the boy. I got 'something's rotten in Denmark', wherever that may be, and that 'the king' wasn't allowing anyone to see 'the princes in the Tower'. She was quite insistent about something like 'the quality of mercy' or other such nonsense."

"Yes," I answered. "She wants us to help Trick, and said that you were the person to speak to."

"Me?!" Auntie May laughed coyly and looked at me out of the corner of her eye while she continued to fiddle with the em-queue-nine. "I don't know why."

"Maybe because you're part of the Dominion," I stated bluntly.

She looked shocked. "Hold your tongue! This isn't the place for such talk! Come inside!"

We both went into the tent, Auntie May clucking her tongue at me. As soon as the tent door was closed tight, she turned on me, her voice hardened and different. "*Never* speak of the Dominion so lightly. There are ears everywhere."

"I-I'm sorry," I stammered. "I didn't even think they were real."

"As real as you and me." She put the music device down on a table covered in tools and coils of wire. "You don't need to know anything more than that."

"But Dee wants to help Trick, and Ceridwen said you'd know how," I protested.

"If Trick *was* a member of the Dominion, then don't you think they would already know where he was and what to do about it?!" Her voice softened. "Tell your sister to leave it be. She's in no shape to go rushing off to Trick's rescue anyway. I've told Ceridwen the same thing. I hope for all your sakes that you listen."

"All right," I said. "I'll let her know. But I can't promise that she won't want to get involved. She blames herself for what happened to Trick."

"I know, boy," Auntie May sighed. "Your sister and you..." She trailed off, then looked at me in a way that puzzled me. "Just stay safe. It's important that you stay safe."

"Well," I said. "I can't promise anything. You know Dee."

Auntie May looked sad. "Aye. That I do. Now get back to her. I'm sure the TastiRum and Lullybies are wearing off by now, and she'll need you there when The Doc comes to check on her." And with that, she opened the tent door and motioned for me to leave. I passed through the door and she fastened it tight against me. She was right though—I could hear Dee stirring in my mind. Time to get back and somehow convince her to follow Auntie May's instructions. And I knew it wasn't going to be easy.

11

Dee

I was dreaming again. The woman with the pale golden-red hair was standing above me crying and a man had her by the shoulders. His back was to me; I couldn't see his entire face, just his profile. He had a scar on his cheek. She was struggling and yelling, "No. I won't!" and he was pulling her away from something. "It must be done," he whispered. Then she broke free and her face came down close to mine. I felt her tears on my cheek. "Hush, love," she said, and then she was pulled away again. The edges of everything blurred and began to glow red as if the world was on fire. I groaned and opened my eyes.

Rogan rushed over to my bedside. "What's wrong? Are you all right?"

"It's so hot," I whispered. "When will it snow?"

"Snow?" Rogan repeated, sounding confused. "Dee, it hasn't snowed for over 50 years. What are you talking about?"

Something didn't feel right. I knew that there was no snow, but now I was starting to shiver. Rogan brought a blanket over and tucked it around me, then he felt my forehead. "Dee, you're burning up! I'm going to get The Doc."

I grabbed desperately at Rogan's hand. "No! Don't leave me—the Frags are coming!" Suddenly, I was terrified—I could hear whispering outside the tent and the sound of pointed teeth gnashing. What was happening to me?

"There aren't any Frags, Dee, I promise. You have a fever, and you sound a little delirious. I'll be right back." He pulled his hand free from mine and ran out of the tent. The whispering was getting louder now and I knew I had to escape. Everything was burning and freezing all at the same time, and I struggled to sit up, gasping with fear. My back was screaming in pain, but I was finally upright. I put my feet on the ground, stood, and collapsed onto the floor. The fiery, scorched edges of the world dissolved into black.

When I opened my eyes again, I was back lying on the cot. I knew that some time must have passed, because The Doc was in the tent. Rogan was sitting tensely in the chair in the corner, looking worried, and The Doc was rummaging through his bag, muttering to himself. Then he turned to me and started pulling the dressings off my back. I couldn't see his face, but I could see Rogan's, and he looked frightened.

"I was afraid of this," The Doc said quietly. "These wounds don't look good." He touched my back gently, but it felt like a thousand knives cutting me. I moaned with the pain.

Rogan jumped out of his chair and came over. "It's okay, Dee. The Doc is here now." He took my hand and said, "What's wrong with her?"

"I'll be honest with you," The Doc answered grimly. "It looks like the start of Mersa."

"Mersa," I croaked. Rogan's grip on my hand tightened. Mersa was a disease that came from infection, a disease that caused your skin to eat itself. If it wasn't caught quickly, the only way to stop it was to cut out the infected skin—or cut off the infected limb. Without treatment, it was always fatal. I whimpered. I didn't want to die *or* be disfigured for life.

"But you can do something, right?" I heard Rogan ask The Doc.

"There are powerful antibiotics that can treat it, but I don't have any. It's not something I usually stock. I've already given her what I have, but they're not strong enough. Good enough for your run-of-the-mill cuts and scrapes, but Mersa — that's different."

"Well, fine then. Where can we get some of the stronger stuff?"

"It's easy enough to find," replied The Doc, "but it's damned expensive, 500 coins at least. That's why I don't normally have any. Just can't afford it. There's a stall in the Hidden Market that sells drugs. Owner's name is Hasban. I hear he has a contact in one of the Fancy hospitals, gets the good stuff, for fun times *and* bad times. He'll have what we need."

"But the Hidden Market isn't for another two days!" Rogan exclaimed. "She can't wait that long, can she?"

Just then, the tent flap flew open and I heard Cee's voice. "Doc?" He paused. "What — what's going on?"

"Maybe we should talk about this outside," The Doc suggested. He was trying to sound calm, but Cee wasn't fooled and neither was I.

"No!" I called out. "Don't leave. If I'm going to die before the sun rises tomorrow, I think I have the right to know."

"Wait — what are you talking about, Dee? She's not going to die, right Doc?" Cee demanded.

The Doc hesitated. "She...things aren't looking good," he answered quietly.

"It's Mersa," I giggled. Why was I laughing? The edges of the world were blurring again.

"Mersa!" Cee gasped. "You can treat it though, right?!"

"The Doc doesn't have the medicine she needs," Rogan answered. "We have to get it from a merchant named Hasban, but waiting for the Hidden Market might be too late."

"Then we don't wait!" Cee said impatiently. "Where can we find this Hasban?"

"Finding him isn't the problem," Rogan replied. "Paying him is. The Doc says the medicine she needs is expensive. I only have a few coins—nowhere near enough to pay what he would ask. We'd have all the coins in the world if it wasn't for that stupid Blue ambush—"

"If it wasn't for that 'stupid Blue Ambush', we wouldn't *need* any coins!" Cee yelled.

"I *told* you I was sorry about that!" Rogan yelled back.

"Keep it down!" The Doc interjected. "The last thing she needs is for the two of you to start going at it again. If either of you has an idea about how to pay for the medication, then feel free to share it. Otherwise, get out of the tent."

Suddenly, the pain was overwhelming and I groaned again despite myself. Cee and Rogan both rushed over to the bedside.

"Do something, Doc!" Cee exclaimed. "Can't you do *anything* for her?"

The Doc handed me some pills and a glass. "Take these," he said. "They'll help with the fever."

I put the pills in my mouth and lifted up my head to sip from the glass, realizing too late what it was. "Not more TastiRum," I pleaded.

"Drink it down," he said gently. "It's all I have. I'm sorry."

I drained the glass as best I could, then sank my head back down into the bed. I started feeling woozy almost right away, and my brain was getting fuzzier by the second. The last thing I remember was Cee saying, "I have an idea..."

Then suddenly, I was in a forest. The trees were dead, their branches dry and close together. The light was dim and shadowy, and there was complete silence all around me. I was scared. "Cee!" I whispered. "Where are you?!"

"I'm here…" His voice sounded faint and far away. "Help me…"

I started running through the rows of trees, feeling the brittle branches snap and cut my skin as I charged through them in a panic. "Where?!" I called. "I can't see you!"

"Dee…" his voice was no nearer. "Dee, I need you…"

The branches flayed my skin as I kept running. Where was he? All I knew was that he needed me and I couldn't reach him. The tears streamed down my face and I felt a terrible sense of helplessness. Then I saw a figure up ahead, a clumsy, dirty figure, and I knew that this wasn't a dream, or a hallucination—this was a memory, an awful memory.

Cee and I had been on our own for over a week. We'd left the workhouse for good, in the middle of the night, and began making our way south, towards the tent cities, where we would be just another couple of faceless, nameless kids, and we could start a new life for ourselves. We'd stolen some food from the kitchen before we left, but our supplies were getting low. We'd hit the dead forest the day before, and moved in a straight line, continually checking the sun's position and hoping that we were maintaining a southerly path. The first night was cold; despite the heat from the sun during the day, the trees had grown tightly together, blocking most of the light and the warmth. Once the sun went down, any remaining heat vanished. We had flint, but we were afraid to make a fire out in the open in case we attracted attention, or burned the whole dead forest down. So we shivered together for hours under our thin blankets, unable to sleep, listening to the night sounds of small creatures scrabbling in the undergrowth, until morning came and enough sunlight filtered through the trees to make walking bearable. By the second night, we were exhausted and just about done in when we came across a small rise. There was a cave in the little hill, big enough for us and our packs to squeeze into, and the rocks had absorbed the day's heat, making it more comfortable than being out in the open. Cee gathered some twigs and sticks; we made a small fire just inside the opening, and that was luxury compared to the night before. After some water and dried meat and fruit, we both fell into a deep sleep. The next morning, I was feeling so much better, and definitely up to exploring. Maybe those night sounds we'd been hearing were edible, some type of small animal good enough for cooking.

Cee was doubtful. "It could be dangerous," he had said. "We should stay together."

"All we've seen for the last two days is dead trees," I reassured him. "There's nothing out there. I was thinking that if I made a little box out of twigs, I could prop it up with a stick, attach one of the pack ties to the prop, and put a piece of dried meat under the box. If I wait quietly, maybe something will come, and I can pull the tie and drop the box on it. We could have a feast!"

"A feast of rats? Yum," he said sarcastically. "Seriously, I should go with you."

"No way," I said. "You need to stay here and keep the fire going. Nobody likes raw rat."

He finally agreed, and we spent the morning making a small box, him gathering the twigs, and me weaving them together. It wasn't pretty but it looked like it would do the job, so I set off. I could feel his worry in my head, but I kept sending back the sensation of calm, as well as a healthy dose of "full stomach" until I could sense him relaxing.

I set up my contraption on one side of a group of closely knit trees, then lay on the other side on my stomach and waited. And waited. Eventually, the sun started to go down. It was getting cold, and I was getting increasingly angrier with myself for being so naïve to possibly think I could catch a woodland creature of any type. The most I was going to catch was a cold. I stood up, shivering, stiff and exasperated, and began walking back in the direction of the cave, carrying my stupid stick box — at least we could burn it. That was when I heard Cee's voice. But the voice wasn't out loud — it was in my head. It wasn't just a sensation or an emotion — I could actually hear his voice, something that had never happened before. And he sounded terrified.

"Dee…Help me!"

"Cee!" I whispered back in my head. *"Where are you?!"*

"I'm here…" His voice sounded faint and far away. *"Help me…"*

Just like my dream that wasn't a dream, I started running through the rows of trees, feeling the brittle branches snap and cut my skin as I charged through them in a panic. *"Where?!"* I called out with my mind. *"I can't see you!"*

"Dee…" his voice was no nearer. *"Dee, I need you…"*

The branches flayed my skin as I kept running. Where was he? All I knew was that he needed me and I couldn't reach him. The tears streamed down my face and I felt a terrible sense of helplessness. The ground beneath my feet had started vibrating like some kind of strange earthquake, making it difficult to move forward. Then I saw a figure up ahead, a clumsy, dirty figure — it was a Frag scavenger. And if there was one, there were certain to be more. It hadn't noticed me yet, and I stopped dead, looking around in dismay for somewhere to hide while I figured out what to do. I slid silently behind the nearest tree and peeked out.

I could still hear Cee faintly in my head. Why wasn't he getting louder? I was frightened, but I tried to reach out to him and let him know I was coming. Then his voice suddenly screamed, the sound bouncing around in my skull, "*NO!! Stay away!!*" That was when I knew he was in serious trouble. But there was no way I was staying away.

The Frag up ahead must be a scout, I thought. Not a very good one, since it wasn't paying any attention to anything, just standing there with its back to me, trying to keep its balance as the forest floor rumbled and shifted, smoking a dirty cheroot. I could smell the tar and creosote, and it was so strong that I knew the Frag couldn't smell *me*. I looked around me for something to use. I could see the outline of a rock buried in the soil at the base of the tree, and I bent down quietly, using my fingernails to pry it out of the earth, never taking my eyes off the Frag. The rock came free and I waited for my chance. The Frag took one last pull on the cheroot, then threw it onto the forest floor. As it ground the glowing end out with its heel, I made my move.

I hadn't intended to hit it hard enough to kill it; I just wanted to knock it out. But when I brought the rock down onto the back of its head, it grunted, then crumpled into a heap and lay still. It wasn't breathing and I was overwhelmed with shame. For all my talk of a rat feast, I'd never killed anything before, and if I *had* caught a rat, I honestly wouldn't have known what to do with it. And now...

My breath caught in my throat as I looked down on the Frag. It was young, or at least not much older than me, but with the wispy hair, ulcerated skin, and missing teeth that come with radiation exposure. Its clothes were filthy rags and it looked like it hadn't eaten for a long time. Then I noticed that its remaining teeth were sharp; I remembered the stories that the Guardians used to tell us in the workhouse to scare us about Frags coming to eat us, and my blood froze. All I had was a rock and a box made out of sticks—how could I protect Cee?! Maybe the Frag had something, some kind of weapon I could use. The thought of getting closer to it made me sick to my stomach, but I knelt down and rummaged through its clothes. Hidden in the folds of its torn cloak was a knife — the edges were rusty, but the point looked sharp enough to do some damage, or at least threaten to.

I took off running towards the cave, too focused to feel my skin tearing against the low hanging branches in my path. Finally, I could see the rise where the cave was and stopped, straining to listen for Cee above the sound of my own breathing.

All I could sense was fear, but I didn't send back anything — the one thing I had going for me in this situation was the element of surprise. There was only enough room in the cave for Cee and one, or at the most, two Frags, and my only hope was that I could drop one of them before they could gang up on me. Then it would be Cee and me against the other one. I snuck up to the entrance of the cave and peered around the edge. Cee was at the back, huddled against the wall, and there were two Frags, one standing and one squatting. The one standing was laughing and saying something to the other one in a low, guttural voice. I didn't understand what it was saying, but from the way the other one stared at Cee and licked its lips, I could guess. I steeled myself, then sprang into the cave, knife out, and plunged it as hard as I could into the standing Frag's back. It fell to the ground, writhing, and the other Frag looked up at me in surprise.

"Cee!" I yelled out loud, as it began to rise, and with that, Cee jumped to his feet and tackled it, slamming its head against the floor of the cave. It lay there, still, and we waited, unsure of what to do for a minute. The other Frag's moaning and struggling began to subside, and after a few minutes, it was still as well. The vibrations beneath our feet stopped suddenly too, and everything was quiet.

"We need to go," I said, not looking at Cee.

"There might be another one out there somewhere. What if it's on its way back?"

"I took care of it," I said quietly. I could feel Cee looking at me questioningly, but he sensed the shame and revulsion I felt and said nothing in response.

"They—they were going to eat me." His voice shook.

"Not anymore," I answered, trying to control the tremor in my own voice. Then we packed up and left the cave.

The memory began to fade, and my mind started to get fuzzy again. Why was I thinking about this right now? For the next little while, I drifted in and out of sleep. After some time had passed, I wasn't sure how long, I woke up to the sound of low voices in conversation.

"What's going on?" I muttered.

"Nothing to worry about," I heard Cee reply with false cheer. "I just came to get my tools."

Rogan's voice interrupted angrily. "I'm telling you for the last time, you're *not* selling your tools. If you do that, how will you be able to support Dee? She won't be able to go thieving until she's well again, and your carvings are the only way you can make money for food. I told you, let me take care of it. It's my fault this happened, so I'll be the one to fix it!"

With that, I heard the tent flap open, and Rogan was gone.

12

Cee

After Rogan stormed out of the tent, I went over to the chair in the corner and slumped down into it. Dee lay there, quiet for a moment, and I wasn't sure if she was awake or if the TastiRum was still affecting her. I was exhausted. It was hard enough trying to control my own emotions, my fear and anger over what was happening to Dee, but her own anguish was always in my head, drowning out my thoughts and making everything twice as hard to manage. I sat there for a while, eyes closed, when Dee finally spoke.

"What did Rogan mean? About fixing things?" she asked. There was a tremor in her voice and her words were slurred.

I couldn't tell her the truth. If she knew what he was planning, it would send her over the edge. She'd probably leap out of the cot and try to stop him, killing herself in the process. It was almost more than I could bear, but I put up a block, a mental wall, so that she couldn't sense that I was lying to her. I'd learned to do that a long time ago. It was difficult, and it took a lot of mental strength to create a barrier that she couldn't tell was there. The best way to describe it was like a screen that came down between what I was thinking and what I wanted her to *think* that I was thinking. The only way to do that was to project images onto the screen, memories or thoughts which seemed calm and normal, while behind the screen, chaos reigned. She didn't know that I could do that, and I was pretty positive that, aside from that time in the Shed long ago, she couldn't do it herself—her mind was pretty much an open book to me, and it was a beautiful mind, full of plans and purpose, as brilliant as a sunrise on a clear morning. I opened my eyes.

"You know he feels responsible for what happened to you. He's gone to Auntie May to see if she can loan him some coins."

"Auntie May?" Dee sounded doubtful.

"Yes. The Doc said she might have something tucked away, and that I could always work it off in repayment. You know—working in her stall, doing extra carvings for her to sell," I assured her, my voice full of mock-optimism. Luckily, Dee was so hopped up on TastiRum and Lullybies that she didn't notice that there was a tremor in *my* voice too.

"Tell Rogan to be careful. I don't want him to get into trouble on my account," she said, sounding blurry and unfocused.

I pushed myself up and out of the chair and went to stand by her bedside. She was flushed, and her eyes were bright. I stroked her forehead. "Don't worry. It's only Auntie May. I'll make sure nothing happens to him. Sarah is going to sit with you now. I'll be back soon with the medicine." I leaned over and kissed her cheek. She sighed, closed her eyes, and slid back into her dreamworld.

I left the tent, my heart hurting as I took one more glance backwards at her.

Sarah was waiting outside. "You can't do this—" she started, but I put my finger to my lips to quiet her and pulled her away from the tent.

"I have to," I whispered. "There's no other way."

"But you've never been thieving before! It's danger-ous! Look what happened to Dee!" She was having trouble keeping her voice down. "You could get a loan from the Caseeno Boys—"

"And owe them for the rest of our lives?! No. This is the best thing to do. Besides, Rogan's one of the best. He can steal in his sleep, everybody knows that. I'll be fine. Just watch Dee for me—I have to go."

With that, her eyes filled with tears and she threw her arms around me. "Be careful," she whispered, then let go of me and rushed in to Dee without another look. I walked up the row of tents to the corner where Rogan and I had agreed to meet. Rogan was waiting, a grin on his face.

"What was that all about?" he asked. "It looks like someone is sweet on you."

"Shut your stupid mouth," I answered angrily, not in the mood for his teasing. "All you need to worry about is the task at hand. We get the baubles, we sell them, and we go to Hasban for the medicine. I'm not interested in hav-ing a conversation with you about anything else. We're *not* friends. And once this is all over, you're going to stay away from Dee. For good!"

He looked shocked and dismayed. He started to say something, then thought better of it, and simply pointed. "This way."

The plan was a complicated one, and it had taken a while to convince Rogan that he needed me to come with him. At first, he was adamant that he would go it alone, that it was too risky to have someone like me along, someone who'd never thieved before. We sat in my tent, Little Jimmy and Nonny watching us, and argued for almost an hour, him convinced that I was a liability, me countering with his need to have a look-out if nothing else. I think we were both feeling guilty, and each of us was trying to prove something to the other.

Finally, Nonny broke in, her gray eyes blazing. "Enough! You're both wasting time with this posturing. Yes, Rogan is a master thief, and yes, Cee's inexperienced, but he's smart and quick. Face it — if you're going to do this, you need each other, so stop jawing and get to planning."

"What *she* said," Little Jimmy agreed quietly. That seemed to settle it.

There was a covered garden in an area called Liberty, about three clicks away, where the Fancies went to walk their little dogs up and down the rows of flowers, be seen in their best clothes, and of course, show off their best baubles. Even the dogs had bejewelled collars, gem-studded leashes, and golden bracelets around their legs. Today happened to be Promenade Day, which is what they called it. The area was heavily guarded by the Blues, and while it would be suicide to attack a Fancy under the circumstances, it wouldn't be hard to run off with one of the dogs. What Blue would chase a couple of Freeworlders all the way into Divinity for a dog? The Blues were notoriously lazy when it came to running after thieves — they preferred to send the Lobots, and with two of us, we could easily distract one, grab it from behind, and smash it to pieces before it could sound an alarm. Then it was just a case of pulling the jewels off the collar or what have you, and selling them. Rogan had an idea that we could sell the dog to the butcher in the Hidden Market as well, although the thought of that made me feel uncomfortable.

"But how do we get all the way to Liberty without being seen?" I'd asked Rogan, once he'd finally resigned himself to the fact that I was coming with him, like it or not. Liberty was east of Old K, and unlike Old K, where the buildings formed a maze of giant ghostly sentinels that offered fair protection against both Blues and Lobots, it was mostly all open territory between Divinity and the gardens, a kind of no-man's-land with few places to hide and a lot of Blue patrols.

"Easy," replied Rogan. "We use the tunnels."

"Tunnels?!" I exclaimed. "What are you talking about?"

"There are tunnels under the entire territory," Rogan explained. "Old Mac says there used to be trains that could take people from one end of the old city all the way out to the Badlands, all underground. Millions of people lived in the Badlands before the Frag Wars, in beautiful houses with grass and flowers and parks — just regular people, not even Fancies. There are still places where you can get down into the tunnels if you know where to look, and I know."

"Fine," I said. "Which way do we go then?" I just wanted to get this over with as soon as possible. I had to admit that I was nervous, and if I allowed myself to think about Dee, my worry was overwhelming. I pushed the thought of her out of my mind — I needed to concentrate now more than ever.

"Do you have the knife?" Rogan asked.

I pulled a carving tool out of my backpack and shoved it at him. "You take it," I said brusquely. "I have no plans to use it for anything but carving."

"It's just a precaution," Rogan said reassuringly, putting the carving tool into the canvas pack that he wore on his back. "Just to scare them if they won't give us the dog."

I didn't answer him. I'd made a vow a long time ago that I would never use my hands for harm again. And if we did get a dog, I wouldn't let Rogan sell it to the butcher — I was keeping it, even if it wasn't what I thought a proper dog should be.

We continued on in silence through the rows of tents, down the main thoroughfare, and out towards the ruined castle until there were no more tents, just broken concrete, piles of brick from buildings shattered by sonic bombs, and overgrown weeds.

"Why are we going this way?" I asked him, concerned. "Liberty is three clicks east of here, and we're moving farther away from it."

"We have to go to Museum," he said. "That's where the tunnel entrance is."

"The tunnel entrance is in a museum?" I'd heard some of the elders talking one day about a museum that used to be in the centre of the old city, a place that housed wonders, things you'd only dream about, like the bones of ancient creatures, and the golden coffins of a race long gone. To explore the museum would be truly breathtaking—think of the carvings I could do after having seen marvels like that!

"No," Rogan said wistfully. "I wish. It just says 'Museum' on the wall down below. It's the closest place to access the tunnel system. Then we have to follow the tunnels to a place called College—it's the nearest exit point to The Promenade, about half a click away."

"So how do we get from this 'College' to the gardens without being seen?" I asked him. "Won't it be crawling with Blues?"

"Not so much on this side of the gardens," Rogan replied, taking the pack off his back and rummaging around in it. "But just in case—here." He pulled out a wadded-up bundle of blue cloth and held it out to me. "This should do the trick."

I shook the bundle open. "This looks like a Blue coverall," I said. "Where did you get it?"

Rogan laughed. "Here's the matching hat." He held out a peaked cap to me, then opened his bag wider to show me another coverall and hat. "Don't worry—I borrowed them from a friend. If anybody sees us, they'll think we're Blues on a break."

"These uniforms look real," I said suspiciously, shoving mine into my backpack.

"Real enough," he replied. "Don't put it on until we get down to College."

We kept walking for another fifteen minutes or so, when Rogan stopped suddenly and pointed to a low mound of shattered bricks, pieces of wood, and other garbage. "There it is."

"There *what* is?" I asked. "All I see is yet another pile of rubble with wooden pallets stacked up against it."

Rogan didn't answer, but went over to the pallets. With one smooth move, he slid them aside. They seemed to be joined together somehow, but instead of being an obstacle, they were mounted on a hidden track that let a person shift them quite easily, like drawing back a curtain. Once they were no longer in the way, a small dark doorway was revealed. "This is Museum," he announced quietly.

13

Dee

I was dreaming again—or maybe hallucinating. Visions of Frags with their mouths wide open were replaced by the woman with the pale, golden-red hair then, just as quickly, she transformed into Ceridwen floating along the ground. Then I could see Trick, shivering on the Tower platform—I reached out my hand to pull him inside but he slipped off the edge and I cried out as I fell too, and everything dissolved again.

"Dee?" I heard an unfamiliar voice.

"I couldn't save him," I murmured. "I tried, but I couldn't reach. I can't see the ground."

"Hush," said the voice. "It's all right—you're safe here."

I half-opened my eyes, but the speaker was someone I didn't know. At least, I didn't think I knew her. She looked vaguely familiar—was she a hallucination, too? "Who are you?" I asked weakly.

She gave me a small smile and pulled the chair closer to the side of the cot. "It's Sarah," she answered. "Nonny's sister. Cee asked me to stay with you for a while."

"Cee? Where's Cee?! The Frags are coming — I need to help him!" I could hear my own voice rising hysterically. Were there Frags? I suddenly couldn't remember. I started struggling to sit up, but the girl, Sarah, stood and put her hand on mine.

"Lie still, Dee. Be calm. Cee is fine — he's just outside. He'll — he'll come in a minute. While we're waiting for him, do you want me to tell you a story?"

"A story," I breathed. A story would be a good thing right now, anything to distract from the irrational fear I was experiencing. The Doc had given me the last of the antibiotics he had, which was keeping the fever from spiking too high, but it was still like I had two minds in my head — one was the normal me that knew I was delirious, and the other was the feverish me, the one that was convinced there was some unknown danger coming.

"OK," Sarah hesitated. "My mother used to tell us stories all the time when we were little. Let's see..."

"Your mother?" I asked in surprise. "You knew your mother?"

"Well, yes," she answered. "Nonny and I didn't grow up in a workhouse. We're from the Lake District south of here, near the big Falls. We only came to Divinity about five years ago. We barely knew our father — he died when I was around two. But then our mother — well, anyway, Gran took us in for a while, except she passed too, so we had no choice. Divinity was the closest tent city, and Nonny and I had no intention of becoming agri-slaves OR going to the Sex House."

"Wait — you knew your grandmother as well?!" I was amazed. It was rare enough to meet anyone close to my age who had known either of their parents, let alone their grandparents.

"Yes," she smiled in fond remembrance. "She was lovely. She did her best with us after Mom, but she was old, and weak from radiation. She'd lived near the border all her life, and that area got hit pretty hard by Dazzlers during the Frag Wars. When she died, Nonny and I had nobody but each other, and it was too dangerous to stay on our own."

"I'm so sorry. But what happened to your mother?" I asked, my natural curiosity getting the better of me. But I quickly added, "You don't have to tell me if you don't want to."

"Oh no, that's OK," Sarah said. "It was a long time ago. Pretty typical story. After The Consortium beat back the Frags, the Lake District, being so far from away from Metro, carried on pretty well as normal for a long time. It was always a tourist area, with artisans and merchants selling goods to people from the cities. Mom had a small store in the town where she made candles, perfumed oils, things like that. We had a garden at home with a greenhouse, and she grew all kinds of flowers and herbs — I can see her now, with a basket, picking out the best blooms for her next concoction. The kitchen always smelled like lavender...anyway, The Consortium left things alone in the outskirts for years, long enough that people forgot about the deal that Adanac had made in exchange for winning the war. Eventually though, The Consortium started making demands, insisting that the merchants sell their businesses to the Fancies who were government favourites. The Lake District held a meeting, and they sent a statement to The Consortium that they were refusing the offer. Well, you can imagine how The Consortium reacted to that. One day, they came, squadrons of Blues with their laser rifles and flash bombs. Before anyone could do anything, they'd garrisoned the town and rounded up the merchants. They were taking over all the shops by force, you see. Nonny and I were at school, and when the teachers heard what was happening, they sent us home. Mom had been saying for months that if The Consortium came, we should pack up what we could carry and run to Gran's. So that's what we did. It took us a long time to get there because we had to keep hiding from The Consortium cavalcades going back and forth on the road."

"But what did they do with the storeowners?" I asked, almost not wanting to know the answer.

"They loaded them up into solar trucks, drove them to the Falls, and threw them all down into the water," she said matter-of-factly. "I guess they wanted to make an example of them."

"That's awful," I said. "I didn't know The Consortium had done that. They don't tell us anything about history at the workhouse."

"Yes," she replied. "As we ran home from school, I could see them all gathered in the town square. The man directing the action was tall, with dead eyes and a nose that looked like it had been broken more than once. I'll know him if I ever see him again. And *he'll* know me." She paused for a moment. I didn't know what to say, and my head was starting to feel fuzzy again. Finally, she spoke. "When I think of my mother, I picture her in the garden, gathering flowers. It helps."

"I never knew my mother," I said. "She abandoned us at a workhouse when we were babies. I—" Suddenly a wave of pain came over me and I groaned. My head was spinning and starting to fill up with flashes of faces and sharp teeth again.

"Easy," Sarah said, concerned. "Enough of this morbid talk. I didn't mean to upset you. Now, you said you didn't learn anything about history at the workhouse. I have a story you might like from the old times. Gran used to tell it because the hero came from the Lake District, a woman who risked her life, travelling through the forest to save the country...."

Sarah began talking. It was nice lying there, listening to the quiet, soothing sound of her voice. The story was a good one. Two olden days armies: one protecting Adanac, the other trying to take it for their own, and the woman who overheard plans of an ambush and then walked 20 clicks to warn of the attack. I drifted in and out, absorbing the details: how she left her children behind, knowing that if anything happened to her, they might perish, how she was helped by a group of noble people called the Mohawks, until finally she reached the camp and told the soldiers what she knew. After a while, listening turned into dreaming, and the woman in the story appeared. She had pale, golden-red hair, and she was carrying a basket of flowers. She turned to me and smiled, then she said, "Don't worry. We're going to win."

"Win what?" I tried to answer, but the words wouldn't come out. She started walking away. "Wait!" I screamed soundlessly, struggling to make myself heard. She turned back for a moment, and I saw that her eyes were filled with tears.

"I'll come back for you, I promise," she whispered, then turned away again. The flowers in the basket started to shrivel up and turn black. As she walked away, the charred petals floated towards me like a dark cloud, getting thicker and thicker, until I couldn't see her anymore. Lightning flashed and terror filled my head like the sound of flies buzzing, getting louder and louder.

"Wait!" I tried to scream one last time, and finally the sound came out. Sarah leaped up. At the same moment, the tent flap was thrown back. The Doc came striding in and moved swiftly to the bed. He was carrying a bottle of pills. Rogan followed close behind him, holding a small dog and looking ashen. Why was he carrying a dog? Was I hallucinating again? The Doc shook some pills out of the bottle and said, "Here. These are what you need. Take them right away." I took them from him and swallowed them down without questioning, then looked back and forth between him and Rogan in bewilderment and fear.

"Where's Cee?" I demanded, the terror in my head growing louder. The Doc didn't say anything. Rogan stared at the ground. "WHERE'S CEE?!" I shrieked. And then I knew why I was terrified.

14

Cee

With one last look around to make sure we weren't being watched, Rogan and I quickly ducked through the opening behind the pallets. The heat of the day swiftly dissipated and we were swallowed by the shadowy gloom as Rogan pulled the fake pallet wall closed behind us. I waited for my eyes to adjust to the strange surroundings. The air was thick and stale. Finally, with the help of the dim light winking through cracks in the pallet wall, I could see that we were standing at the top of a flight of stairs leading down into darkness. Rogan moved beside me and reached into his pack, removing a solar lantern.

"This has enough charge for the trip," he whispered, turning it on. The glow of the lantern reached down to reveal the bottom of the stairs, and a patterned floor beyond it.

"Why are we whispering?" I asked. It seemed unlikely that anyone could hear us from the street.

"I don't know," Rogan laughed nervously, then said in a normal voice, "I always get a little spooked when I'm in the tunnels. I've never seen anything except the occasional rat, but there are stories—"

"Save your stories for later," I interrupted harshly. "We don't have time."

"Right," he answered. He held the lantern out in front of him and grabbed the metal handrail attached to the wall with the other. "Be careful on the stairs — some of them are crumbly." Without a backwards glance, he started to go down, picking his way carefully to avoid any sections that were damaged. I took hold of the railing and followed his path.

When we got to the bottom, I looked around. It was dark but I could tell that I was in an open area, littered with paper and other garbage. Rogan swung the lantern around, looking for something, and I could see a glassed-in booth and barricades.

"This way," Rogan directed. He climbed over one of the barricades and moved towards another flight of stairs.

"How far down are we going?" I asked. I'd never been underground at all, and I was feeling a little claustrophobic.

"Maybe about 20 metres?" Rogan shrugged his shoulders. "Not really sure. It's just down one more set of stairs, then we'll be at the tunnels. Come on."

When we got down the second set of stairs, which were metal, ridged and uneven, my jaw dropped. We were standing on a long platform, with columns rising to the ceiling that were carved into fantastical shapes — animals, strange-looking humans, and some decorated with symbols. On the wall in tiled yellow letters four feet high was the word 'MUSEUM'.

"What *is* this place?" I breathed.

"People used to wait here for the trains. I don't know what the carvings are for. Maybe from the ancient peoples, but whoever made them is long gone now. We need to go down onto the tracks." He moved to the edge of the platform and then leapt into a dirty crevasse with metal rails leading off into the darkness of the tunnel.

I made a mental note of the columns and the figures on them. If I could replicate some of them later, I could earn quite a few coins. I jumped down after Rogan, giving the columns one last look before we entered the tunnel.

We walked in silence for a long time. There was no noise except for the sound of our feet kicking up dust and the scrabbling of what I could only assume were rats. I wondered if this was where the meat at Blawblaw's came from — it certainly seemed like it would be the perfect hunting ground for their Friday Night Special. It felt like we'd been walking for hours, but finally Rogan stopped.

"There's a tunnel that branches off coming up soon. The track will split into sections," he said. "Keep your eyes open for it — we need to go east."

Sure enough, in a few minutes, we came to the junction. As we got closer to the point where the tracks divided, I gasped. "What is *that*?" I exclaimed. It looked like metal containers joined together on wheels, just sitting there up ahead.

"That?" Rogan laughed. "That's one of the trains. Do you want to see? It won't take a minute."

Even though I knew we were on a tight schedule, I couldn't resist. "Maybe for a minute then…"

Rogan laughed excitedly and started jogging at a brisk pace. "Just wait — it'll be worth it," he called over his shoulder, as he ran down the length of the containers to the front, me following close behind.

We slipped through the gap between two doors leading into the train. I followed him up to the front, where we entered the cab where the driver must have sat. It reminded me of the solar trams that the Fancies use to bring them into town from the Quay. A lot of the Fancies live on The Island and come across the lake when they want to shop in Liberty or the Hidden Market, or to get medical treatments — both necessary and cosmetic. The latest fad, so Dee told me, was to have their eyelids surgically altered to look like the bigwigs in The Consortium. Most of the higher-ups were from mainland Chin and Jan, and there were pictures of the Founders in the books we had to read in the workhouse, men and women with almond-shaped eyes that the Fancies were desperate to emulate. But unlike the solar trams that brought the Fancies, which were luxurious with velvet seats and the finest food and drinks, this train was dirty and broken down. The red seat covers were ripped, and the metal bars were rusted.

Rogan pointed to a console with what looked like a hundred buttons on it. "Listen to this," he said eagerly, and pushed one.

Suddenly a crackling noise filled the air, and a woman's voice echoed, "Please st...clear...doors."

I jumped at the sudden sound. "What was that?!"

"I don't know," he said. "She says all kinds of things, things about stations and the names of the access points. I wish the trains still worked, but they ran on hydrocells, and the rails are broken in a lot of places. There's a little juice left, enough to make her talk, but not enough to run the trains. Sometimes I think about all the people who used to ride these trains every day, before the wars, coming in from the Badlands to work in the core, and what their lives must have been like, not having to steal or eat 'stew', seeing snow every year, actually having families to go home to."

"Yeah," I agreed. "I wish I could see snow. Old Mac remembers it, says it was beautiful."

We stood, lost in thought for a moment, then I remembered abruptly what we had come down here for, and that Rogan wasn't my friend. "We're wasting time," I said roughly, and strode out of the cab, down the aisle, and back onto the tracks. "Which way?"

Rogan must have sensed my anger—he simply pointed and started walking. We continued on, coming to another junction and turning south. We passed a platform but he didn't stop. After another half-click, we came to a second platform. This time, he put his hands on the edge, and hoisted himself up. I followed suit. The sign on the wall said "College". This access point wasn't as ornate as Museum, but there were faded paintings on the wall of figures in uniforms, holding sticks and wearing shoes with what looked like knives on them.

Rogan saw me staring as we walked by and said, "There used to be a game that was played on ice, with sticks."

"Ice?" I echoed in disbelief. "I would have liked to see that as much as snow." I filed the images on the wall away with the ones I had seen in Museum. I had a lot of work to do when we got back, but I could carve in the tent while Dee got better.

"It's time," said Rogan. "Put on the coveralls and hat. If no one sees us up close, we'll be okay. Then we can get near enough to the gardens to snatch a dog."

We got dressed in silence. My coverall was a bit big, so I rolled up the sleeves and pant legs, hoping that if I was seen from a distance, I wouldn't look too strange. I was starting to get really nervous, and Rogan didn't look at ease either. We climbed the stairs up from the platform to another area, similar to the previous access point with a glassed-in booth and barricades. Another flight of stairs, and we were at the top. This time, instead of pallets and a pile of rubble, there was what looked like a solid metal wall at the top of the stairs.

"How do we get out?" I asked.

"Look closer," Rogan replied, holding the lantern up to the wall. In its light, I could see seams, and a flat bar that looked like it might be a handle. Rogan turned the lantern off and put it in his pack. As the light faded, I saw him grab the bar and tug. A door-sized rectangle in the middle of the wall swung open a few inches. Rogan peeked out. "I don't see anyone. Let's go. Fast!"

We slid out onto the concrete walkway outside the door, and Rogan pushed it back in — once again it appeared to be solid. "We're about half a click away, so keep an eye out," he warned. "Let's aim for that building up ahead, then take it from there."

The building looked intact but abandoned. There was a faded sign hanging crookedly from the front that read "Intertransactions Here". It must have been one of the places where people could go to reload their wristwallets — banking chips embedded in their wrists — but now, only the Fancies had wristwallets, and they could reload them at home. The only people who used actual coins were the Freeworlders, or the Fancies when they came to the Hidden Market since none of us had what they called "Scanbank". Personally, I preferred the solidity of a coin to air money.

We scurried forward, heads swivelling in every direction, on the watch for Blues. We made it to the building without being seen. "What now?" I asked in a hushed voice.

"There's a row of old storefronts up ahead on the next block. We can skirt around them — it's not far now."

Again, we crept up quickly, bent over at the waist like we were running inside a low tunnel. There was still no sign of any Blues. We stopped and Rogan pointed at an ancient stone structure ahead with a pointed roof. "Last stop. Then it's time to act."

My stomach was doing flips as we continued forward. I was concentrating so hard on keeping up the mental wall between me and Dee that I almost ran into Rogan's back when he stopped suddenly. I looked past him — there were two Fancies, a man and a woman and their Blue guards up ahead, two Lobots whirring around them. "Act normal," he said. "Pretend we're just hanging out here, having a conversation."

"What the hell do we talk about?!" I hissed at him. "The weather?!"

"Wait — they're going the other way," he answered back. "Stop acting so nervous — we're almost there. It won't be long before we have the dog, the baubles, and the medicine. Keep focusing on *that*."

He moved forward, keeping a consistent distance between us and the group up ahead. Finally, they turned right, onto a path that led to a huge complex constructed of glass and metal. I could see dozens of sim-masked Fancies with their tiny dogs, the men with their shaved and tattooed heads and the women with outrageously coloured wigs, strutting around outside the main building and disappearing into it. The whole structure was surrounded by a large hedgerow, which seemed like the perfect place to hide and wait. Rogan and I tucked ourselves into a gap in the bushes, scrutinizing the crowd and waiting for the moment that one of them was separated off. Then a Fancy, a woman with bright blue hair and new trendy eyes, started walking towards our hiding spot. She was focused completely on a little white dog with a beautifully jewelled collar, speaking to it as you'd speak to a baby, bending over and giving it little morsels that she took from her purse, while the dog panted, spun in circles and leaped up for the treats. The Blue with her looked intensely bored and was more interested in the people going into the glass atrium than he was in what she was doing. She was moving closer and closer to us. Suddenly, without warning, Rogan stepped out of the bush, ripped the diamond-studded leash from her hand, and scooped up the dog. The Fancy shrieked, the dog started barking a shrill, high-pitched bark, and the Blue guard turned to see what the commotion was about.

"Run!" shouted Rogan, tucking the dog under his arm and pushing past me through the hedgerow to the other side. I turned to follow him, but my right foot got tangled in the pant leg of the coverall, which had somehow unrolled on the way here without me noticing it. I took two steps, then fell onto the concrete, my feet still in the hedgerow. I felt something clamp onto my ankle. Rogan turned and saw me — he hesitated and started to turn back.

"No!" I screamed at him. "Keep going! Leave me!" He gave me one last agonized look, then ran down the street towards the access point, the tiny dog squirming and squealing under his arm. The clamp on my ankle grew excruciatingly tighter as I was yanked to my knees by my hair. A rough voice said, "Gotcha, you piece of Freeworld shit," and a hand slapped me hard across the ear. A hood was thrown over my head, and I felt a pinch as the Lobot attached to my ankle injected me with its tranquilizer dart. The wall in my mind between me and Dee crumbled and fell, then the world went black.

15

Dee

I looked wildly around the tent. "Where's Cee?!" I shrieked again. "What's happened to him?!" I struggled to push myself up to a sitting position on the cot. I could hear rain outside, hammering against the tent in the empty vacuum of silence after my screams.

Rogan shuffled his feet, looking like he was about to cry. The dog he was holding under his arm starting squirming and broke free of his grasp. It launched itself onto the floor and ran under the chair in the corner, where it whimpered and shivered.

"Dee, I—" Rogan began, but The Doc interrupted.

"You need to calm down and listen," he ordered in a gruff voice. "Stay still before you hurt yourself."

"Just tell me what's going on!" I cried. "I know something's wrong. He was scared and in pain, but now I can barely feel him." I started sobbing.

"He was captured by the Blues," Rogan said quietly, looking down at the floor. I stared at him in disbelief. "I didn't—I didn't want him to come with me," he stammered. "I told him 'No', but he wouldn't listen."

"Come with you where?!" I asked. "You were at Auntie May's—how did the Blues get him there?!" None of this was making any sense. If the Blues were in Divinity, then we were *all* in danger—we should be running, not just sitting here.

"Auntie May's?" Rogan looked confused. "That's what he told you," he muttered under his breath, then said out loud, "No, I went thieving to get money for the medicine you need. I told him not to come, that it was dangerous, but he insisted. He was only supposed to be the lookout...."

"Why are *you* here, then?" I demanded. "Why weren't you captured too?!"

"I turned back to help him, but he told me to run. I had to get you the medicine, you understand, Dee? I didn't want to leave him there, but I had no choice!" Rogan's voice was full of anguish. "But he was alive when I ran, and I'm sure he still is. The Lobot probably stuck him with some knockout drugs."

I'd stopped sobbing, and now I looked at Rogan coldly. "And what happens when he wakes up, Rogan? Do you think they'll just let him come waltzing back to us? How could you, Rogan? You know he's no thief."

"Don't blame Rogan," interjected The Doc. "We all tried to talk Cee out of this. It was no use. He's as stubborn as you are, in his own way."

"What?!" I was furious. "You mean you *all* knew about this and no one told me? That's it—I'm going to get him." Despite the pain, I jumped up from the cot. I took two steps, and then the world started to go fuzzy. I grabbed wildly at the chair next to the cot but missed, and The Doc caught me before I hit the ground.

"You're not going anywhere. Not for a couple of days, at least. Now lie back down and be sensible. We don't even know where Cee is right now."

"Then we need to find out," I said flatly. The world had stopped spinning, but I'd realized that The Doc was right—I would be no use to Cee in this condition. I needed information, and I needed to think. "Rogan, get Ceridwen. She might know something. And tell Auntie May what happened."

"Done and done," he replied. "She's already sent Ceridwen out to see if her contacts at the Sex House and Caseeno know anything. She'll come back when she has information. And then we'll have to decipher her riddles." He sighed.

"Cee is the only one who truly understands her," I said. "Ironic." My eyes were starting to get heavy, and the pain in my back was throbbing in time with my heartbeat. I groaned involuntarily, and The Doc looked concerned.

"It'll take a couple of doses before the Mersa meds start to kick in. Meanwhile you need to rest."

I laughed derisively. "Rest? How am I supposed to do that, with everything that's going on?" Yet, despite myself, I felt my eyelids getting even heavier. I heard The Doc say, "Maybe because I slipped a sleeping pill in with the meds," and then everything went dark.

I flickered in and out of consciousness for the next while. I don't know for how long, but I measured it by the number of times I asked, "Is Ceridwen here yet?" And each time, the answer was "No". Whenever I woke, The Doc was there to give me another dose. The pain was starting to ease, and I no longer felt feverish, just exhausted. The fact that my sleep wasn't restful didn't help—I kept having terrible dreams: Cee in the cave with the Frags, Cee being beaten by Blues, Cee falling off the platform just like my dream about Trick. I still couldn't hear him in my head, and it terrified me. I had to hold on to the hope that Rogan had offered, that Cee was simply unconscious. I'd heard stories about the potency of the Lobot's stinging tranquilizer darts, and I was glad if that was the case. The longer Cee was asleep, the less time he would have to suffer until we could get to him. "How" was another story, of course. Finally, I woke up completely for the first time in ages and felt a little more clear-headed. I could still hear the rain pounding outside, one of the tropical winter storms that we got more and more often. *Was* it winter? It was hard to say, since everything was just hot, hotter, and excruciatingly hot in this part of the country. People said that winter used to be very cold, freezing even, but that was a long time ago. At the workhouse up north, it was easier to tell the seasons apart—the temperature got slightly lower towards the end of the monsoon season but stayed basically the same level of warmth the rest of the year, which made it the perfect place to grow crops. Down here, though, the only things that grew were the weeds, thanks to the hot rain and the even hotter sun that evaporated the rain.

As I lay there, I noticed that my back had stopped burning—it still felt bruised and swollen, but not on fire like it had before. I turned restlessly, then tried to sit up. As I did, I realized that Rogan was in the chair in the corner, the tiny dog curled up at his feet like a white ball of fluff. He rose, came over to the bed, and tucked some extra cushions behind my head.

"You're awake—how are you feeling?" he asked, concern in his eyes.

"Actually," I answered, "I'm starving." He went quickly to a cooler in the corner and pulled out a can.

"Think you can stomach a little stew?" He waved the can at me.

I grimaced. "Stew. Yuck. But I'm so hungry, I'm pretty sure I can choke it down." The little dog in the corner sat up and whimpered. "So what's the deal with the dog?" I asked.

Rogan looked embarrassed. "That's how I got you the medicine—I mean I sold the baubles on its leash and collar to pay for it. Don't worry about the dog. I'm taking it to the butcher later, and we can use the coins for something better than stew."

"No, you're not!" I exclaimed, so forcefully that Rogan took a step back and the dog scuttled under the chair in fear. "Cee's coming back, and he's always wanted a dog. We're keeping it!"

"Dee—" he started, but then thought better of it. "Fine. We're keeping the stupid thing."

"I'm glad that's settled. Now tell me the whole story. I can't believe your grand plan was to steal a dog."

"Well, why not?" Rogan answered, insulted. "It was an easy snatch. The Fancy's Blue didn't care about the dog. We would have been fine if Cee hadn't gotten his feet tangled up and fallen."

"Don't blame Cee for this. You knew he was too inexperienced to go out thieving."

"What did you want me to do?! Beat him senseless? Tie him up? Anyway, he was pretty good at sneaking—it was just bad luck...."

But I'd stopped listening to his protests for a minute. I was starting to feel something in my head, faintly at first, but growing louder. "Hush for a minute," I said. I focused on the feeling. "It's Cee!" I exclaimed, my heart racing. "I can feel him! He's scared—but...he's angry too! That's a good sign!" I smiled at Rogan with relief.

"I've never understood how the two of you do that," he said, shaking his head, "but I'm glad you can." He passed me a plate of 'stew' and I started shovelling it down. "Take it easy," he laughed. He took a small spoonful from the can and put it on the ground by the chair. The little dog's nose started to twitch. It looked cautiously at us, then crept out from under the chair and started licking the spoon. Rogan saw me staring at him. "What?" he said defensively. "If we're keeping it, we have to feed it."

We sat there a moment in silence. Suddenly, the solar lamp flickered, blinked out, then came back on. At the same time, the tent flap opened silently and Ceridwen swept in with the rain, Auntie May following close behind.

Ceridwen strode over and planted herself on the chair next to the cot. She drew back her hood, brushed a few tendrils of translucent hair from her cheek, and stared at me intently.

"Hail, brave friend," she said in her low, lyrical voice.

"Ceridwen," I breathed. "I'm so happy to see you. What news?"

"Lend thy serious hearing to what I shall unfold," she said, cryptic as always. "Your brother's death, I know, sits at your heart."

"But he's not dead, is he? I can feel him!" Against my will, tears began to form in my eyes under her steady gaze. "Tell me he's still alive!"

"I saw your brother, most provident in peril, bind himself to a strong mast that lived upon the sea where, like Arion on the dolphin's back, I saw him hold acquaintance with the waves."

"Cee is on a boat somewhere?! That doesn't make sense!" Rogan exclaimed. "I don't understand."

"Stop trying to take her literally," Auntie May said. "She speaks in symbols. 'Peril' means danger, but Cee is strong and can survive."

I sighed with relief. "He's alive! But where is he? Do you know?"

Ceridwen looked grim. "With a heavy heart, go I unto the Tower."

I gave a half-sob and put my head in my hands. "What will they do with him?" I cried. "Is he inside, or outside?" If he was inside, it was bad enough—letting the crowd decide what body part to take. But if he was outside...

"Upon the platform where we watched," Ceridwen said gravely.

Rogan slammed his fist into his hand and turned away. "But why? He was only caught stealing. And he didn't actually steal *anything*. The platform is for real criminals, for fights to the death—it's unprecedented!"

"The offence is not of such a bloody nature; only myself stood out, for which, I shall pay dear," Ceridwen intoned. Then she got up and stood by the door, like a ghostly sentinel. Auntie May took her place.

"What the girl means," she said, "is that The Consortium is sick of these brazen attacks. The Fancy, the one you stole the dog from, is the Mistress of one of the Second Founders. They're going to make an example of Cee, a demonstration of their power over the Freeworlders. Even though he didn't steal anything, he was there, and he was caught."

"But we can't just leave him there! And Trick, too— we have to do something. And I'm coming. No arguments." Nobody argued.

"I can't say too much right now," Auntie May said quietly, looking around at us. "But there is a plan. Cee is now part of that plan. And we'll need all the help we can get."

Ceridwen smiled a broad, beaming smile from the doorway. "Let's march without the noise of threatening drum."

"I assume from what she's saying that the plan involves a sneak attack?" Rogan asked, his back still to the room. "That's kind of my specialty—maybe I can help." At the sound of his voice, the little dog gave a tiny bark, and jumped up against his leg. He looked down and said, "Stop it, stupid dog. I don't have any more stew for you."

Ceridwen looked over at the dog in wonderment. Crossing the tent, she crouched down in front of it. "In peace and honour live Lord Titus long." She stroked the soft white fur on the dog's head—he stood up against her knees and licked her hand.

Rogan, Auntie May and I looked at each other. "Titus?" I said.

"I guess so," Rogan answered.

"It's a good enough name as any," Auntie May agreed. "Although I thought you were going to take him to the butcher—"

Suddenly she stopped when she saw me grow pale and my eyes widen. "What's wrong?!" she asked.

"I—I don't know. Cee was angry before, but now—now he's furious! I've never felt anything like this from him before!" And then the ground began to shake.

16

Cee

One minute, the world was dead. The next minute, I was
wide awake and shivering. I gasped, and took in a huge
lungful of air, then realized that I couldn't see anything—
everything was pitch black. I looked from one side to the
other and felt fabric rustle against my skin. There was a
hood over my head—why was I wearing a hood?! Then it
all started coming back to me—the Fancy, the dog, tripping
and landing hard on the concrete, the Lobot's sting—where
the hell was I? I could feel the cold curve of a wall against
my back, and a cold, smooth floor beneath me. My wrists
were in front of me on my lap, tightly encased in metal
cuffs. Then I didn't have to wonder where I was—I knew. I
was in The Tower.

    I stifled the panic rising in my mind, stilled my
breathing, and listened. I could hear the faint rumblings
of what I assumed was a generator, and muffled, faraway
voices. I strained to hear what they were saying, but I
couldn't make out anything except for a low murmur and
occasional laughter. The Tower. Strangely, I wasn't scared,
not yet. I was more angry—angry at Rogan for getting us

into this situation in the first place, but more angry at myself for being so clumsy and stupid. Rogan was right—I was no thief. If I'd stayed in the tent with Dee, carving, I would have been much more use to her than I was now. Now though, I was a liability. I'd heard stories about the way the Blues got prisoners to talk, and suddenly my stomach did a flip. Would they do that to me? Would I be able to hold out, or would I crumble and tell them everything, leading right to her and Rogan?!

I shivered again, this time not so much from the cold as from the fear I was beginning to finally feel. Then I heard a sound that was much closer—the distinctive click of a door being opened. The door closed again, and I heard heavy footsteps on the concrete, coming towards me. They stopped in front of me, and a low voice said, "Well, well. What do we have here?" He sounded young, and slightly amused. For some reason, while the voice was precise and formal, it seemed vaguely familiar, but I couldn't place it. Then the hood was snatched roughly off my head. I blinked hard against the sudden brightness—the person who spoke was in silhouette, backlit against the unobstructed light pouring in through the windows. Then he moved closer and came into view. I looked up and realized how I knew the speaker.

"Songe?" I asked, incredulous. He certainly bore a striking resemblance to the workhouse Guardian I used to know, the miserable piece of shit that had hurt Dee. But there was something strange about him. The last time I'd seen him, he'd been missing an eye. Yet now...

"Look at you," he said, smiling broadly at me, almost affectionately. "What *have* you gotten yourself into? You know, you were so out of it that I was worried you were going to slide right off the platform before we could have a chance to speak, so I had you brought in. Isn't that lucky?" His voice was a soft purr, but there was something hard beneath it, something malevolent.

I stared at him, and he stared back, with that same amused look on his face. Finally, he spoke. "It's been so long. The last time we met, I believe you had *me* at a disadvantage. We certainly do live in interesting times, do we not? I never thought I'd see you again, let alone under these circumstances." The casual tone of his voice contradicted his next action, which was to violently grab me by the collar and haul me up to my feet. He towered over me—I could feel his rapid breath on my face and his hands at my throat. I turned away from him. "Oh, don't look away," he said quietly, almost cajolingly.

I slowly faced him again and was struck with wonder. The eye that I'd taken in exchange for what he'd done to Dee was now back. There was still scarring on his cheek and around the socket from the laser pruner, but the eye... I looked closer and all at once, I understood.

"Isn't it remarkable?" he whispered, then threw me back down hard onto the floor.

I lay there in pain for a moment, but summoned what courage I had left. I had no interest in playing his games and said angrily, "Stop screwing around and just get it over with!"

He laughed, an expansive laugh that filled the room. "Get what over with?" he asked. "You don't really think I'm going to kill you, do you? Why would I do *that*? Trust me, I'm saving you for something much more special. And after all, if it wasn't for you, I wouldn't be where I am now. I'd just be another half-dead agri-slave instead of the Lieutenant-Governor. Do you want to know what happened?"

I sat up and pushed myself backwards across the floor into the corner of the room, him moving forward with me, and we stared at each other again.

He crouched down in front of me and said in a low voice, "It was a miracle." Then he stood up and walked over to a chair in the opposite corner. He pulled it into the middle of the room, then backed away closer to the door, leaning his shoulder against the doorjamb. "Come. Sit," he offered generously.

Using the walls for leverage, I slid up the corner until I was upright. I felt unsteady, and I stumbled as I walked towards the chair. His eyebrows shot up and he smirked, but I regained my balance and sat down slowly, cuffed wrists on my lap. I didn't say anything—I just waited as he examined his nails and picked invisible lint off his uniform. Finally, he spoke.

"As you know, after your little...outburst, I was unceremoniously packed off to the Breadbasket to finish my days as an agri-slave. Oh, I hated you for a long time. And why wouldn't I? You'd robbed me of my sight, but more importantly, my position, *and* my future. And now, what was my life? Up before the dawn, breathing in chemicals all day, working until the skin shredded from my fingers, coughing all night, continually defending myself against those who thought I was *weak*—but I always knew I was destined for great things. And one day it happened."

He paused and looked at me. "Oh, come on! Don't just sit there—participate!" There was a slightly maniacal edge to his voice and I realized that he just might kill me after all if I didn't play along.

"What happened?" I asked, trying to sound interested.

He beamed at me. "That's better. Well. One day, out of the blue, I was called into the Ag Office. I came in, all grubby from the field, skinny from the rotted food they gave us, and wheezing from the effort. I was brought to a room, a beautiful room with silk curtains and real leatherskin furniture, and told to help myself to the buffet that was laid out on a large, wooden table. I'd never seen so much food! I was in the process of stuffing myself with whatever I could before I was either killed or sent back to the fields, when a man walked in. Guess who he was?" He paused again.

Right on cue, I asked, "Who was he?"

Songe smiled. "Very good! You'll never believe it though—it was my father!"

"Your father? I didn't think you knew your father."

"Well, I didn't. But he knew *me*! Turns out, his efforts to have children over many, many years had been highly unsuccessful. Except for me. I was the only one. And what with him being a rather important Chin official with a lot of holdings and investments, it began to bother him that he had no one to pass his wisdom, and his vast wealth, over to. So he tracked me down—it wasn't hard because, thanks to you, I'd become quite...notorious. Then what do you think happened?" He paused again, waiting for me.

I was getting angry again, sick of the game, but I said, "What happened next?"

"After a quick DNA check, he whisked me away from the Breadbasket. Well, his servants did—I haven't seen him since. But it was truly wonderful. Not only did he completely rehabilitate me—lungscrape, genetic mods, education, elocution, but most importantly, a new eye. And not just any eye."

"Cybernetic?" I asked.

"Even better!" he exclaimed cheerfully, coming closer and leaning over me. He smiled, then looked down at my hands. Suddenly a narrow red beam of light shot out of his eye, hitting my thumb. The pain was intense, and I jumped and yelled.

He snickered and straightened up. Then his face grew dark. "Such a neat little tool," he said coldly. "So useful for so many occasions. I could actually cut your thumb right off if I really wanted to. All it takes is a few more seconds of concentrated photonic energy, and no more carving for you."

I must have looked shocked at how much he already knew about me because he smiled and waved his hand dismissively. "Don't be so surprised—I saw them bringing you in and I made...enquiries. By the way, how *is* your sister?" His smile faded. "There isn't a day goes by that I don't think about her."

With that, the anger that had been slowly simmering in me turned into outrage. "Don't you dare talk about my sister, you bastard!"

He smirked again. "Not a bastard any more, I'm afraid. In fact, because of my father, and this splendid new eye, I've risen up the ranks quite quickly. So not only will I be the one deciding what happens to you, I'll be seeing your sister very soon as well. I can't wait. I'm sure she's going to be thrilled to see me again too, and we can pick up where we left off. And I'll make sure you're still able to watch when I—"

"Shut UP!!" I screamed, and The Tower began to vibrate and sway. My head was filled with violence and I tried to stand up, but Songe pushed me back down into the chair. The rumbling intensified.

He looked around, intrigued. "Interesting. Maybe I'm not the only one with a special talent. Well, perhaps a few more days on the platform will cool you down."

With that, he grabbed the hood off the floor and shoved it down over my head. I felt his hands pull my wrists up, then I was being dragged across the room and out the door. My shoulders felt like they were being ripped from their sockets. I struggled and he kicked me viciously in the ribs, not saying anything. I heard another door open, and a cold wind hit me hard. Songe quickly took the cuffs off my wrists, then, using his foot, he rolled me through the doorway onto freezing cold metal. I could hear him laughing as he slammed the door shut behind me. All I could hear was the howling gale that whipped around my body, chilling me to the core. My fury grew, and the metal beneath me began to shake and buckle as I roared my rage into the cyclone.

"Stop!" a voice screamed. "Calm down!"

"Who's that?! Who's there?!" I shouted over the screeching of the wind. The hood was gently eased off my head. A small figure sat shivering in front of me, his dark hair disheveled and his clothing torn.

"It's me," he said. "Trick."

17

Dee

The rumbling finally stopped. Auntie May and Ceridwen looked at each other knowingly.

"There are more things in heaven and earth, Horatio, than are dreamt of in your philosophy," Ceridwen whispered to Auntie May, who smiled.

"What are you talking about?" I demanded, struggling to sit up straight. "Do you know something about what's happening to Cee?!" The effort was too much, and I collapsed back against the cushions again.

"Assume for the moment that he's fine," Auntie May said. "Well, not 'fine', but not in any immediate danger. What we need to do right now is stay calm and gather our resources."

Rogan laughed suddenly. Everyone turned to look at him. "Our resources," he said sarcastically. "What's the plan? The four of us are going to storm The Tower? I'm sure the Blues will be shaking in their boots."

"Mind yourself!" Auntie May responded sharply. "You know nothing about it, boy." Then she said quietly, "The Dominion is involved."

"The Dominion?!" Rogan laughed again, incredulously. "A rag-tag group of old Freeworlders and a couple of sonic bombs? Give me a break."

Auntie May straightened up and looked as if she was going to slap him. Ceridwen chuckled softly and said, "There is no darkness but ignorance."

"Who are you calling 'ignorant'?" Rogan exclaimed angrily. "You can't even talk like a normal person. This is ridiculous." He turned to leave the tent.

"Rogan, where are you going? Please stay — I need you!" I pleaded, distraught. This was getting worse by the minute. I didn't have Cee right now, and if I lost Rogan too...

Rogan turned, his eyes angry. "I'm going to gather my *own* 'resources'," he answered. "There are plenty of people in Divinity who'd be willing to help. Everyone's sick to death of the Blues, the Fancies, The Tower and The Dome. The Baby Gang is just dying to do something, and Little Jimmy said even the Caseeno Boys are ready to take action."

"For a price, I'm sure," said The Doc, stepping into the tent. "And the Baby Gang are just children, Rogan. Do you really want to put their lives in danger?"

"People want to do *something*!" Rogan responded. "Anything is better than living our lives this way, scrounging for food, constantly worried that you'll be swept off to be mutilated in The Dome, or even worse, killed, just for trying to survive! All this talk of the 'Dominion', as if a fantasy is going to save us — we need more than that!"

"The Dominion is no fantasy," The Doc answered gravely. "It's no 'rag-tag' band of rebels either. The Dominion is a highly organized group who've been orchestrating attacks on The Consortium for months now. And they're coming."

"I'll believe that when I see it," Rogan sneered, turning to leave.

"Doubt all you want," Auntie May replied angrily. "But who do you think blew up The Dome in Mont Royal last month? Huh, boy? Frag ghosts?!"

"So the rumours are true?" I asked. "And King's Town too?"

"Aye," said Auntie May, "and I'll tell you about it if you'll sit and listen."

"I don't have much choice," I said. "Rogan, please don't go. Listen to Auntie May." He was still at the door of the tent, his back to us. Then he turned slowly and sighed.

"Fine," he said, going back to his chair in the corner, "but if it's just more Freeworlder nonsense, I'm leaving. I'm sick of wasting time." As he sank into the chair moodily, Titus gave a whimper. He picked the little dog up, walked over, and placed him on my lap, where he settled comfortably. I reached out a tentative hand and stroked the soft fur between his ears. Titus wriggled happily and moved up so that he was lying on my chest. I put my arms around him, and Rogan looked at me, stifling a grin. "Looks like you've made a friend," he said.

"He's keeping me warm, that's all," I protested.

Rogan reached out and scratched Titus behind the ear. Titus wagged his tiny tail and nestled in more comfortably. "Sure," Rogan whispered to me, and winked. His hand moved from Titus's ear to my arm, where it lingered. We looked at each other as if this was the last quiet moment we would have together before everything changed. Then I took a deep breath, cleared my throat and broke the silence.

"Tell us about the Dominion," I said to Auntie May. "When did it start?"

"About seventeen years ago," she began, "when a boy named Darv Bouchard was sentenced to The Dome for stealing.

"Darv Bouchard was about the same age as Cee and you when he became a freedom fighter. He lived north of

Mont Royal in Kabac province with his mother, in a tent city called Terrebonne. It was a hard life, as it is for any Freeworlder in a tent city, but Darv and his mother made the best of it. She had been crippled in a Frag attack and couldn't walk, but she was an accomplished weaver, and Darv, who had always been good with his hands, had made her a loom so that she could create blankets and clothes that Darv could trade for food. Anything she had left over, she fashioned into dolls and other little toys that she gave to the children in Terrebonne. Darv himself spent his days scavenging for yarn or pieces of fabric down by the shipyards in the great heaps of refuse that were dumped there by EastInd freighters. The Fancies, or as they called them in Mont Royal, the Bijoux, consumed and then discarded, shredding everything including clothing, but leaving enough that Darv's mother could work her magic and weave the scraps back together into something useful.

"But Darv grew more and more dissatisfied and angry when he looked at the waste, at the sadness and sickness in Terrebonne compared to the luxury and excess of the Bijoux. He became involved with a group called Les Coquins, a gang not unlike the Caseeno Boys. Despite his age, he quickly became their leader, and moved them away from extortion and gambling to a much higher purpose — hijacking solar transports on their way from the docks outside of Terrebonne to Mont Royal. Whatever they stole — food, medicine, clothes, weapons — they either gave away to the Freeworlders in Terrebonne, or they traded on the black market.

"They had a good run, but eventually, The Consortium had had enough. They infiltrated Les Coquins by way of a spy named France DuLac in order to gather information. France DuLac was a beautiful young girl, and Darv fell in love with her, never knowing that she was a Consortium agent. He involved her in everything, and in turn, she told The Consortium everything. One night, while waiting to ambush a shipment of medical supplies destined for the private Bijoux hospitals in Mont Royal, Darv and his fellow Coquins were attacked by Blues and taken prisoner. There were sixteen of them, all seasoned rebels, and the word quickly spread that the Dome Master had announced a Grand Tournament. They would be paired up to fight to the death, each winner going on to fight again, until only one remained. And that one — well, the crowd would decide his or her fate. There hadn't been a Grand Tournament at The Dome in Mont Royal for years, and the Bijoux were as excited as the Freeworlders were sickened. Tickets cost a fortune but they sold out within minutes.

"The sixteen were kept in isolation, none of them knowing who would fight who. When the day finally came, they had been beaten, starved, and were desperate. The fighting began, and it soon became apparent that they were more than willing to cooperate, using weapons on each other fiercely, even if they had tears in their eyes. Soon, it was Darv's turn to fight. His opponent was a much older man named Seguin, who had been in Les Coquins for years. Seguin was weak and emaciated — he could barely hold the blade the Blues had given him. As they circled each other, Darv made a decision. He rushed in, disarmed Seguin, then threw down both Seguin's blade and his own weapon.

"'I refuse!' he screamed. 'Je refuse!' he said again in the old tongue. The other members of Les Coquins were standing on the sidelines waiting their turn. Without hesitation, they threw down their weapons in alliance with Darv, and echoed his scream: 'Je refuse!' Darv looked up into the stands. The Bijoux were protesting, clamouring and yelling at the glassed-in skybox where The Consortium leaders sat. He could see the Dome Master rise to his feet, a man with dead eyes and a crooked nose. He gave a signal. Before anyone knew what was happening, the Blues began firing on Les Coquins until only Darv was left standing. He looked around in disbelief as the crowd roared its pleasure.

"'Je refuse,' he whispered once more, and he clenched his fists, waiting for the inevitable. But then he looked up again, into the glassed-in box, and saw something he hadn't expected. France was there with The Consortium leaders. She was yelling and crying, gesturing wildly and pushing the Dome Master who had given the order to slaughter Les Coquins. The man grabbed her arms and spoke sharply — she crumpled to the floor, sobbing. Then he paused for a moment and turned away. When he turned back, he spoke into a microphone so that all could hear:

'Mercy Rule. Crowd, what say you?'

"There was a sudden hush. Then the crowd began to chant, 'Eyes! Eyes! Eyes!' The man in the booth signalled again, and a Blue grabbed Darv. He was holding a laser scalpel, and with one quick move, Darv was half blind. But just as the Blue was about to take the rest of Darv's sight, there was a commotion. Dozens of people with laser rifles had begun pouring down the aisles to rush the floor of The Dome, firing as they went. It was the rest of Les Coquins, there to save their leader and anyone else who had survived. Some were killed by the Blue onslaught, but Seguin and several others were wounded but still alive. In the chaos, they were able to make their escape into the tunnels beneath the city, never to be seen by The Consortium again.

"Over time, Les Coquins grew and gathered more members, not only from Kabac province but from across Adanac, and they became the Dominion. Their goal is to completely overthrow The Consortium and restore power to the citizens of Adanac. And 'Je Refuse'? That became their motto."

"But how are they planning on doing any of that?" I asked. "Everyone knows that The Consortium controls — well, just about everything! How can an underground organization possibly get rid of The Consortium? It doesn't make any sense. I mean, it's one thing to steal food from transports or blow up a couple of buildings, but a government coup?"

"Don't underestimate the Dominion," The Doc responded. "And don't forget—if The Consortium could infiltrate Les Coquins…"

"Then the Dominion could have agents within The Consortium?" I sat, pondering this while Titus snuggled deeper into my arms.

Rogan snorted. "All right. That was a nice story, but how much of it is true and how much of it is just legend? It sounded a bit too much like a fairy tale to me."

Suddenly Titus jerked his head up from his nest within my arms and gave a low growl. Ceridwen looked towards the tent's opening and said softly, "Look where it comes again, in the same figure, like the king that's dead."

Titus's growl turned into a sharp bark. He leapt down from my lap and ran back under the chair where Rogan was sitting as the tent flap was thrown back. A man stood there, one green eye blazing, the other covered by a black patch.

"Not dead yet, ma chère," he said.

18

Cee

I stared at Trick for a moment. He looked terrible—there were dark circles under his eyes, his lower lip was cut and swollen, he was covered in bruises, and his clothes were torn. A wave of shame came over me when I remembered how adamantly I'd refused to consider helping him. Then I happened to look past him and realized with horror that behind him, all I could see were sulphurous yellow storm clouds gathering in the dark, brooding sky—where the edge of the platform ended, there was nothing but open air, and we were both within inches of that edge. I scrambled backwards as quickly as I could until I could feel the solid wall of The Tower behind me.

Trick stared at me with a slight air of amusement. "Afraid of heights?" he asked.

"Apparently," I said. "I've never been on a 'height' before."

"Well," he answered, "I won't lie and say you'll get used to it. Luckily, it doesn't bother me quite as much. You're Cee, aren't you? Dee's brother?"

Despite his small stature, and his haggard appearance, he had an air of quiet confidence and a manner of speaking that made him seem older than I knew he was. "Yes," I said. "We've never met, but I know who you are."

"Your sister—how is she?" He looked concerned and moved closer to me, pulling his knees up against his chest for warmth. "She's been much on my mind these last few days."

"She's—" I started to respond, then my voice caught.

"What is it?" he asked anxiously. "She's not—"

"No," I said, my voice full of anguish. "But she has Mersa. I was caught trying to steal from the Fancies to pay for the medicine she needed. I have no idea if Rogan was able to get it to her or not, or if he even made it back to Divinity. All I can tell you is that Dee's still alive, but without the drugs, who knows for how long." I slammed my fist against the platform. "I feel so useless! I should be there to help her!" The platform began to vibrate with a low hum.

Trick reached out his hand and placed it on my fist. "Stop," he said. "This isn't your fault. And Rogan would go to the ends of the earth to make sure your sister survives. I can guarantee that." The vibrations subsided and Trick sat back. "That's better," he said under his breath. "Now, let's discuss the plan."

"Sure, the plan," I said cynically. "Oh, I have an idea—all we need to do is grow wings and just fly down from here. Problem solved."

Trick looked at me for a moment, then continued on as if I hadn't spoken. "Obviously, you and I are going to fight to the death in The Dome," he said matter-of-factly. "I really have no interest in killing you, and of course, I'd prefer it if you didn't kill me. I'm hoping you feel the same way."

"Fight to the death? I don't understand. Why is The Consortium trying to make an example out of either of us? I didn't actually steal anything, and you—you're just a kid!"

Trick laughed, a light, happy sound that echoed against The Tower. "That's very true, I am!" he replied, still chuckling. Then he grew serious. "Why do you think I'm here then?"

"Well, you're a fence, I know that."

"So are a lot of other people. No, it's not the stealing that made them beat me for days. They know I have information that they desperately want. But I'm not going to give it to them, and they've finally realized it. They could have just thrown me off The Tower, but the crowd needs to be entertained. That's where you come in. Get it?"

I still didn't understand what he was trying to say. "But why a fight to the death? I mean, I don't know who would have won, and I'm not excited about losing a hand or foot, or worse, but this? Why?"

Trick sighed in exasperation. "Do I really need to spell it out for you? They want to send a message to the Dominion."

Then it finally dawned on me. "You're in the Dominion?"

"Je refuse," he said ironically. When he saw the look on my face, he said it again. "'Je refuse'—the rallying cry of the rebellion. Really? You don't know it? You're not just playing with me, are you? You, of all people."

This was getting more confusing by the minute, but just as I was about to ask him why he said me "of all people", the metal door flew open and slammed against the wall of The Tower. A Blue guard stepped out onto the platform. He was wearing a tether that was attached to a bracket inside the door.

"They're such cowards," Trick snorted. "They offered me a tether on the first day if I told them what I knew. I laughed in their faces." He turned to the Blue and yelled, "I'd rather fall off this damned Tower than wear a leash like a big baby!"

The guard scowled and yelled back, "We'll see how brave you are when you're back in the box, Thaddeus. Let's go!" He started moving towards us. I jumped up and stood between him and Trick.

"Don't bother," Trick said, turning to me. "They'll just drag you in too. I'll be fine." He sounded brave, but I could see the fear in his eyes before he turned back to the Blue and began walking towards the door. "I'm coming, Durand—I wouldn't want you to worry about the wind blowing you over the edge. Although the thought of you dangling in mid-air does make me laugh—"

The Blue guard, Durand, cut him off with a slap to the head. Trick reeled for a second and staggered backwards, blood trickling from the corner of his mouth. I ran forward, but Trick steadied himself and waved me off. The guard snickered and grabbed Trick by the arm, hauling him inside. Then he pulled the door shut, slamming it into its metal frame, leaving me alone on the platform.

I huddled against the wall, trying to escape the wind, but it was everywhere. The sun had finally appeared from behind the bank of dark yellow clouds in the sky, but it wasn't making any difference. You'd think being this much closer to the sun would make the platform warmer, but the wind—the wind never stopped. It came howling from all directions, and there wasn't one side of The Tower where it wasn't blowing relentlessly. No wonder people went Tower-mad if they stayed up here too long. I shivered and tried to pull myself into an even tighter ball, my chin tucked into my knees and my hands under my crossed arms. Every so often, I looked up to see the progress of the sun across the sky. I was trying not to think about Trick, and what might be happening to him right now. Despite his maturity, he was still more a child than a man, and it sickened me to think of him being interrogated and beaten. I reached out in my mind to Dee, to see if I could tell how she was feeling, but all I got back was a faint presence, just enough to let me know that she was still alive. It was comfort of some kind, I supposed. There was so little I could think about without making myself crazy—I reached into my pocket and pulled out the wooden bead that I carried with me. I rolled it between my fingers, and then focused on carving to pass the time, dismissing the thought that I might not survive to ever create another figure. What could I carve next? I let my mind drift until an image began to form and take shape. It was the little dog, the one we stole from the Fancy. Why was I thinking about it? I was sure that it was either dead, along with Rogan, or in the best case scenario, Rogan had sold it to the butcher. But still—I could see the tufts of hair on the top of its head as clear as day, and its little stub of a tail wagging ferociously. I was wishing more than anything that I had a carving tool and a block of wood when the metal door opened again with a loud clang.

Trick rolled out onto the platform, semi-conscious and bleeding. Behind him came Songe.

"We meet again, old friend," he said jovially, looking at me as he kicked Trick in the ribs. Trick groaned and then fell silent. "I'd just thought I'd 'pop by' and make sure the accommodations were acceptable."

I leapt to my feet, ready to take action. Unlike Durand, Songe wasn't wearing a tether. How easy it would be to overpower him, send him hurtling to his death. As if he could read my mind, he casually put his hand on the doorframe.

"Oh, you're such an open book," he said, smiling venomously. "Save your energy. I have no intention of putting myself in harm's way. My father would be so disappointed at the waste of coin. I mean, look at me—state-of-the-art technology and all that. It would be quite an expensive death, I assure you. But tell me—are you and your little friend enjoying your stay? The only thing that *he* would say was 'Je refuse'. How very tedious he's becoming."

I stared at him coldly, rage beginning to build inside me. Songe stared back at me with curiosity. "Dare I mention your lovely sister?" he asked softly. "And she *was* quite lovely, if I recall. Those sweet lips, crying out for you…"

The rage turned into blind fury and The Tower began to shake. "Ah, there it is," he said. "Curiouser and curiouser." He backed up towards the door as the shaking got worse. The platform was starting to buck as the ground below heaved. "Well," he said, "I'm afraid I must leave you now. Try not to fall over the edge."

With clenched fists, I charged at him, but he was too quick. With one swift move, he disappeared inside The Tower and slammed the door closed behind him, just as I reached the spot where he had been standing. I pounded my fists against the door and screamed, "I'll kill you! If it's the last thing I do, I will END you!!"

In the chaos of the shaking and buckling of metal, I heard Trick groan again. Then, suddenly, I felt the sensation of someone squeezing my hands, a sense of comfort and reassurance flooding over me. It was Dee—she was there and she was alive. I inhaled sharply, then exhaled slowly, letting the rage dissipate, letting it be replaced by her calm. The platform stopped moving and I sank to the floor. Trick pushed himself slowly up onto one elbow and looked at me.

"You really need to learn to control that, you know," he said. "The last thing either of us needs is to be shaken off here like a couple of rag dolls."

"Control what? What are you talking about?" I was confused, but his response filled me with dread.

"The rumbling and quaking, of course. Who did you *think* was causing it? Did you think it was just a coincidence that every time you get really angry, or frightened, the earth starts shaking? I can't believe they haven't contacted you, that they haven't told you *anything*." He saw the bewilderment on my face, and the fear. "It seems not," he said, more to himself than to me. "Interesting."

"Who are 'they'?!" I demanded. "Who hasn't told me 'anything'?"

Trick looked concerned. "Why, the Dominion, of course. You're their greatest weapon."

19

Dee

There was complete silence in the tent, as we all stared at the figure before us. He was tall, with dark, flowing hair, and was dressed completely in black, from his hooded jacket right down to his heavy boots — the only exception was a small red leaf sewn onto his sleeve. Despite his rugged appearance, he was young, no older than thirty-five. His one good eye roamed around the room, taking each of us in. He lingered on me for a moment; his eyebrow seemed to arch subtly in surprise before his gaze moved on and rested on Ceridwen. He moved towards her and took her hands in his. Smiling, he said softly, in a slightly accented voice, "Like him that travels, I return again, just with the time, not with the time exchanged."

Ceridwen raised his hands and placed them against her cheeks, which had become faintly pink. "I am glad to see you well," she replied.

They gazed at each other fondly for a moment, then The Doc cleared his throat loudly. "It's good to see you, Darv," he said, "but it's getting crowded in here and I've got patients to tend to."

Darv turned from Ceridwen, releasing her hands, and grabbed The Doc in a bearhug. The Doc looked uncomfortable, but patted Darv on the back awkwardly before he broke free.

"Of course," said Darv. "We'll speak later." With that, The Doc slipped out of the tent, and Darv Bouchard turned his attention back to us.

"Introductions would seem to be in order," he said, his one eye moving from me to Rogan. "I'm Darv Bouchard."

Auntie May broke in. "This is the girl I was telling you about, the one whose brother is in The Tower." She sounded nervous, hesitant, and very unlike her usual scrappy self, as if being in Darv's presence intimidated her.

Darv smiled kindly at her. "Thank you, Aunt," he said, and she relaxed visibly. "And who is this one?" he continued, staring first at Rogan, then down at Rogan's hand, which was still on my arm.

Rogan subtly slid his hand back to his side and said, "I'm Rogan. I'm a...friend of Dee's."

"Ah," chuckled Darv. "The skeptical friend. Well, let me assure you that I'm no more a fairy tale than The Tower behind me. And right now, her brother, along with one of my best soldiers, is up there. This is no bedtime story, but a hard reality. The time has come to act. To fight," he said forcefully.

"To fight?!" Rogan exclaimed scornfully. "You and what army?"

"Rogan, stop!" I cried, but Darv just laughed. He didn't seem bothered by Rogan's insolence; in fact, he looked like he was rather enjoying it.

"You remind me of someone I know, sure you do," he said, holding up his hand to Auntie May, who had stepped forward, her eyes flashing. She was about to scold Rogan, I could tell, but she stepped back and stayed silent. "You want to know about an army, hmm?" Darv continued. "Well, they're out there. And they're waiting."

"What army?!" I asked, with more hope than dis-belief. "Surely the Dominion doesn't have anywhere near the numbers to take on The Consortium here."

"Not the Dominion itself, but we're not the only ones who want to see The Consortium taken down. We've formed an alliance with the Frags. And they're fiercer and more bloodthirsty than anything you could imagine."

"The Frags?!" I exclaimed in disbelief. "Are you out of your mind? The Frags are monsters, something out of nightmares. I've seen them up close — all they care about is killing, and eating what they kill — Consortium, Freeworlder, or Fancy — they don't care!"

"Now, *that's* the stuff of fairy tales right there," Darv laughed. "The Frags are more clever and organized than you think. It's been decades since the radiation and the Dazzle bombs — they were weak then, but they're stronger now, and determined to right the wrongs of the past."

"And you trust them?" Rogan scoffed. "Not me. Not for a minute."

"I'm with Rogan," I said. "I've — " Suddenly the ground began to rumble. The solar lantern on the table tipped over and fell to the floor with a crash. Titus began barking, a shrill, high-pitched yelp. My head was filled with fury, a blind, black rage that was building as the tent shook and started to twist. It was Cee. I could feel him in my mind, raging like a storm. I wrapped my arms around my head, rocking back and forth as the waves of violence flowed over me. I reached out to him and battled with him, sending thoughts of calm, of "home", until gradually, I felt the storm subside. The tent stopped shaking, and Titus ran over to Rogan, who scooped him up and tucked him inside his jacket, where the little dog shivered.

"What the hell?!" Rogan exclaimed, moving closer to me and putting his arm around me protectively. "Are you all right?"

My head was spinning, and I felt faint. "I — what was that? It's the second time in the last 24 hours that I've felt as though the earth was going to split in two. Is it a new Consortium weapon? Is the planet dying?" I looked up at Rogan, pleading. "What's going on?"

Auntie May and Darv were standing by the doorway, but they were still close enough that I could hear them. "The boy's finally coming into his own," Auntie May said quietly.

"Whatever it is, it's taking a lot to push him," Darv answered. "I'd hoped for more by now."

"Well, he's a good soul," she answered with a small smile, reaching up to pat his cheek in a motherly way. "Slow to anger. Too much like his father, if you ask me." As the words came out, Darv pulled back from her caress and gave her a sharp look. She gasped, covering her mouth with her hands. But it was too late—both Rogan and I had heard her.

"His father?" I said slowly. "What are you talking about?" Darv looked uncomfortable, anxious. I continued, "*His* father is my father. Someone better start talking right now and explain this. Who is our father? Who?!"

"This isn't the time," Auntie May said. "There's too much to be done without these kinds of distractions—"

"Distractions?!" I yelled. "You call this a DISTRACTION?! Well, let me tell you—NOTHING is going to get done until someone tells me exactly who our father is!" I pointed at Darv. "Is it you?! Is that what she meant?!" Darv remained silent, staring off into the distance. "How long have you known?!" I insisted. Still nothing. Then it slowly dawned on me and I said quietly, bitterly. "You've always known, haven't you? How dare you come here now?"

"This wasn't the way I wanted it to be," Darv answered, looking back at Auntie May, anger in his eyes.

She dropped her gaze and whispered to him, "Forgive me."

"Forgive *you*?!" I was beside myself with anger, struggling to leap out of the cot. Rogan tried to hold me back, but I shoved him aside and stood upright for the first time in days. "What about him?! Just showing up here 16 years after the fact, after everything we've been through, with a grin and a 'We have an army', and 'Oh, by the way, I'm your long-lost dad'! Is this some kind of joke? Do you have any idea how we've suffered?!" The silence in the tent lingered on painfully while I waited for him to reply. Auntie May turned away, wiping a tear from her eye. Rogan simply stood behind me, in solid support.

"I was trying to protect you," Darv finally said, with a shrug of resignation, still staring out into the distance.

"Oh, well that's all right then," I said sarcastically. "And fine protection it was, too—if you didn't count the beatings, the humiliation, the days in the Shed without food, the complete lack of any kind of human affection, being constantly told we were worthless—at least Cee and I had each other, because we certainly didn't have *you*!" I took a step forward, and was overwhelmed by dizziness. Rogan caught me as I started to go down, but I straightened up and turned to him, my back to Auntie May and Darv. "I'm all right. Just make him leave. I never want to see him again." Rogan put Titus down onto the cot and gathered me in his arms. I pressed my head against his chest, trying not to weep.

"Get out," Rogan said. "Do what she's asked of you and get out."

Darv sighed. "I can't," he said. "Unless the two of you come with me. It isn't safe. The Blues are coming. We need to get to the haunted city and fast, if we want to survive and save your brother. Be angry, be furious, hate me, want me dead—whatever you like. Just pack up and let's go."

"Let's go?" asked Rogan in disbelief. "Dee can barely walk, let alone make it all the way to Old K!"

I pulled away from him and looked him in the eye. "Don't worry about me," I said. "I'll be fine as long as you're with me. Cee is all that matters right now. My life isn't worth much if anything happens to him." I paused. "But first we need to go back to my tent, to put Cee's tools somewhere safe, gather supplies and tell Sarah what's happening. She deserves to know the truth. Plus we can't take Titus with us—hopefully, she'll be willing to look after him."

"I'm sure she will, but—are you certain about this? You're still so weak. I could take you to the tunnels and we could wait there..."

"Wait in the tunnels?!" I laughed harshly. "You and I both know that neither of us is cut out for hiding. Where's the fun in that? I'd rather have a Lobot on my tail any day than slink around in the shadows, and so would you." Rogan grinned in agreement, and I turned to Darv. "Meet us at the edge of Divinity. We'll be there in an hour."

Darv nodded, still not looking at us, then left the tent. Auntie May sighed heavily. "He did what he thought was best at the time. He was so young—"

"I don't want to hear it," I interrupted her. "Come on, Rogan, let's go."

I gathered up Cee's toolbox, grabbed the meds The Doc had left me, and pushed past Auntie May out into the afternoon sun, Rogan following with Titus under his arm. We walked down the row of tents in silence, my thoughts blazing. Rogan left me alone for a few minutes, then suddenly burst out, "Why are you so angry?"

I stopped dead in my tracks and turned to glare at him. "What kind of question is that?" I demanded. "Why shouldn't I be angry?!"

"I don't know," Rogan shrugged, pushing the hair out of his eyes and looking back at me calmly. "Haven't we all dreamed of the day our parents would come back? I know I have. It was the only thing that kept me from crying myself to sleep every night in the workhouse. You know, the hope that one day, my mother or father would come and save me—"

"But he didn't come back and save me, did he?!" I shouted back. "It's too late for that now!"

Rogan looked confused. "What do you mean, too late? I don't understand."

"Nothing," I muttered. "Come on. We don't have time for this." I stomped off, Rogan following behind at a distance.

We finally reached Cee's and my tent. I set the toolbox on the ground then turned and took Titus from him. "Stay here—I'll be right back." I put Titus down gently, pushed open the flap of the tent, and went inside, the little dog following at my heels. Sarah was in a chair in the corner, sewing something bright. She looked up and gasped when she saw me.

"Dee! It's really you—are you better?" She put down her needlework, came over and hugged me, then her eyes filled with tears. "Cee—" she started.

"I know," I replied. "Don't worry. We're going to save him. I promise. But I need you to stay here. Can you look after this one?"

I pointed at Titus and her eyes lit up. "Ohhh," she breathed, "He's just like a Fancy dog." Titus wiggled his tail and stood up on his back legs. Sarah picked him up with a small cry of delight and hugged him to her chest. "Of course I can take care of him," she cooed. Then she looked back at me, tears still threatening to spill over. "But Cee—what's going to happen?"

"The Dominion is here," I said, sounding slightly resentful. She gave me a strange look, and I tried to say it again without sounding bitter. "No, really. There's a plan. Rogan and I are meeting with them today. Everything will be all right."

Sarah looked doubtful, but then Titus gave a tiny yip, and she focused back on him. "So sweet," she murmured to him. I reached out my hand and scratched him behind the ear.

"Cee's tools are by the door—put them somewhere safe. If you need any food, there are a couple of carvings in the box under Cee's bed that you can trade. I—I hope to see you soon." I didn't wait for her reply; I fled the tent before she could see the tears forming in my eyes. I hurried past Rogan. "Come on," I said brusquely.

He followed in silence as we marched down the rows of tents towards the edge of Divinity where my would-be father was waiting. Finally we saw him in the distance, standing in the shadow of a tent, Ceridwen next to him. As we got closer, I saw that he was talking to S-Sam. When we reached them, S-Sam looked at us silently but intently.

"Well?" I challenged Darv. The urge to lash out at him was strong; I was hoping that he would say something, anything, so that I could yell at him again, as if that would make me feel less betrayed.

But all he said was, "Get ready to meet the Skeleton Army." Then he turned and started walking towards Old K.

20

Cee

"Weapon? What are you talking about?!" I asked Trick, incredulous. "How am *I* a weapon for the Dominion? They don't even know who I am, and I've certainly never met any of them! And despite what Auntie May says, I doubt they even exist! If you think that I'm the one causing the quaking, then you've gone Tower-mad. The earth shifts all the time — it has nothing to do with me."

"I'm no more Tower-mad than you are," Trick replied, coughing weakly, "and it's more than just 'the earth shifting'." He pushed himself up, wincing, so that he was resting on his elbows. He stared at me hard. "You really don't know anything? About who you and your sister actually are?"

"We're a couple of workhouse kids who ran away and became Freeworlders. What else is there to know?" Trick tried to sit up. Suddenly, he gasped and his face contorted with pain.

"What's wrong?" I asked, my concern for the small boy overshadowing my confusion and curiosity. "Are you all right?"

He breathed in slowly through his teeth. "I think one of my ribs is broken, that's all." I started to say something, but he waved me off dismissively. "I've had worse," he said. I watched as he slowly manoeuvered himself so that he was sitting with his back against The Tower wall. Holding his arms around himself stiffly, he said, "Right. Well, I don't know when the Dominion was planning to bring you 'into the fold' as it were, but I think for both our sakes, I should fill you in before something happens to push your buttons again and we're both launched into space."

"Sure," I said skeptically. "I can't wait to hear all about it. Let me guess: you're the head of the Dominion, Dee and I have magical superpowers, and together, the three of us are going to overthrow The Consortium."

Trick laughed suddenly and sharply, then immediately gasped. He wrapped his arms tighter around his ribs as he continued to alternate peals of laughter with cries of pain. When he finally calmed down, he looked at me. "Well, it sounds strange when you say it like that, but you're not far off."

"You *are* mad," I said, shaking my head at him. "Or delirious from pain. One or the other." I turned away from him and looked out at the sky. The clouds were dark yellow and foreboding—another hot rain was coming soon. It would be a relief. Aside from not having eaten since I couldn't remember when, I was dying of thirst. I pictured myself laying back on the platform, mouth wide open, catching those steaming drops of water on my tongue. I could almost taste the bitter acidic tang of the rain, when Trick interrupted my daydream.

"I'm sorry," he said quietly. "I'm sorry that they didn't tell you, but you have to know. The Dominion *is* real."

I sighed. "Fine. The Dominion exists. *Are* you the leader?"

"No," he laughed, then clutched his ribs again. "Just one of many foot-soldiers. My main role is to act as a liaison between Dominion forces and Dominion Loyalists, like Auntie May, in Divinity, as well as across Trillium Province. I take information back and forth, use my business to help them buy weapons, things like that. It's not much, but I do what I can."

"OK," I said. "So where do Dee and I come in? And why don't either of us know any of these other 'Dominion Loyalists' if we're so important?"

"It wouldn't be much of a secret underground movement if everyone knew who the rebels were, would it? Auntie May is one, yes, but there are many others. You actually *do* know some of them—you just didn't know they were Loyalists. As far as you and your sister are concerned, it was more about protecting you, I think. I don't have all the details, but I'll tell you what I know."

I could hear thunder rumbling in the distance. The hot rain was getting closer. Then the thought occurred to me: what if there was lightning? The Tower was the tallest structure in the city, in the country probably. What a way to end it all—barbequed on the top of The Tower. I shivered.

Trick followed my gaze into the sky, and as if sensing my thoughts, he said, "Don't worry. The Tower is well-protected. There are grounding rods buried all around the base that draw electricity away from it. We're perfectly safe."

"Safe?" I laughed harshly. "I suppose—if you don't consider the possibility of falling off here, our upcoming fight to the death, or dying of hunger or thirst first. Anyway, how does a kid I've never met know so much about me?"

Trick pondered for a moment. "The same way I know about a lot of things," he finally said. "There's an advantage to being so young and small. It has its many disadvantages, of course, but it's very easy to sit in a corner and be ignored by people who would underestimate you. I should probably start at the beginning."

"Why not," I sighed. "It's not like we're going any-where anytime soon. Please, enlighten me."

Trick wriggled around, wincing noticeably, until he was in a semi-comfortable position. He pushed his dark hair out of his eyes and said, "Like most people our age, I was abandoned at a workhouse before I could walk and—"

"When you said 'beginning', you really meant it," I interrupted, rolling my eyes. He gave me a sharp look, and I felt immediately chastised. "Sorry," I muttered.

Trick nodded and continued. "I was put into the care of a Guardian who was an absolutely sadistic monster. His name was Claude, and he was most likely traumatized by his own past, but he made sure he took out his anger on me any chance he got." He swivelled around and pulled his thin shirt to one side to reveal a criss-cross pattern of thick, raised scars running across both his shoulders and down his back. I took a deep breath; he shrugged indifferently, then let the shirt fall back into place. He continued. "He had a special belt buckle, and he would use it on me for any rea-son, no matter how minor. No one was terribly concerned about it, as long as he didn't kill me."

"Sounds familiar," I said, nodding.

"As a result, I never spoke unless I absolutely had to. I'd learned the hard way that if I could blend into the background, make myself invisible, I stood a much greater chance of surviving. I got very good at watching and listen-ing, especially for the sound of the buckle singing through the air behind me. Then, right before my Seventh Drop-Off Day, I happened to overhear one of the Protectors talking about a solar transport trailer that was leaving in the mor-ning, taking fresh produce and other supplies from our workhouse near the border to the Island. I snuck out of the sleeping ward and onto the transport, hidden among the crates. That was the last I saw of the workhouse. I spent days eating raw potatoes, barely able to move for the infer-nal heat inside the trailer, but it was worth it. I crept out of the transport once it got near Old K, and made my way to Divinity."

"I'll bet Claude caught it for not keeping a better eye on you," I snickered. Guardians could be as kind or cruel as they wanted, but to actually lose a small child that he was in charge of would have meant days in the Shed for Claude.

"He most likely would have," Trick replied, "but I killed him before I left."

"You killed him?! You were six years old!" I exclaimed, shocked.

Trick shrugged his shoulders. "I was…precocious," he replied.

I was stunned — the thought that Trick was so cold-blooded at such an early age was a little disturbing, although understandable given the circumstances. I was torn between not wanting to know and morbid curiosity. Finally, I asked "How did you do it?"

"I waited until he was asleep, then I looped the belt around his neck, pulled it tight and used his headboard for leverage. When he stopped thrashing around, I took the buckle off the belt and shoved it as far down his throat as it would go." He looked at me and smiled faintly. I understood in that moment that underestimating Trick was the worst thing *anyone* could do.

We both sat in silence, then he cleared his throat and continued. "Once I got to Divinity, it was hard. For the first few months, I scavenged what I could during the day and slept behind the bins at Blawblaw's, safe from anyone who'd try to take advantage of someone young and vulnerable. One night, I was going down a row of tents, looking for scraps of food, when I heard a woman's voice. She sounded frightened. There was a man's voice as well. I crept closer and heard him say, 'Give me what you owe, or I'll drag you to the Sex House myself.' I peeked through an opening in the tent flap and saw her. She was…lovely." He sighed long and hard as he turned away and looked out towards the horizon. He said nothing for a few moments, until I spoke.

"Who was she?" I asked quietly.

He turned back quickly, as if I'd startled him out of a reverie, a beautiful dream that he didn't want to wake up from. "Her name was Sylvie Blaine," he said. "She had a stall at the Hidden Market. He was a Caseeno Boy, come to shake her down for protection money. I watched as he grabbed her arm. She cried out, and I stepped into the tent. 'Why are you hurting my momma?' I asked. He turned to me, surprised to see a little boy standing there, and while he was distracted, she grabbed a knife from the table and stabbed him in the back. Some of the neighbouring Free-worlders came and helped her get rid of him."

Despite my initial skepticism, I was finding Trick's story fascinating. I could see him in my mind, a tiny figure in the doorway silhouetted against the dark night, and her, grabbing the knife and plunging it into the back of the man who would hurt her. It felt...incredibly satisfying. "What then?" I asked eagerly.

"She took me in," he said simply. "She was as much a mother to me as any woman could ever have been. She was also a Dominion Loyalist, and over the next two years, I went with her everywhere, to every secret meeting, to every rendezvous with rebel leaders, where I sat in a corner, playing with a toy like a good child. But I watched and listened, until I knew everything I needed to know."

"Two years?" I asked. "Why two years? What happened after two years?" I wanted this story to have a happy ending, but deep down, I knew that it didn't.

"She became ill," he said. "Radiation sickness. She wasted away and there was nothing I could do. Once she was gone, I was on my own again. But at least I had the Dominion. I began working for them, creating a network of spies, and using my resources to fund them, until a traitor had me ambushed and I ended up here."

"The Baby Gang?" I asked, shocked. "They're all part of the Dominion?"

He nodded. "And many more."

"But who's the traitor?" I asked. "Is that who got Dee hurt too?!"

"I don't know who it is. Yet." Trick's face became dark. "But I have my suspicions."

"I'd put my coin on that S-Sam," I said. "There's something about him I don't trust."

Trick chuckled. "No, not S-Sam. He's a loyal soldier. I have no doubts about him. No, it's someone else, someone desperate with nothing to lose. Someone who's willing to sell out his friends for coin."

I sighed in exasperation. "Fine, but where do Dee and I come into this?"

Trick took a deep breath. "OK. I need you to stay calm. It's very important that you don't—'freak out' when you hear what I have to tell you. *Very* important. Trust me."

"I'll do my best," I said slowly, trying to still my rapidly-beating heart. "What is it?"

"Your father—yours and Dee's father—is Darv Bouchard, the founder and leader of the Resistance." I gasped but he continued, oblivious. "When you were born, The Consortium was closing in, thanks to having infiltrated the Dominion by way of a spy. Darv had you taken to the workhouse, where he thought you'd be safe. I know how awful that must have been for you and Dee, but he did the only thing he could to protect you—hide you away."

"I...I have a father?" I was astounded. "I mean, obviously there was a 'father' involved, but you mean he's still alive? And out there?!" This was a dream. There was no other explanation. I sat, staring into space, trying to figure out how I could wake up.

"I know this is a lot to take in." Trick touched my shoulder gently and I turned to him. "But there's more." I stared at him, dumbfounded, unable to speak. "Right after you were born," he continued," and before you were left at the workhouse, you were taken to a special facility. You were given a cybernetic implant."

"What kind of implant?" I whispered. I was trying to do as he said, to stay calm, but my mind was in chaos.

"It's some kind of sonic device—triggered by an increase of noradrenaline in the brain—that's the flight or fight response. Whenever you're terrified, or furious, the implant activates and causes enough sonic energy that everything around you starts to vibrate. Including the tectonic plates under the ground. Those earthquakes we've been feeling? That's not nature. That's you, and you're getting stronger. Strong enough to rip the world apart."

21

Dee

Darv Bouchard strode on ahead, not looking back. Ceridwen seemed to float along silently, her cloak flowing around her, having no difficulty with his pace. S-Sam was trying to keep up with him, but was struggling to make his way over the rubble that littered the ground between Divinity and Old K. Every so often, S-Sam would glance behind at us, a look of quiet concern on his face. Rogan and I walked side by side in silence for a while, Old K looming ahead of us and getting closer by the minute. Suddenly Rogan stopped and grabbed my arm, pulling me over to him. The movement shot a bolt of pain through my back, but I didn't let him see me react.

"What is it?" I asked. He looked tense and worried, but let go of my arm.

"This is a bad idea," he answered.

"What part? The part where we follow my so-called 'father' into the haunted city, the part where we join an underground rebel army, or the part where we overthrow The Consortium?" I didn't mean to be sarcastic with him, but it seemed a little too late to start questioning things now.

"All of it!" he said, gesturing broadly at the shells of the scrapers ahead of us. "Remember the last time we were in there? It wasn't exactly a Fancy Promenade. What if this is another ambush?! I mean, the guy hid the fact that he was your father for years—what are the odds that he's hiding other things now?"

I thought for a minute. What if Rogan was right? But then something occurred to me. "I think someone like Darv Bouchard might be able to fool The Doc, or even Auntie May. But I don't believe that Ceridwen would trust him for a second if he was a traitor. She seems to have a sense about these things—I'm sure she could tell if he was lying."

Rogan considered that, and his face relaxed a bit. "Okay, so Darv isn't going to murder us as soon as we cross into Old K, but what about the rest? You've heard the same horror stories about the Frags that I have—who's to say they won't simply capture us and turn us into their next meal?" He shivered at the thought. I tried not to visualize the Frags in the forest that day, so matter-of-factly considering eating Cee.

"I can't tell you anything but this," I said. "I need to save Cee. And if going into Old K and battling it out with a group of southern cannibals is what I have to do, then that's what I'm going to do. If you don't want to come, if you're scared, then you don't have to be here." I meant it kindly, but Rogan's eyes flashed.

"I'm not scared!" he said, offended. "I'm worried about *you*. A few hours ago, you were still lying on a cot, trying to recover from Mersa. Now, you're going full force into what may be a trap, at the bidding of a man you've never met before, who tells you he's your father. Excuse me for being cautious!"

I started to respond, but then another bolt of pain went through me. I couldn't stop myself from wincing, and Rogan's face immediately softened. "Hey," he said quietly, "I'm sorry. Are you all right? Are the pain meds wearing off?"

"Seems like it," I said. "Maybe time for another dose of the Mersa drugs too." I fumbled in my backpack, and found the pill bottles The Doc had left me. Rogan pulled a water flask from his pack and held it out to me. We'd stopped at the Tap before we left Divinity—who knew if we'd be able to find clean water in Old K. The Tap was the only solid structure in the entire tent city, a low brick building that housed latrines, sinks, and showers. It was a meeting place as much as anything, where people could socialize, gossip, and relax for a few minutes while they got fresh water or cleaned up. In the evenings, people would gather, some with make-shift instruments, and a band would suddenly form. Then the call would go out: "Band Night—no squatting!" and the music carrying up into the sky and over the tent city would draw Freeworlders young and old, come to dance and forget their troubles for a few hours. Luckily, the Tap was just as crowded during the day, so no one had noticed us hurriedly filling our flasks. I wasn't sure whether the Tap had been there first and Divinity had sprung up around it, or whether it had been built after the first tents started to go up so many years ago. Either way, it made life in Divinity a little more bearable, and I was glad for the water right now. The sun was getting lower in the sky as the afternoon moved towards dusk, but it was still hot enough that the walk was making both of us sweat. I swallowed the pills with a mouthful of the water. It tasted slightly metallic, but it was refreshing. Just as I handed the flask back to Rogan, we heard Darv yelling at us from up ahead.

"What are you doing? Let's go!" he shouted, gesturing at us to come on. Ceridwen put her hand on his arm and said something to him, then they both turned away and kept walking towards Old K. S-Sam hung back, waiting for us to catch up.

I gave Rogan a weak smile. "Last chance to go back to the comforts of Divinity," I said.

Rogan sighed, then gave me a broad grin. "Not me. Last one to Old K is a Frag dinner."

I laughed despite myself. I would be lost without Cee, but if anything happened to Rogan, I didn't know what I'd do either. It occurred to me that maybe I thought of him as more than a friend too, then I quickly pushed that thought aside. Maybe in another time or place, but this wasn't the moment for sentiment or romance.

We caught up quickly to S-Sam, who looked at us questioningly. "Everything's fine," I said. "My shoulder was just hurting a bit." S-Sam nodded, and the three of us walked together through the piles of broken bricks, crumbled mortar, and shards of glass that marked the path to the haunted city. When we finally reached the border, we all stopped at the same time. Darv and Ceridwen had disappeared into the shadows without a second thought, but Rogan, S-Sam and I hesitated. We all remembered our last visit to Old K, the chaos, the violence, the pain, and everything that had happened since. It seemed appropriate to take a moment. I wasn't one to pray to the old god, and I didn't think Rogan or S-Sam did either, but I felt compelled to look up to the sky and whisper, "Keep us safe." Beside me, I heard S-Sam echo "K-Keep us s-safe". Rogan simply took my hand and gave it a squeeze before letting it go. Then we stepped into the shadows.

Immediately, the temperature dropped and I felt a chill come over me. Rogan pulled a light jacket out of his backpack and handed it to me. "Take it," he ordered. "The last thing you need after being so sick is to freeze. Don't argue," he finished, cutting off my protest.

As much as I hated to be babied, I put the jacket on. I would be no good to Cee if I had a relapse. As it was, I was feeling a little weak and dizzy, but I put that down to the pain pills The Doc had given me. Who knew what was actually in them? I was just happy it wasn't Lullybies and TastiRum.

We made our way down the main thoroughfare of Old K. Everything was completely silent in the dim light, broken only by the occasional piece of concrete falling from one of the decrepit buildings somewhere off in the distance, and the sound of our feet on the hard pavement. Darv had stopped up ahead and was waiting for us. As we got closer to him, I heard a noise, barely noticeable at first but then growing louder. It sounded like hundreds of people whispering. I could tell that Rogan and S-Sam heard it too, by the way they were looking around. It seemed to be coming from far away and right beside us all at the same time. "What *is* that?!" I said in a low voice, too afraid to speak normally.

"Ring the alarum bell," Ceridwen said softly and cryptically.

Darv looked up at the scrapers blocking out the sun. "The Skeleton Army," he said. "They know we're here."

"W-Why…w-why…w-why," S-Sam sputtered, his fear making it more difficult than usual for him to speak.

I instinctively knew what he wanted to ask. "Why are they called the 'Skeleton' Army? Are they — are they undead?" The thought of it made my skin crawl, but Darv just laughed lightly.

"No, they're not 'undead', chère. When they first came to us, they were starving, to the point where they looked like skeletons. The Frags aren't able to grow much food for themselves below the border, just like we can't here. But unlike us, they don't have the Breadbasket. Since they've come up here to join us, we've been trying to fatten them up a bit, but it's no good. No matter how much they eat, they still look emaciated. Maybe it's the radiation — who knows? At any rate, they've embraced the term. Their uniforms are quite…intimidating."

"That doesn't explain the noise. And I'm *not* your 'chère'," I said. Darv dipped his head slightly in acknowledgement at the last statement, not seeming offended. I didn't care if he was anyway — he had no right to use a term of affection with me.

"The Frags have no technology — that was stripped away from them by The Consortium after the Water Wars — so they communicate by passing messages along orally, person by person. There are Frag soldiers stationed about every 30 feet above us." He laughed as Rogan, S-Sam and I all looked up at the same time in shock. "The sound you're hearing is simply them passing the word along that we are welcome guests and not their enemies. Be grateful that we are — their numbers are larger than anyone could guess and they are fierce warriors. I pity any Blue who might have followed us."

Ceridwen nodded silently in agreement. They turned and continued to walk down the thoroughfare, the three of us following and glancing up occasionally as the whispering sound increased in intensity. It seemed like we'd been walking for hours. My legs were starting to feel wobbly, and my head was getting fuzzy. I was desperate to sit down for a moment, but I kept going, not wanting to show any weakness. Finally, it seemed that we'd come to the heart of Old K, the buildings crowding in on us in a claustrophobic way. Darv halted in front of the ruins of a scraper taller than any of the others, and the whispering abruptly stopped.

"We're here," he said, stepping through a doorway that once had glass doors. Now the doors were wide open, careening off their hinges, glass shattered on the ground around them. Even through the gloom, we could see a stairway going up to the next level and one disappearing down below. "Come on."

Our footsteps echoed on the floor, a marble expanse that would have, at one time, been very luxurious. Now it was covered in debris and dust. We made our way over to the stairs leading down and followed Darv to the bottom. Instead of getting darker, the air seemed to brighten slightly as we descended. At the bottom, Darv pointed to the left, and we followed him along a wide corridor wordlessly. It still felt like we were being watched by a hundred eyes, even though there was no one to be seen. Finally, after a series of twist and turns, we came to an intersection and Darv paused. "We go this way." He pointed right. "Are you ready?"

We all turned the corner, and I gasped. Nothing could have prepared me for that moment. I heard Rogan next to me inhale sharply, and S-Sam swallowed hard. We were on the brink of a huge, cavernous underground chamber. It stretched back for what seemed like a couple of clicks, crisscrossed by other sets of stairs going up and down in the distance. Standing silently below us within that chamber, lit only by the dim glow of the solar lamps that lined the walls, were hundreds of people, all wearing black hoods that covered their faces except for their eyes, and long black coats, or black pants and shirts. Painted on the hoods were white skulls, and their clothing was decorated with stark white bone bodies. We stared at each other in silence, the skeletons completely motionless — they might have been gruesome statues for all we knew. Then the crowd began to silently part, as one of them came towards us. He was taller than anyone I'd ever seen, and the skull on his hood was painted red. He was so thin that I could see the real bones under his flesh jutting out through his clothing as he came closer. He climbed the set of stairs two at a time, rising powerfully and commandingly. Then he stopped, a few feet from us, and took off his hood, revealing a ravaged face, and sharp, filed teeth. In stark contrast to his dark skin, his hair was white, and gathered into a multitude of short braids that jutted out from his head in all directions. He looked at Darv and Ceridwen, and then back at us.

"I'm Malachi Thorn," he said in a low, dangerous voice. "Don't you look tasty?"

22

Cee

"That can't be right," I said to Trick, shaking my head slowly in disbelief at what he had just told me. "It doesn't make any sense. There have been plenty of times that I've been angry, or scared, and there hasn't been so much as a vibration in the ground, let alone tectonic plates shifting!"

He was silent for a moment, watching the clouds continue to roll in and thinking. Finally, he said, "Maybe there's another factor involved. Think back to the last few times it's happened. What do they all have in common?"

"Well, I don't know," I said. "If it's true what you're telling me, then right now, the thing that's triggering it is Songe. I'll never forgive him for what he did to Dee. Taking his eye wasn't enough! I—"

"Stay calm," Trick warned. "OK, so what about other times?"

"Last week when I realized that Dee was hurt. I could hear her scream in my head, and then the shaking started. But it was when she was in the haunted city. I was still terrified that she was going to die when I saw her in The Doc's tent, but nothing happened then."

The hot rain began to fall, pinging against the metal platform. I leaned my head back and opened my mouth, hoping to catch a few precious drops. Trick said, "Hang on," and he disappeared around the bend of The Tower. My mind was racing. Trick's story sounded preposterous, but what if it *was* true? What if I really *could* cause the earth to vibrate hard enough to cause some kind of damage? I thought back to all the little earthquakes of the past. It didn't just happen when Dee was hurt—there was the time I got caught in a cave by some Frags. I was terrified that they would kill me and eat me, but then Dee showed up and saved me.

Another time, I was about Seven. I got lost in the fields—I couldn't find my way back to the workhouse, and I was too far away to let Dee know. It was getting dark, and I could hear the coywolves howling. I remember crying, and the ground shaking. Finally, one of the Thirteens found me and brought me back. Dee was beside herself, crying too, but the second I could feel her in my mind, the shaking stopped. Suddenly Trick reappeared, carrying a shallow metal bowl. He put it down on the platform.

"We can use this to catch some of the rain." He gestured at the bowl. "I keep it around the other side. I told Durand if he wanted it back, he'd have to come out and get it. Luckily, his little leash doesn't reach that far." He paused and scrutinized my face. "You look like you might have discovered something. A pattern, maybe?"

"I'm not sure," I said. "But it seems to me that every time one of these 'earthquakes' happens, it's when I'm furious or terrified, but Dee and I are away from each other. The greater the distance between us, the harder it is to 'hear' each other. When we're together, it either stops, or it doesn't happen at all."

Trick raised his eyebrows. "Interesting theory. Maybe that's *her* superpower then. You can rip the world apart, and she can stop you from doing it."

It had started raining harder. The bowl was filling up and Trick gestured again at it. "Help yourself," he said. I picked it up and drank deep. The water was hot and acidic, but it was a relief to my parched mouth. I took half and handed the bowl to Trick. He drained it and then put it back down to collect more rainwater. We were soaking but it felt good after so many hours of the wind and sun drying out our skin. Trick was just saying, "You know, I wonder —" when suddenly the door flew open and clanged hard against the metal of The Tower. We both turned quickly, prepared for whatever was coming out. I could see two figures silhouetted against the light inside the door. One was tall and imposing, and the other was bent over, snivelling and crying. Then the tall figure wordlessly shoved the second out onto the platform, and pulled the door shut behind him. The newcomer screamed and scrambled as the momentum pushed him towards the edge of the platform. He managed to catch himself and threw himself back towards safety. Then he collapsed and curled up into a fetal position with his arms wrapped around his head, moaning. Trick looked at him with a kind of detached curiosity and then sat back down. I watched for a minute as he moaned and rocked, then I crouched down next to him and put my hand on his shoulder. He stiffened, but the moaning stopped and he lay still.

"It's okay," I said. "You're safe now." I could hear Trick behind me, trying to suppress a snicker at the irony of what I had just said. Then the newcomer took his arms away from his head and I stepped back in shock. "Little Jimmy?!" I exclaimed.

"Cee, is that really you?" Little Jimmy pushed himself up into a sitting position and wiped his face with the back of his hand. "Everyone thought you were probably dead by now."

There was only one thing in my mind, one thing I was desperate to know. "Jimmy, how's Dee?!"

"Dee?" he echoed blankly. "Oh, she's OK. Rogan got the meds to her in time."

I sagged back against The Tower in relief. Everything that I'd gone through wasn't for nothing. I sent a silent message of gratitude to Rogan for saving her. Hopefully one day I could thank him in person. I smiled to myself—the faint sensations I'd been getting from Dee, alternating between anger and fear, were making sense now. She was probably furious that she was still stuck in bed while I was who knew where. I could see her now, railing against The Doc, hating the fact that she was too weak to help me. But that's exactly what I wanted—it was safer that way. She knew I was still alive, and that was enough. Suddenly, Trick's voice rang out through the rain. "I know you," he said. "You're Jimmy Diamond."

Jimmy looked at him nervously, then said with false bravado, "That's right. Little Jimmy Diamond, cuz when the chips are down, I always put my money on diamond."

Trick stared at him hard. "So to what do we owe the pleasure of your company, Jimmy Diamond?"

Jimmy looked confused for a second, then said, "Oh! You mean, how did I get here? The Blues made a surprise raid on Caseeno, rounded a bunch of us up. I wasn't having it, took a swing at the Lieutenant-Commander. Next thing I know, I'm tossed out here like a sack of hammers."

"Jimmy! That wasn't very smart!" I wasn't surprised, but at the same time, I couldn't believe he was stupid enough to leave Nonny all alone.

"I guess I just let my temper get the best of me," he said, sounding ashamed. Then he brightened and said, "But I'm out here with you two, so it won't be so bad, right?" I stared blankly at him and he continued, "Because we'll be rescued, right?" He looked at us hopefully.

"Rescued by who?" Trick said slowly, punctuating each word in a dangerous way that Jimmy was too oblivious to understand.

"Well, I—I mean, you're...you're important," Jimmy stammered.

"Important to who?" Trick pressed him, speaking again in a low, malevolent voice. Suddenly, it dawned on me what Trick was getting at.

"Jimmy, why are you *really* here?" I asked. "Don't try to tell us that you're going to fight to the death over sucker-punching a Blue. They wouldn't have bothered, just shot you on the spot. What's going on?"

Jimmy looked around desperately. "No, no, I don't know anything," he said. "The guy inside—"

"What guy inside?!" I demanded angrily. "Tell us!"

"Whoa, wait!" Jimmy put up his hands. "Calm down, Cee, please. Stay calm!"

Trick stood up and loomed over Jimmy, whose hands were still up, trying to ward off our scrutiny. "Why do you want Cee to stay calm, Jimmy Diamond? What do you know? What did they ask you to find out?!"

Jimmy started snivelling again. "Please. They said if I got any good information, they'd let me go. I have a wife at home!" He stood up, unfolding his lanky frame and facing us, back against the sky.

"Why you, Jimmy? Of all people, why you?" I asked.

Trick answered for me. "Because he might bet on diamond when the chips are down, but he loses every time. You'd think he'd learn, but no. Exactly how much do you owe the Caseeno Boys, Jimmy? Enough to betray your people?" Trick took a step forward, and Jimmy took a step back, glancing nervously over his shoulder at the precipice. "I always wondered who tipped the Blues off that I'd be in Old K. What did they give you? Enough coin to pay your debts? Is that all we're worth to you?" Trick took another step forward. Regardless of the difference in their sizes, Jimmy took another step back despite how close he was getting to the platform's edge, obviously intimidated.

"They said they'd kill me," Jimmy whispered. "Forgive me."

"Forgiveness is overrated," Trick said coldly.

"Trick, NO!" I yelled, but it was too late. He launched himself at Jimmy, planting his hands squarely in the middle of Jimmy's chest. Jimmy screamed as he was propelled backwards. There was a moment, a fraction of a second when Jimmy's heel caught on the edge and he flailed his arms, trying to use the air to pull himself forward to safety, but it was no use. With one last scream, he disappeared over the edge, the scream fading as he fell. Then there was nothing.

"Why?!" I yelled at Trick.

He turned to me and shrugged his shoulders in resignation. "They would have killed him anyway. He wasn't clever or cunning enough to make an effective spy."

The door to the interior of The Tower flew open again and Durand came out, his tether disappearing around the inside of the door.

"Thaddeus!" he called. "It's time for you and your friend to come inside. Fight's tomorrow. We need to get you ready."

"Why don't you come out here and get me?" Trick taunted. Then Durand was shoved aside, as Songe strode out from behind him, his cybernetic eye flashing red as he looked at us.

"You killed my spy," he said blithely. "That wasn't very nice." At the sight of him, I could feel my anger starting to build, but I tried to do what Trick said, to control it. There was a slight tremor in the metal of the platform, but I put up a wall, blocking the hate, the same way that I could block Dee from feeling my true emotions. The tremor subsided and Songe raised an eyebrow but merely said, "You have a simple choice. Come in now, or I'll slice you in half."

Trick and I looked at each other. He shrugged, and we both moved together towards the door, shoving past

Durand and into the bright chamber beyond. We were taken up two flights of stairs and into a circular hallway that ringed The Tower. There was a series of rooms in the interior. Songe said, "You'll stay here for a few hours. Then you'll be taken down to The Dome to prepare. Personally, my money is on Trick. He's certainly much more mercenary than you are, dear Cee. And of course, if anything happens to you, I'll be sure to take good care of your sister...." He paused, waiting for my reaction, but I steeled my mind and the wall held. He looked faintly disappointed. Durand shoved Trick into the room hard enough that he stumbled and hit the floor. Durand laughed, but Songe gave him a sharp look, and he stopped and looked down at his feet.

"Don't damage the goods," Songe said softly. He took my arm and gestured towards the room where there was a table set up with food. My mouth immediately started watering. But just as I was about to step inside, I caught movement out of the corner of my eye. I turned, in time to see a figure disappearing around the bend in the hall. It was a woman in a blue uniform, a woman with hair the colour of a golden sunset. She glanced back at me quickly and I realized that she looked exactly like someone I'd seen before in my dreams. Exactly like our mother.

23

Dee

My heart leapt into my throat. Rogan moved towards me protectively as Malachi Thorn took another ominous step forward. Then his ravaged face, with its filed, sharp teeth, crinkled in a strange way, and I realized that he was trying not to laugh. With that, Darv stepped in and said, "For the sake of the old god, Malachi, knock it off. You're terrifying them!" Then they both started roaring with laughter, clapping each other on the arms and embracing. I glanced over at Rogan and S-Sam, who looked like he was about to faint. Rogan just shook his head in bewilderment and shrugged his shoulders.

Malachi let go of Darv and looked at us, still shaking with laughter. "Your faces," he said in a low, thick voice. He sounded as if his throat was full of gravel. "Don't worry," he continued. "We don't eat our allies. Only our enemies." He paused, and despite the great number of people in the chamber below, all was silent. The Skeleton Army remained motionless. Ceridwen came forward, and he took her hand in a strangely chivalrous way. "White Witch, we meet again."

"On your attendance, my lord; here," she said, smiling.

"And who is this scruffy lot?" Malachi asked Darv, gesturing at me, Rogan, and S-Sam.

Darv pointed at me. "This is my —" he began, but thought better of it when he saw the angry look I shot him. "This is Dee, and her friends Rogan and Sam. They're important to the cause."

Malachi nodded. "Well met. It's good that you're all here now. There's news and plans to be made. Come — there's a gathering place towards the back of the chamber where we can sit and parlay."

We all descended the stairs. When we reached the bottom, the Skeleton Army once again silently parted, allowing us to pass through them. We were in what looked like some kind of underground city. There were empty storefronts lining the chamber, their signs ambiguous and foreign.

"Who is Victoria, and what's her secret, do you think?" Rogan whispered to me as we went by one shop that stretched back into darkness. There were plastic statues of people in some of the windows or lying on the floor, featureless, their eyes blank.

"What *is* this place?" I asked. I'd never seen anything like it before. There were areas around Divinity where the streets had once been lined with stores and businesses, but they were mostly rubble now, after the Water Wars. Anything left standing had been looted, and it looked like this empty underground city was no different.

Malachi looked surprised. "You've never seen a mall before?" he asked.

S-Sam shrugged, but I laughed sharply. "Uh, no. Rogan and I were both abandoned at workhouses far up North when we were babies. We'd never even seen a city before coming to Divinity." I put special emphasis on 'abandoned', watching Darv to see if it sparked a reaction, but he kept walking purposefully and didn't look back.

"There were malls like this everywhere where I come from," Malachi said. "But they were all shut down by The Consortium."

"Shut down?" I asked. "You mean destroyed during the Water Wars?"

Darv gave me a sharp look, and Malachi snorted in derision. "Water Wars," he said. "Is that what they teach you here?"

Darv looked apologetic. "They were raised in workhouses," he said. "All they know is the propaganda spewed by The Consortium."

By this time, we'd reached an open area that had tables and benches, ringed by what looked like food counters. A sign labelled it "Food Court". Malachi motioned to a table, and said, "Maybe it's time they learned the truth. Then they'll understand why we're here. But first, let's break bread together." We sat down on the hard, plastic seats, looking at him expectantly. He gestured silently, and suddenly, out of nowhere, hooded figures appeared, carrying trays of steaming bowls and cups that they placed in front of us. The cups were filled with clear water that smelled sweet and tangy, and the bowls contained what looked like some kind of stew.

Ceridwen looked at her tray and chuckled to herself. "Although the cheer be poor, 'twill fill your stomachs."

"She has a keen sense of humour *and* irony," Malachi Thorn said to Darv, then looked at the rest of us. "Dig in. I promise it's all safe for human consumption."

I took a sip of the water. It was hot and savoury. "Mm," I said. "What is it?"

"It's lemon balm tea," he replied. "It's one of the few herbs that can grow in very dry conditions. The stew, on the other hand, is made with synthetic protein. It's not the most tasty stuff in the world, but we can make it look more appetizing than the square cubes it comes in."

S-Sam was already devouring it hungrily. He looked up and said through a mouthful, "I-I-It's r-really g-good!"

I was shocked. If someone had told me last week that I'd be sharing a meal with a Frag, and that I *wasn't* that meal, I would have called it insanity. What was happening was a direct contradiction to literally everything I'd ever heard of or experienced with Frags. They were supposed to be animals, uncivilized cannibals who lived like nomads. The three who'd tried to attack Cee and me were certainly evidence of that. But Malachi and his army, despite their intimidating appearance, were different. First of all, they seemed highly organized and disciplined. As for "uncivilized", I'd just been handed a cup of lemon balm tea — not exactly the drink of barbarians. While I was mulling this over, Rogan said very pointedly, "So you were talking about the truth — what did you mean?"

Malachi scooped up the last of his stew and swallowed. Then he put down the spoon carefully, put his hand over his eyes and quietly said, "Thanks to the earth and what it grows. Thanks to my kin and what they sow." Then he looked up and began. "The truth. One man's truth is another man's history — or woman's, of course. In this case, the truth of my people is the history of yours, or to say more rightly, what The Consortium has told you all these years. That we're savages. That we're monsters. That we attacked you to take what was yours. But to understand the truth, we have to go back long before what you call the Water Wars. Many years ago, we were very much like you, a country struggling with the changes to the earth that we all know of. Strange weather, more severe storms, rising oceans that drowned the coast, and drought that dried up the nation's interior had caused what was left of our people to start moving North, away from the desert and starvation. Our only water source was the ocean — we built thousands of clicks of pipeline that transported the ocean water to huge desalinators that removed the salt, making it drinkable. But unlike you, we had decades of leadership that refused to acknowledge the need to change. While your country was developing solar tech and building wind farms, ours was still using fossil fuel and hydroelectrics. Once the oil dried up, we were an easy target."

"A target for who?" I asked. This was completely different than anything I'd ever been taught, and, true or not, it was fascinating.

"The Consortium," he replied. "We relied on them for trade. It was a relationship that benefitted both sides. But one day, they sent envoys who demanded that we shut down all production and become a consumer nation. No more exporting. They wanted to take over our economy and make the relationship completely one-sided. In exchange, they would…leave us alone."

"What do you mean, 'leave you alone'?" Rogan asked. "That sounds like a threat."

"It was," Malachi replied. "One that our leadership was too arrogant to understand. Of course, they refused The Consortium's 'generous' offer. Two days later, we were attacked. They targeted our desalinators, blew them out with EMPs, then leveled them with sonic bombs. All usable water production stopped."

"That's when you started rioting and attacking us," I interjected.

"We had no choice," he responded. "We were desperate, dying of thirst. The Consortium left us like that for 6 months, and then their envoys came back with another offer."

"This was the most unkindest cut of all," Ceridwen said sadly. Malachi sighed and nodded.

"W-What was the o-o-offer?" S-Sam asked. We all leaned forward, on the edge of our seats. Even Darv, who already must have known the story, was fixated on Malachi, who drew a deep breath and then continued.

"They took the children," he said, his voice catching. "In exchange for water, the government agreed to hand them over as slave labour for Consortium factories."

There was a long pause, then Darv said, "You see? We're not so different from each other; despite the stories you've heard, the Frags aren't zombies, deathwalkers, ghosts, or evil spirits."

"Not so different at all," I said ironically. "Except the Frags had their children stolen. We just abandoned ours to the workhouses."

Darv's eyes flashed angrily and he was about to say something, when Rogan interrupted. "I have to ask," he said. "If you're not really cannibals, why do you file your teeth like that?"

Malachi laughed. "I'm an old man," he said. "If I didn't look like this, would you be afraid of me at all?" Rogan laughed as well, and Malachi continued. "We don't have any sophisticated weapons or technology, but we try to look as intimidating, as barbaric as possible. The Consortium envoys come every year to take whatever children we have. The least we can do is make sure they don't stick around for anything else."

"Why don't you stop having children then?" I asked. "Wouldn't they leave you alone after a while?"

"We tried that at first," he said. "And then they set up breeding farms. That was worse. They don't take the children until they're five years old, so at least we have a few years with them before they're ripped out of our arms. You see all these people?" He made a sweeping gesture towards the silent Skeleton Army, patiently waiting. "This is not only an army of trained soldiers—they're also mothers and fathers, some of them even grandparents like me. *Show*!!" he commanded suddenly. With that, the army turned as one, and they all removed their skull-painted hoods. Some of the soldiers were younger, but most were middle-aged men and women, or even older; the one thing they had in common was that they all looked fierce and determined.

"You see," he said. "Our strength comes from the fact that we have nothing to lose. We will help you fight, and win."

"OK," Rogan said slowly. "But what's the plan? We can't just waltz up to The Tower, knock on the door, and ask The Consortium nicely to give us back our country, and your children."

Darv laughed harshly. "We won't be waltzing—it will be a much more delicate dance than that. But let me assure you that by the time we're done, all the Towers, from coast to coast, will be taken."

"And then what?!" Rogan insisted. "The Consortium just leaves? And what's to stop them from retaliating?

"I think they have bigger problems right now." Malachi smiled broadly, his teeth glittering in the low light.

"What do you mean?" I asked.

Darv laughed lightly. "Consider the way The Consortium treats the people here. Do you really believe they treat their own citizens any better? Our sources tell us that the people of EastInd have already risen up and overthrown their government, and that Jan is on the verge of doing the same. The Consortium has its hands full, and frankly, I think we're the least of their concerns. Outside of the main city centres, there are very few Blues—they're all being moved back to mainland Chin to support The Consortium in their home countries. The time is right for us to strike."

"But what makes you think they'll give all the children back?!" I turned to Malachi. "What's stopping The Consortium from just…killing them all?!"

Malachi's eyes darkened. "They won't. Not if they want to see *their* families again."

Ceridwen said softly, "I cannot but remember such things were, that were most precious to me."

Hearing her words, Malachi sighed and sat back in his chair. "We love our children," he said quietly. "And The Consortium loves theirs."

"You mean 'hostages'," said Rogan flatly.

"We have no choice," replied Darv. "A lot of the Bijoux, or what you call the Fancies, are members of powerful

Consortium families. Some of the Blues too. We believe that we can negotiate."

"OK, fine." There was a cynical edge to Rogan's voice. "Say we take The Tower *and* destroy The Dome, and we get the Frag kids back and everyone is happy. What do we do then? How do we survive without The Consortium?"

"We rebuild," Darv said. "It won't be easy, but we're strong. We were independent once; we can be independent again."

"There's just one problem," I said. Everybody turned to stare at me, and I suddenly felt very uncomfortable, but I continued on anyway. "I've seen the weapons the Blues have, and I've seen what we have. The Consortium has us completely outgunned."

"That's where you're wrong," Darv answered, smiling. "We have something that the Consortium isn't counting on. Your brother."

24

Cee

With a look of disgust, Durand slammed the door behind us, leaving us alone. Trick stood up slowly, wincing from the pain in his ribs, and brushed himself off. He regarded me curiously. "What is it?" he asked. "You look like you've just seen a ghost."

"Not a ghost," I said slowly. "More like someone from a dream."

"Well," Trick responded, "why don't we start eating before we run out of time, and you can tell me all about it? I don't know about you, but I'm starving, and until I get something in my stomach, I won't be able to concentrate anyway."

It sounded like a good plan, since I needed some time to thoroughly process what I'd seen, or at least thought I saw. I nodded. We went over to the table and my eyes grew wide at the assortment of food laid out before us. There was bread and meat, fruit that I'd never seen before, bowls of vegetables and rice, and a tray of tiny dark squares that were decorated with fancy swirls of a creamy substance.

"I don't understand," I said to Trick, loading up a plate. "Why are they doing this? I mean, they've starved us for days, and now a banquet?"

Trick laughed and shoved one of the little squares in his mouth. "Mmm," he said. "Chocolate cake. You've got to try this before anything else." He held one out to me, and continued, "They want us healthy and happy before the match, I imagine. It wouldn't be much of a spectacle if the two champions were barely able to move from hunger, would it? But go slow—you don't want to make yourself sick."

I took the cake from him and popped it in my mouth. A sensation like nothing I'd experienced before came over me. "Chocolate? It's—amazing!" I exclaimed, closing my eyes in sheer delight. It was almost enough to make me forget for a moment where I was—but not quite.

"Have some of the other food now," Trick ordered. "You need to keep your strength up. You can have more of the chocolate later." He smiled at me like an indulgent parent, and suddenly I was overwhelmed with tremendous sadness at the thought that, in less than 24 hours, we would be fighting to the death, me and this small boy.

As if sensing my thoughts, he said, "Never mind anything else now. Let's sit down and eat, and you can tell me about your dream."

I loaded my plate and sat down. "All right. Well, Dee and I were left at a workhouse too when we were only 3 months old—"

"Starting at the very beginning, I see," he snickered, reminding me of my earlier joke. "Sorry, I couldn't resist. Carry on."

"I guess I deserved that," I said, laughing too through a mouthful of meat and bread. I swallowed and continued. "We never knew our parents. The only evidence we had was a note pinned to our carrier that said, '*Take care of them. I can't*'. But as I got older, I started to have...I don't know if you'd call them dreams or visions...about our mother. I could sense her in that moment, her despair and grief at having to leave us, and as I grew older, I was able to get a sense of what she looked like. It was always very vague, but I know that Dee saw her too, and because of that, I was able to put together a really clear picture of her."

"And?" Trick prompted, putting his fork down and leaning forward in anticipation.

"And...and I think I just saw her outside in the corridor. In fact, I'm positive it's her. But it doesn't make any sense. She was wearing a Blue uniform, a Regional Commander. How could that be our mother?!"

Trick thought for a moment. "It makes sense in a way," he said finally. "We know that Darv Bouchard is your father, and we know that Les Coquins, his first rebel movement, was infiltrated by a Consortium spy, a young woman. What if she took her role more seriously than anyone could have guessed, and she became pregnant? There's no way her family would have let her keep the baby — or babies, as it turned out. And she was *very* young."

"Somehow that makes me feel worse," I sighed. "I always liked to imagine that our mother gave us up for less selfish reasons, like she just couldn't afford to keep us, and that it was terrible for her. If what you say is true, we were simply an embarrassment to her."

"I don't know about that," Trick said. "She left a note, didn't she? That's more than I got. And the note makes it sound as though she didn't have a choice and was doing what she hoped would be the right thing for you and Dee."

"I wish I could believe that, but if she'd really cared about the right thing, she would have come back for us. And if what you say is true about this cybernetic implant I'm supposed to have, then obviously she knew about that. So why *didn't* she come for us? The workhouse was bad enough for me, but it was ten times worse for Dee. I—"

Suddenly a voice blared out of a loudspeaker in the corner. "Five more minutes!"

"Five more minutes until what?!" I exclaimed, looking around wildly.

"Five more minutes until they separate us, I imagine, to get us ready for the fight tomorrow," Trick said quietly. "Have some more cake now."

I looked at Trick, young, vulnerable, bruised and exhausted, sitting there holding out a piece of chocolate cake to me like a younger brother, and I fought back the tears that were threatening to form. "I won't kill you. I don't care what they do to me," I declared adamantly.

Trick smiled sadly. "I appreciate the sentiment, but I doubt that you'll have much choice. I refuse to kill *you*, so if you don't satisfy the crowd, they'll just have us both slaughtered. I'm ready to sacrifice myself for the Dominion, for the greater good. It's for the best."

"Nobody's sacrificing anything!" I insisted. "We just need a plan. We—"

Then the door swung open and Durand stood there smirking. "Time to clean you pathetic maggots up," he laughed harshly. "The crowd wants to see sparkling young warriors, not beggars." He nodded to two Blues behind him, and they grabbed each of us, taking us in separate directions.

I took one last look at Trick. "Choose your weapon wisely!" he called out, tapping his temple three times.

"Good advice," the Blue holding Trick's arm snickered. "Although it won't take much to send *you* into the next life." Then he dragged Trick around the corner and out of my sight.

"Don't underestimate him," I muttered under my breath, wondering exactly what Trick meant.

The Blue holding me, an older EastInd man whose name badge said 'Varma', gave me a sharp look and pulled me towards a set of doors. "We're going down this way," he said, and pushed a button next to the door. I heard a strange whirring noise that sounded like it was getting closer, then suddenly the doors opened onto another tiny room. Varma wordlessly manoeuvered me into the room, and the doors shut behind us. Inside there was another bank of buttons. He pushed one, and the room gave a shudder. We were moving. I looked around nervously, and he laughed. "Never been in an elevator before, Freeworlder?"

I shook my head and we continued the trip downward in silence. I jumped slightly when the elevator came to a stop and the doors opened again, this time into a foyer leading to a glassed-in bridge that arched away into the distance. He took my arm and steered me towards the bridge.

"Where are we going?" I asked him.

Varma snorted and said, "To The Dome, of course. Where do you think? They'll clean you up, give you a weapon and a good night's sleep, then it's a fight to the death! No offense, but I put my coin on the little guy. He might not look like much, but he can take quite a beating, and give it out too. When we first got him here, he bit off one of his guard's ears! We had to shock him five times to make him spit it out! Heh heh." He chuckled, shaking his head in amusement. I said nothing, but I laughed inwardly too at the thought of anyone being fooled by Trick's size.

By this point, we were half-way across the glassed-in bridge. I looked out, and could see the solar cruisers in the water, travelling back and forth between Metro and the Island, dropping the Fancies onto the mainland to do their shopping and show themselves off, while the rest of us struggled to survive. On the docks, there were men with shaved and tattooed heads in light-coloured suits and women dressed in bright colours like peacocks, tiny dogs and children between them. Even from this far away, they all seemed pre-occupied, wandering aimlessly. Varma saw me watching, and he snorted again. "Look at them!" he said derisively. "Strutting around in their finery while they listen to propatainment streaming through their implants. I don't know how they stand it, having voices jabbering in their heads constantly, talking about the latest gossip, what to wear, which Consortium bigwig was seen with new eyes — it's sickening. The sooner we're rid of them—" He broke off suddenly, giving me a sideways glance then quickly changing the subject. "So," he continued heartily, "what weapon are you thinking of? I bet the little guy goes for a knife over a shocker — he has a taste for blood, I think."

"I don't know," I muttered distractedly, still wondering about how much he seemed to despise the Fancies on the dock. I always thought the Blues were loyal, trained to protect them, but maybe they were unhappy about the state of things as well.

"Never mind," he said. "You'll choose soon enough. Here we are." He stopped in front of a red door and pushed it open. Inside were storage lockers, and in the back, I could see a large open room full of showerheads. It looked kind of like the Tap back home. He went to one of the lockers, opened it, and took out some fresh clothes, towels, and a couple of small bottles. "Go on in there," he ordered. "Get washed and then put these on." He shoved the stack at me and left, locking the door behind him.

I put the clothes down on a wooden bench in front of the lockers, got undressed and wandered back into the shower room. It was cavernous, with a concrete floor, and about twenty showerheads ringing the walls. I hung the towel on a hook and looked at the tap on the wall below one of the showerheads. It was labelled "H" and "C". Was it actually possible that there was hot water here? I turned on the tap and waited for a moment. Sure enough, the water quickly became warm, then hotter. I adjusted the temperature and then turned the shower on. Standing beneath the luxurious spray, I was almost able to forget why I was there. I hadn't had a hot shower since we'd left the workhouse, and even then it was only ever lukewarm. I scrubbed myself clean, washed my hair, and then just stood there for a few moments, letting the water run over me. Finally, not knowing when Varma would be back, I reluctantly turned off the tap. I dried myself, then went back into the locker room to get dressed. The clothes weren't particularly special—light blue shirt and dark pants—but they were made from the same solprotectant material that the Fancies used and the fabric was softer than anything I'd ever worn before. I was sitting on the bench, facing the lockers, fingering the silky collar of the shirt when I heard the door unlock. I didn't look around—Varma could just wait until I was ready. The door shut and I heard the lock click again. There was silence for a moment, and then I heard a small sob. I spun around quickly, and there she was—the woman from our dreams. I jumped to my feet and she flew towards me, wrapping her arms around me tightly.

"It's really you!" she gasped. "Thank the old god!" We stood there for a moment in silence, then I took her by the shoulders and pushed her away so that I could get a good look at her. She was older now than the woman in my vision, but with the same golden-red hair as Dee and me, and the same green eyes that Dee stared into while tears dropped from them onto her cheek.

"I know you," I said slowly.

"Yes," she answered. "You do. And we have so much to talk about."

25
Dee

I was shocked, outraged — I couldn't believe the story Darv had just told us. "You mean to tell me," I shouted, "that not only did you abandon us to the workhouse, you used Cee like a human experiment first?! A cybernetic implant that can cause earthquakes — is this some kind of sick joke?!" I was on my feet, screaming at him at the top of my lungs. Malachi fidgeted awkwardly in his seat, Ceridwen sighed deeply, and Darv held his hands up in the air as if to ward off my fury.

"You don't understand!" he said. I started to turn away, and he grabbed my arms. Something snapped inside me and I went wild, ripping myself away from him, leaping over the table and putting it between us.

"I hate you!" I shrieked at him. "Stay away from me!"

Darv started towards me, but Rogan jumped up and blocked him. "Don't," he ordered harshly. "Don't touch her. Cee's the only one, and sometimes me, but nobody else. You don't know what she's been through."

Darv looked shaken and turned to Rogan. "What are you talking about?" he demanded.

"No," I yelled at Darv. "Don't you *dare* pretend to care now!"

I turned my back on all of them, and stormed away, walking blindly through the empty mall. The Skeleton Army watched me silently. Their scrutiny was making me feel worse, so I ducked into a darkened store. It was littered with plastic body parts and broken shelving. I made my way to the back where there were tiny rooms with doors. I went into one, slammed the door shut and locked it, then sat down on the bench inside, breathing fast and heavy, hot tears on my face. The tiny room was pitch black and cool. It was comforting somehow to just sit there in the dark, listening to my own breathing while I struggled to sort this mess out in my head away from everyone else. I tried to reach out to Cee, but he was too far away — all I could sense was the faint hum of his presence, nothing more. I stifled an anguished sob and pressed the heels of my palms hard into my eyes to stop the tears from coming again. I missed Cee so much. I'd never had to deal with anything frightening or infuriating without him there to comfort me or calm me down, and now I was scared *and* furious.

I remember when Cee and I first arrived in Divinity — it wasn't easy, but it was such a relief after the years of the workhouse, then having to make our way down south, avoiding Frag nomads and the roving homeless gangs they called The Dead Kids, or TDK for short. TDK were people of varying ages who'd run away from the workhouses, ag farms, and slave factories, but who were too damaged to function in a tent city, so they banded together and survived as best they could. The Consortium and the Fancies considered Divinity, and places like it, barbaric and uncivilized, but they weren't. Divinity was our first real home, and it was the first time that either of us had felt really safe. Tent cities had their own unwritten sets of rules and codes of behaviour, the most important of which was that everyone was equal, something that the

Fancies would never understand. If you wanted to live in a tent city, there were three rules that you had to follow:

1) "What's mine is mine and what's yours is yours."

2) "Don't play if you can't pay."

3) "If you have a problem with the first two rules, take it to Tribunal."

Those first two rules covered just about everything, and if they didn't, Tribunal would decide. Being on Tribunal was voluntary; if there was a dispute that couldn't be solved any other way, word would go around that three impartial people were needed, people who weren't relatives, or had no interest in the outcome of the conflict. I stepped up for it once. It was the case of a newcomer named Liam who had stolen dyes from a stall owner at the Hidden Market, and then used them to create beautiful paintings that he himself sold for a huge amount of coin to the Fancies. The stall owner, Koyo, argued that he should receive all the money that Liam had made, since the dyes were his but couldn't be returned because Liam had used them all up. Liam argued that the only reason the paintings sold so well was because of his talent, so he should only have to pay back the cost of the dyes. Then, to complicate things even more, it came out that Liam had taken the money he made to Caseeno and lost it all.

At Tribunal, we agreed that Liam had broken Rule 1 but not Rule 2, which was lucky because the Caseeno Boys usually took care of Rule 2, and Liam could have ended up with two broken arms instead of a hearing at Tribunal. After a lot of discussion, we gave them a choice: Liam could work at Koyo's stall until his debt was paid, or he could give Koyo something of equal value, or he could leave Divinity. Well, Koyo didn't want a known thief in his stall, but he *did* admire Liam's paintings, so he took the last one as payment. I'll never forget what Koyo said in his final statement: "Not only is the painting beautiful, but I will always smile when I think about the Fancies who believe they are better than us, but whose walls are no more lovely than mine." Then, in an interesting conclusion to the whole thing, Koyo offered to become partners with Liam, providing him with the supplies he needed for his paintings and letting him share the stall in exchange for part of the profits. As far as I know, they're still together, even sharing the same tent now. So Tribunal works, at least most of the time. The times that it doesn't—those are the people who end up part of TDK, living rough and marauding.

Thinking back to Tribunal gave me some comfort. I remember being up there on the platform, my opinion actually mattering, and Cee watching, so proud of me. Would he be proud of me now, sitting here in the dark holding back tears? Suddenly, there was a soft knock on the door. I paused—I wasn't in the mood to talk to anyone.

"Whoever it is, go away," I said. I knew who it was though, and I knew he wasn't going anywhere.

"No," Rogan said through the door. "Are you okay?"

I sighed, got up and leaned against the door with my palm flat on it. I could sense him on the other side, full of concern. "I don't know. Yes. Maybe." I sighed again. "I'm just tired."

"Darv wanted to know why you got so upset."

"What did you tell him?"

"The truth. I said I didn't really know, just that something had happened when you were younger, and that being touched by someone you didn't trust sent you out of your mind. Do you remember the first time I put my hand on your shoulder?"

I laughed wearily. "The first time we went thieving together, yes. I would have walked straight into a group of Blues if you hadn't grabbed me to stop me from turning the corner."

Rogan laughed as well. "And in return, you almost broke my nose. I grew up in a workhouse too. I know terrible things happen. Who was it? One of the Protectors?"

I hesitated. I'd never told anyone about that day. Cee was the only one who knew, and I didn't have to tell him in words. But Rogan was my best friend, and he'd saved my life in Old K—in fact, he'd saved my life more than once. He deserved to know the truth. I clenched my fist against the door and took a deep breath. "It—it was a Guardian. He caught me stealing candy. He said he might be persuaded to overlook it if I—" I paused, remembering the repulsive feel of his touch on my skin. I swallowed hard and continued. "I told him I'd rather die. He smiled at me, this awful smile, and said, 'Be careful what you wish for'. Then he dragged me to the Shed and threw me down. I hit my head. I don't remember much after that, except the pain. When...when he was done, he stood up, laughed and said, "Sweets to the sweet." Then he threw the candy at me and left me there. It was right before my Fifteenth Drop-Off Day." I could feel my fingernails digging into my palm. I shoved away the memory of Songe's leering face and tried to quell the wave of nausea that had come over me.

I heard Rogan breathe in sharply. "What was his name? Where is he now?" Rogan's voice on the other side of the door sounded low and dangerous.

"Don't worry," I said. "Cee took care of it."

There was a pause, then Rogan said, "Cee? Our Cee? I don't believe it! What did he do?"

"I don't know all the details, but it involved a laser pruner. The Guardian was sent up north to an agri-station and I never saw him again."

Rogan was silent for a minute, then he said, "After you were hurt in Old K, Cee told me that if you died, he would kill me himself. I guess I got off lucky."

"Cee said *what*?!" I was shocked.

"He was serious," Rogan replied. "As serious as I've ever seen him."

We were both quiet for a moment, then Rogan said, "Let me in."

I unlocked the door, then sat back down on the bench. The door swung in slowly; Rogan was silhouetted against the dim light from the store. I patted the bench beside me and he came in and sat down next to me with a sigh. I leaned my head on his shoulder and he took my hand. I breathed in deeply — he smelled like Divinity just before the hot rain came, a mixture of spice and canvas and swirling dust, and before I knew what was happening, I was sobbing into his jacket. He said nothing, just put his arm gently around me and let me cry, for Cee, for myself, for a home left behind, for a father who'd abandoned us and a mother we'd never know, for everything we'd lost, and the fear of what we could still lose.

Finally, I had no more tears left to shed. I sat up straight, sniffing, and wiped my face with my sleeve.

Rogan turned to me and asked, "What now?"

"Now?" I answered. "Now we go back. We have work to do."

26

Cee

She was wearing a Regional Commander's uniform, and her hair was shorter than in my visions, but there was no question that it was her. I looked at her in stunned silence. She took my arm, looking around nervously, and pulled me towards the bench. When she said, "Come and sit down," I suddenly realized that she hadn't actually spoken to me yet.

"Am I hearing you in my head?" I asked, amazed.

She smiled and answered again without speaking, "Is it clear? Loud?"

I nodded slowly. It was, as clear and distinct as if she was talking directly to me. "That's wonderful," she finally said, using her voice for the first time. It was a soft and low voice with a slight accent.

"Who are you?" I asked. I felt as though I already knew, but I needed to hear it from her.

Her green eyes met mine. She hesitated for a moment, then took my hand. I could feel her trembling, a tremor that ran through me and gave me chills.

"My name is France DuLac," she said. "I'm your mother." She gripped my hand tightly, as if guarding

against me pulling away. I didn't. I just sat in wordless re-
straint, trying to think of something to say. Finally, I said
the only thing I could think of under the circumstances.

"Where the *hell* have you been for the last 16 years?"
I was trying to keep the anger out of my voice but I wasn't
very successful.

She let go of my hand and stood up, sensing my
emotion and turning away from me. "You have every right
to be furious, but at least let me try to explain."

I wanted to hate her, to order her out, but I didn't
for three reasons. First, because I was curious. I had so
many questions — why did she leave us at the workhouse?
Was Darv Bouchard really our father? Where was he? Did
he even know what had happened to us? Second, because
I was in a pretty dire position right now, and, call me mercenary, but maybe she could use her position to help me
and Trick. And finally, and most importantly, because
when her voice was in my head, there was something else
there too — a sense of terrible loss and loneliness, kindness
and determination that made me want to give her a chance.
I nodded, and she sat back down next to me on the bench.

She took a deep breath and began. "When I was
born, it was right at the end of the Water Wars. My father
had been a commander in the Adanac military, as limited
as that was, and when The Consortium forces helped us defeat the Frags, he was the key liaison with their leaders. In
exchange for his help during the war, he was made Governor-General of both Kabac and Trillium provinces. My father
was a hard, cruel man, and he supported The Consortium
as they systematically dismantled Adanac society and re-
made it in their own image. I lived with my mother, a meek
and dutiful woman, and I rarely saw him. But my mother
died when I was fourteen, and I went to live with my father
in Mont Royal where he presided over The Dome there. A
small rebel group called Les Coquins had been making his
life miserable for years, and while he'd caught a couple of

them, torturing them and then letting the crowd do as it pleased with them in The Dome, he was never able to determine who the leader of the group was. Then one day, just after I'd turned sixteen, he called me in and told me that he was sending me to Terrebonne, a tent city outside of Mont Royal, to infiltrate Les Coquins and find out the identity of the leader. I didn't want to go, I begged him not to send me — but he gave me no choice. His plan was to dress me in rags and have me tossed unceremoniously outside Terrebonne to fend for myself as a Freeworlder. But first, he subjected me to experimental treatments with Consortium designer drugs, treatments which he believed would mutate my DNA to increase my perceptive abilities and make it easier for me to gather information."

"You mean he made you into — what, a telepath?" I asked, incredulous.

"Yes," she answered. "It was his dream to create a new generation of people with enhanced abilities. But his experiments on me came with a side effect that he never intended. Not only could I sense what other people close by were thinking, I could see the truth of who my father really was, a hateful person who had abused my mother for years, and took pleasure in the torture he inflicted. I decided to go to Terrebonne, but instead of becoming a Consortium spy, I would simply disappear. Then the worst thing happened."

"The worst thing?" I asked. I couldn't think of anything worse than your own father experimenting on you with drugs and then sending you off on your own to survive in a tent city.

She smiled sadly. "The worst thing. And the best thing. I met your father."

"My father?! Who was he?" I didn't mean to phrase it in the past tense, but for some reason, I'd always believed that our father was dead. Dee never had any sense of him, and neither had I, so I just assumed that he had passed a long time ago.

France's sad smile became a look of pride and affection. "He *is* Darv Bouchard, the leader of the resistance. The very man I was supposed to trap was the man I fell in love with. We were together for almost two years before Les Coquins were betrayed and he was sent to The Dome. My father was furious when he found out that instead of working for him, I'd been working for the resistance and feeding The Consortium false information for months."

"What did he do to you? I can't imagine that he just let you get away with it."

"Oh, he had a fine punishment in store for me, I'm sure, but what he didn't know was that I was pregnant, and that Darv had already arranged for my escape, regardless of what happened to him. I convinced him to show Darv mercy, pledging to continue my work as a Consortium spy. After Les Coquins attacked The Dome in Mont Royal, Darv and I fled, going into hiding until I gave birth. But we knew that if my father found out about you and Elysia and the powers you had, he would hunt us down, never stopping until he had you both."

"Elysia? Who's Elysia?" I asked, confused. "And what powers are you talking about?!"

France laughed. "Elysia's your sister, of course. I know you call yourselves Cee and Dee now, but you were born Niko and Elysia. As for powers, it became pretty obvious not long after you were born that you'd inherited my 'perceptive abilities'. You never cried—neither of you. When you were hungry, you just...let me know. You're aware of your cybernetic implant—it was an attempt to try and channel those abilities in a way that could be useful."

I stood up quickly, walked over to the bank of lockers and leaned forward, resting my head against the cold metal. It was too much to take in, to even believe. Was this how Songe would finally get his revenge, by sending in this woman with her fantastical story to get my hopes up? Any second now, I expected him to appear, that leering grin on his face, and say "Gotcha!"

From behind me, France sighed. "I know it sounds fantastical, but it's true. Songe has nothing to do with this—as far as he knows, I'm just another Regional Commander that he has to grudgingly obey."

I looked around at her sharply—I'd forgotten that she could basically read my mind. "Fine," I said cynically. "So you took us to the workhouse. And right before you abandoned us, you had me fitted with some kind of cybernetic device so that years later, I could be used as a weapon. Tell me, how are you any different from your own father?"

She came over and put her hand on my arm. "All I can do is tell you I'm sorry, which is more than my father ever did for me. Luckily, he was more concerned about his reputation, saving face with The Consortium, so when I came back and lied to him that Darv had abused me and forced me to work for him, he accepted that, and I was able to continue secretly providing information to the Dominion as I rose up through the ranks due to his influence. Now, as Dome Master, I—"

"Dome Master?!" I exclaimed, shocked. "*You're* the Dome Master?! How could you do that?" I shrugged her hand off my arm in disgust and turned my back to her, but she grabbed my elbow forcefully and pulled me around to face her.

"Niko, listen to me," she said intensely. "I *know* this is a lot to take in. But as awful as everything sounds, I need you to put it aside. Everything I've done was absolutely necessary, no matter how much I hated it. There are bigger issues at stake—rescuing you and Trick is only part of a much greater plan to bring down The Consortium once and for all. Your father is coming. He's bringing your sister, and an army with him."

Before I even had a chance to react to what she had just told me, the door suddenly opened and Varma was standing there. I moved instinctively in front of France to protect her, but she stepped around me and went to Varma. He saluted and said, "It's time. I have to take him."

"I just need five more minutes," she replied. "We're almost finished."

"Fine," said Varma, "but no more than five—you don't want that little weasel upstairs getting suspicious. He's beside himself right now. I don't know what this one here did to rile him up so much, but he's up there on the skydeck, pacing around like a coywolf and shooting that damned eye at anything that moves—he's killed five birds already! I'll be waiting outside." With that, Varma left the room.

"We have more support than you could imagine. You'd be shocked if you knew how many Blues are on our side," she responded to my stunned stare. "But I need to ask you this, and it's very important. The implant—I know you can use it, but can you control it?"

"I—yes, I think so. Why?"

"Because when the Dominion comes, they'll need a diversion, something big, to distract the Blues who are still loyal to The Consortium long enough to give the Dominion time to strike and secure The Tower—an attack on The Dome will certainly get their attention. Show me," she ordered. "I need to see it."

I concentrated. It wasn't difficult. All I had to do was let loose my anger at what was happening right now, everything she'd told me, and it was enough. The floor started vibrating beneath our feet.

"Good," she said, an impressed look on her face. "Now stop before it draws any unwanted attention."

I put up the mental wall the way I'd taught myself to do, and the vibrating stopped immediately.

"Excellent," she said. "But what happened the other night? I felt you—The Tower was literally buckling."

"Songe isn't the only one who's 'riled up'," I answered curtly. Then she was in my head, moving around, searching. I quickly put the wall back up to try and block her, but not before she saw what I didn't want her to see.

She inhaled sharply, and she blinked back tears. "We were promised you would be well taken care of," she said, her voice catching.

"People break promises all the time," I answered. My voice sounded harder than I'd meant it to, and her face crumbled.

"I know you can never forgive me for everything I've done," she whispered. "But I did it because I love you."

I said nothing. Then Varma came back into the room and took me by the arm. "Let's go, my young warrior."

"Wait!" I said. "There's just one more thing." France came close, a pained look still on her face. "You said we inherited your 'abilities' and that I got the implant to what—magnify mine? But what about Dee? Does she have an implant?"

France reached up and touched my cheek gently. "Your sister has her own power," she said. "She doesn't need one."

27

Dee

Rogan and I made our way back through the dim store, stepping over the plastic limbs, torsos, and heads that littered the floor. Suddenly, I had a terrible vision of Divinity, with real bodies lying on the ground and I gasped. Rogan looked at me, concerned.

"What's wrong?"

"I—I think I'm just realizing how dangerous this all is. I know it sounds stupid, but I've been so focused on finding Cee that I really haven't given much thought to the bigger picture. Rogan, people could die. *We* could die!"

Rogan sighed. "I know. I had that same feeling when we crossed into Old K. But we can't turn back now—there's too much at stake."

We were almost at the edge of the Frag army, who were still standing silently, waiting, so I whispered, "I know. I don't want to turn back. I just don't know if I trust Darv. I mean, I trust that he's on the right side, that he's not a traitor or liar—but I think he's so consumed with destroying The Consortium that he doesn't care how many people get hurt in the process. Look what he did to Cee. Can I trust that he won't sacrifice me as well when the time comes?"

"I can't believe that," Rogan whispered back. "He's your father. I'm sure he won't let anything happen to you."

I laughed quietly. "I think I'm the last of Darv's concerns, unless he can use me for something. History has proven that one." I waved off Rogan's attempt at protest, then punched him lightly on the shoulder. "Enough. I'm tired and my back is really starting to ache. Time for some more pain meds. Let's go see if there's any of that tea left."

Rogan nodded and we walked back into the Food Court. Darv was over by the counters talking to a Frag soldier, and when he saw us, he raised his eyebrows questioningly. I resisted the urge to make a rude hand gesture, shrugging my shoulders instead. He nodded slightly and went back to talking to the Frag. I sat down on one of the hard plastic chairs at a table beneath a mammoth staircase and sagged forward, my head on my hands.

"Is the pain bad?" Rogan asked.

"Some. I'm tired. What I'd really like to do is just sleep for a little while."

"I'll go grab your pack and see if I can find something for you to drink," Rogan said. "Then we can look for a spot to get some rest." He disappeared around the corner. I sat quietly for a moment, thinking about how I was going to move forward. I was furious with Darv, but the fury was exhausting me as much as the pain in my shoulder and back. The fact was, as much as I tried to hate him, I admired him. He was confident, steadfast, made allies out of enemies, and commanded a force of rebels all fighting for freedom. People respected him, looked up to him, so why couldn't I? Then I felt a slight breeze brush against my cheek. I lifted my head up from my hands. Ceridwen was sitting at the table across from me, silently watching me. I smiled weakly at her. She smiled back wearily and said, "I am made of the self-same metal that my sister is."

"Well, I don't know about you, but I'm feeling a little 'rusty'."

Ceridwen laughed, a light crystal sound. Then she stopped and looked solemn. "Thou..." she hesitated. "Thou hast a careful father."

"Is he?" I answered derisively. "I wouldn't know. You've known him longer than I have."

"He's a good man," came a gravelly voice from behind me. It was Malachi. He sat down with us and continued sternly. "He brought us out of the darkness. He gave us hope. And I can tell you this: I would rather have hidden my only daughter in a workhouse than lost her forever to The Consortium, to die as a Consortium slave. Put your anger aside—he's paid the price for his actions. And you're luckier than some."

Ceridwen's piercing blue eyes glistened and she said quietly, "I would give you some violets but they wither'd all when my father died."

I reached out and touched Ceridwen's pale hand. She smiled wanly at me. "I'm sorry," I said.

"Sorry for what?" Rogan asked, reappearing from around the corner, my pack in one hand and a large cup in the other.

"Nothing," I answered, sighing. Rogan looked at Ceridwen and me curiously, but didn't pursue it.

Malachi stood up and said, "The moon is high. Try to rest. Morning will come soon and then we move." He and Ceridwen left together, his long stride keeping pace with the way she seemed to float along, her hooded cape flowing around her.

Rogan looked at me again with his eyebrows raised, but I gestured at the floor and said, "Malachi's right. We should try to sleep and this looks like as good a place as any. Where's S-Sam?"

"He's asleep in the main concourse with some of the Frags. They don't say much and that suits him fine—he seems really comfortable around them, believe it or not." Rogan laughed and handed me the cup and a pill. "Now take this and lie down."

I did as I was told. Rogan lay down on the floor next to me, our packs under our heads for pillows. Within seconds, Rogan's eyes closed and he drifted off. It took me a while longer, thanks to the dull throb in my shoulder and the thoughts that were racing through my mind. Could I really leave the past behind? Darv said he'd done what he did to protect Cee and me, and he wasn't much older than us when he'd left us at the workhouse. Would I have done things any differently if I'd been in his position? Maybe it was time to give him a chance, or at least stop being so awful to him. I thought about how he'd react if I suddenly called him "Dad", and then laughed at myself for getting sentimental. Finally I fell into a deep, dreamless sleep.

I woke abruptly to the sounds of whispering and the rustle of movement. I looked over and Rogan was sitting up, looking alert and eating a bowl of some kind of thick paste. "What's going on?" I asked.

"You slept all night—so did I. About half an hour ago, word came back that the sun was up and it was time to get ready to go. Here," he said, pushing another bowl towards me. "Have some oatmeal. It's kind of bland but it's filling. Oh, and I found a place a little further down kind of like the Tap. You can get cleaned up if you want."

I took a tentative taste of the oatmeal. It wasn't impressive but Rogan was right about it being substantial. It felt like it was sticking to my ribs and it warmed my insides in a satisfying way. When I was finished eating, he took me to the washrooms and left me to go find S-Sam. I got partially undressed and looked at my stitches in the mirror on the wall. The gashes were healing nicely now but they were still tender. I cleaned up as best I could, then got dressed and went out to look for Darv and Malachi.

I found them deep in conversation at the bottom of the giant staircase. "Good morning," I said.

Malachi smiled to himself knowingly. Darv looked surprised, but said, "Good morning." Then he added cautiously, "I hope you slept well."

"Yes," I answered politely. "Rogan says we'll be moving out soon. What's the plan?"

Darv seemed relieved to not have to make any more small talk and got down to business. "Our sources outside say the streets are deserted. Still, we'd best stay underground, so we'll be taking the Path to Un-Station." He stopped when he saw that I didn't know what he meant, and explained, "Un-Station is a hub, a place where all the tunnels converge. We have contingency forces coming from all over Adanac. Les Coquins from Kabac crossed the border three nights ago into the Badlands and are making their way to Un-Station as we speak. The Inuksuk—"

"The Inuksuk?! They're coming?" I was shocked but excited. The Inuksuk were another legend, a resistance group from the far North, where there was still ice. Old Mac said that the Inuksuk had incredible technology and that they kept hidden from The Consortium by erecting giant stone statues that deflected infrared and sonar.

"Yes," Darv said. "The Inuksuk from the North, members of both the Wheat Kings and Rising Sun from the West, and a host of Ceridwen's people from The Rock in the East."

"Ceridwen's people?" I was astonished. "Do they all look like her?"

"No," Darv smiled. "She's unique in that way."

"Please tell me they don't all *talk* like her!" The thought of an entire resistance force that spoke in cryptic riddles made my head spin.

"Thank the old god, no, chère—" Darv laughed, then stopped and hesitated. "Sorry. I know you don't like it when I call you that."

"Uh, no, it's all right," I said with false nonchalance. Darv looked surprised again, but I steered the conversation back. "So why does *she* talk that way then?"

"All I know is that her mother died when she was a baby and that her father was a scholar, a real professor of words, who raised her until he was murdered by The Consortium Anti-Intellect Squads. They're the ones that closed down all the universities. She made her way to Terrebonne and that's where I met her. She was around ten years old then, and mute from the trauma of seeing her father die. She never spoke a single word for the first two years that I knew her, then suddenly one day, she looked at me square and said, 'Let come what comes; only I'll be revenged most thoroughly for my father.' I took her at her word, and after Mont Royal, I sent her as a kind of informant, to gather information about what was happening in Metro. She's been here ever since, and started watching over you and your brother once you came to Divinity."

"Is she really Fey?" I asked.

"Never doubt it for a moment," Darv answered, winking at me with his one good eye.

Suddenly I had a new-found respect for Ceridwen. Fey or not, difficult to understand or not, she'd suffered like the rest of us and survived.

Rogan and Malachi reappeared and joined us. "Is it time?" Malachi asked.

Darv nodded, and Malachi turned and whispered something seemingly into the air, but the whisper began to amplify and grow until it filled the hall. I realized that whatever he had said was being passed along like a wave, and as it reached each level of the underground city, the Frag army started to melt away. The hundreds that had been standing like silent sentinels were disappearing almost imperceptibly. I blinked and almost half were gone; I blinked again, and there were only dozens remaining in the concourse. I looked at Rogan, and when I looked back, the concourse was completely empty. The whispering stopped, and the only sound now was S-Sam's footsteps echoing as he made his way towards us.

When he reached us, his eyes were wide with awe. "S-Spooky," he said.

I nodded in agreement, then Darv announced, "All right. Grab your things. Ceridwen has gone with the advance party to Un-Station. We have a cache of weapons there already, and the Blues who are loyal to us have laid sonic charges all around The Tower. Once everyone is inside The Dome watching the fight, that's when our forces will come up to ground level. Then we just have to wait for your brother to provide us with the distraction we need. Once the quake starts and the Blues run out to defend The Dome, we set off the charges and take The Tower."

"Wait!" I said. "I don't understand. Why can't we rescue Cee and Trick first? If Cee has the power that you say, he can cause the quake when he's with us!"

"No," Darv responded. "We need all eyes on him. That's the plan. The Inuksuk have run thousands of simulations, and their tech is never wrong—there's no margin for error. It has to be this way." He shouldered his pack and started walking away.

I was furious. I ran after him, yelling, "How can you just sacrifice him like that? He's my brother! He'll think I've abandoned him. He doesn't know about *any* of this!" I stopped and my voice caught. "He's all alone."

Darv turned to look at me. "No, chère, he's not alone. He's with your mother. And he knows about everything."

28
Cee

"Does Dee know?!" I demanded. "Does she know about her power?"

France—my mother—stepped back slightly. "No, not unless she's discovered it for herself. Your father wouldn't say anything to her."

"If it's not an implant, then what is it?"

Varma interjected. "Commander, you have to go," he warned. "It's been too long already."

"He's right," France said, moving quickly towards the door. "Stop worrying about your sister—she's fine. Just stay focused on the plan. We can't afford any mistakes, not when we're so close. The next time you see me, I'll be in the skybox. Pretend you don't know me."

"That won't be difficult!" I answered forcefully, turning my back to her. I heard her sigh and hesitate, but then the door opened and closed again. She was gone.

I turned around and stood there, staring at the door that she had just disappeared through, clenching and unclenching my fists, trying to control my anger. Varma looked at me steadily.

"Save it for later," he said. "She's doing what has to be done. If circumstances had been different—"

"We'll never know though, will we?" I interrupted. "Anyway, it doesn't matter. I've managed this long without a mother. What's the rest of my life—short as it may be?" I laughed bitterly, and Varma looked uncomfortable. He went over to the bench and bundled up my old clothes.

"I assume you aren't too attached to these rags?" he asked, moving towards a garbage bin.

I shook my head, but then remembered. "Wait!" I called out. "There's something in one of the pockets that I'd like to keep."

His eyes narrowed suspiciously and his grip on the bundle tightened. "Not some kind of weapon, is it? You're only allowed to use sanctioned ones. As much as I'd like to give you a leg up, it would tip off the bigwigs if you ran into The Dome with a ripper—only straight blades on the fighting floor, you know."

"Check for yourself," I replied. "I promise, it's nothing dangerous. Just something…sentimental. It's in the front pocket of my pants."

Varma hesitated for a moment, then shrugged, and started rummaging around. "Is this what you're after then?!" he asked with a grin, pulling out the finely polished wooden bead and holding it up towards me.

"That's it," I said. "Just something to remind me of home." Varma passed it to me, then tossed the rest of the clothes into the bin.

"All right," he said, motioning to the door. "Time to get some rest. You'll be up early enough."

"I thought Trick and I weren't supposed to fight until noon," I said. "Why the rush?"

"Yeah, well, they like you to watch some of the earlier bouts," he answered with disgust in his voice. "They think seeing the crowd go crazy, choosing a hand or a foot, all the blood, gets the death fighters desperate and jittery.

Makes for better entertainment." He sneered. "I'd like to see any one of them take *their* chances in The Dome. Now *that* would be entertaining."

My stomach did a flip at the thought of all the gore and screaming, but I tried not to show it. Varma directed me out of the room to another room further down the hall. This one was small and stark, with a metal cot. The mattress looked thin and hard. There was a side table with a solar lamp and nothing more. Off to the side was a washroom with a toilet and washbasin.

"You'll spend the night here," he said. "I'll be back in the morning. Pleasant dreams, my young warrior."

With that, he left, locking the door behind him. I was immediately plunged into complete darkness, and had to fumble my way over to where I remembered the side table being. I groped for the lamp and turned it on. The light was weak — the lamp hadn't been charged for a while — but it would do. I sat on the edge of the cot and put my head in my hands, breathing deeply and trying not to let the despair I was feeling overwhelm me.

There was a very good chance that by the same time tomorrow, I would be dead. It was a horrifying thought. I wasn't even seventeen years old, and although my life so far hadn't been much, I wasn't ready to give up on it yet. The last year, in Divinity with Dee, had shown me that there was good in the world, and that happiness was a possibility I wanted to know more about.

When Dee and I had first arrived at the tent city, we were exhausted and starving. We'd run out of food two days before and our water packs had dried up overnight. We literally stumbled into Divinity, desperate and filthy, not knowing what we would find. No one was surprised to see us — teenagers arriving in our condition from the workhouses were pretty commonplace. A woman gave us some bread, and a man directed us to the Tap. Their faces are still a blur but I remember their voices, kind and helpful. It was the first time anyone had spoken to us like that. Then, as we made our way through the maze of tents, we got hopelessly lost. I was afraid to ask for help, but Dee was having trouble walking, so I stopped in the middle of a crossroads, looking wildly for some indication of the right direction. Suddenly I felt a hand on my shoulder. I whirled around and an older woman was standing there. Her name was Shaheera. She brought us straight to the Tap and for the next few weeks, she took care of us. She and her husband, a man called Natu, had been in Divinity for just a little over a year. They were making their way across Adanac, from one tent city to another, trying to get back to The Rock where Natu's family had come from originally. Shaheera said, "We're getting old. He wants to see the ocean again before it's too late."

Shaheera invited us to stay with her and Natu, even though their tent was small. They treated us like family, or at least what Dee and I had always hoped family was like. It wasn't long before we were both healthy again, thanks to Natu's wonderful cooking. They didn't have much, but they shared it with us. In the evenings, when the air was a little cooler, we would sit outside the tent and the neighbours would all gather to hear Shaheera sing in her beautiful, clear voice, or listen to Natu tell funny stories about life on The Rock. I asked him once why he ever left The Rock and it was the only time I saw him unhappy. "I thought there was a better life for me out west," he had said. "But I was wrong. The only good that came of it was Lady Shakes there." That was his affectionate name for Shaheera, especially when he'd had a bit of the TastiRum.

After a while, Dee and I both started feeling guilty about living with them but not contributing, so that was when Dee first went out thieving, before she met Rogan. She joined a small gang and began doing what they called "snatching", waiting for a Fancy to come by and then grabbing their bag or whatever else they might be carrying before the Blues knew what was happening. As I've said before, Fancies don't normally use coin; they have Scanbank wristwallets, so most of the time her score was something to eat or sell. When Shaheera found out, she wasn't thrilled, but she said, "Well, it's one way to make a living. Better than the Sex House anyway."

Then one day, Shaheera and Natu sat us down for "a talk". I could feel Dee in my head, all panic and confusion; we were both convinced they were fed up with us at last and were going to ask us to leave. But no—they were the ones leaving. The time had come, Natu said, for them to be on their way. They were heading to King's Town and then Mont Royal, making their way East.

"No!" Dee had protested. "It's not safe! There are Frags out there, and The Dead Kids gangs!"

"Oh, don't you worry," Shaheera smiled. "Natu is no stranger to a blade, and I can handle myself. We haven't made it this far on our good looks alone, you know."

And then, shockingly, they said we could have their tent. "It'll just go to squatters otherwise," Natu had said. "And we couldn't leave without knowing that you had somewhere to call home."

They packed up the next morning, and then they were gone. It was one of the few times I've ever seen Dee cry. As for me, I was sad, but I had this feeling in the back of my head that we would see them again. I didn't know where or when, but I was pretty sure about it and it was a comfort to me as I watched them disappear into Old Metro, making their way to the Badlands with all of their belongings on a small solar wagon following behind them.

Our time with Shaheera and Natu had shown us that people could be decent and caring, and even fun. We'd never experienced any of that in the workhouse. Even "Drop-off Day" was bittersweet. Sure you got candy sometimes, but it was still a reminder that no one had wanted you badly enough to keep you. Yet this last year in Divinity made me realize that it was possible to see a future, with friends and maybe even families of our own. I ached when I remembered Sarah holding me—I would give anything to feel her arms around me again. Maybe there was nothing to it, but I'd never even know. And Dee—how could I leave this world without seeing her face one last time? How could I leave her alone?

I could feel the floor beneath me starting to tremble, and it took all my strength to stop it. I was sure that somewhere that bastard Songe was grinning. Well, if this was my fate, I was taking him with me. They wanted a quake? I'd shake Metro to its core and bring The Dome down around his head if it meant never having to look at his sneering face again.

The battery on the solar light finally lost its charge and the room went black. I lay back on the hard cot, but there was no way I could sleep. It took everything I had to keep the wall up in my mind—there was no point in letting it all go now, wasting the one opportunity I might have. Eventually, light began to seep under the door, and finally, I could hear footsteps. The door opened, and Varma was silhouetted against the morning sun.

"Wake up," he said. "It's time."

"I wasn't sleeping," I answered, sitting up and stretching my back, stiff from the hard mattress.

"I'm not surprised." He stood back and let me move past him through the door. "We're going down."

He took me back to the elevator, and I braced myself as we seemed to drop for ages. Finally, we stopped and the doors opened onto a foyer at ground level. I could see The Dome through the glass doors and my heart started to beat faster. We went outside into the heat of the day, and I could see people, Fancies, streaming into The Dome through the main entrance about half a click ahead and up one level. They looked so strange in their light-coloured, shimmery clothing, their pale sim-masks and modified eyes, the men with their shaved and tattooed heads and the women with hair of every colour imaginable. Even from here, I could see that they all seemed somewhat distracted, no one actually speaking to each other. Many of them had their heads perpetually cocked to one side as if listening to something interesting—must be those propatainment implants that Varma told me about. I wondered what they were saying about me, about the death match.

Varma saw me staring. "Don't worry about those idiots," he said. "We're going in here." He gestured towards a tunnel across the concrete courtyard in front of us. I looked over and saw a figure waiting there. It was the Blue guard, Durand.

I stiffened, but Varma leaned in close. "I should probably tell you," he said quietly into my ear. "Durand? He's one of us."

29
Dee

I hadn't spoken a word since Rogan had asked me, "Are you okay?" and I had waved off his concern with a terse, "I'm fine." There was nothing else to say. Cee was with our mother. I had finally started to make my peace with Darv, and now this. Darv was up ahead with Malachi; he had seen the look on my face when he made his pronouncement and he was smart enough to leave me alone to absorb what he'd told me. He probably thought I was furious with him again. Strangely, I wasn't. I was too exhausted, too worried to be angry. In fact, I was more curious than anything, and I wished that circumstances were different, that I could ask him questions about her. What was she like? Did I look like her? I certainly didn't look much like Darv, with his dark hair and swarthy skin, although my eyes were the same colour as his. Green eyes used to be more common, but they were unusual now.

I walked in silence, by myself, thoughts of Cee and our mother whirling around in my brain. Was she as mercenary as Darv? Was she fine with using Cee as a weapon, or was she as frightened as I was? I still couldn't quite hear

Cee in my head; there was just a hum, a presence that told me he was out there. I couldn't wait to get close enough to really sense what he was feeling—it shouldn't be long now. We were underground, on the so-called Path that ran from where we'd started at the "mall" to Un-Station. It was dark, lit only by the dim light of the solar lamps that Darv, Malachi, and a few of the Frag contingent were carrying. Rogan was up ahead, knowingly giving me time to think. There were empty storefronts down here too, an eerie ghost town in the half-light. Shadows swooped in and out as we passed by, moving with the lamps like spectres, making me jumpy. Suddenly, a large figure appeared beside me—for a moment, I thought it was a Blue, maybe the beginning of an ambush, and my heart lurched. But it was only S-Sam.

"Are-are you all right?" he asked.

I sighed. "Yes. Well, as all right as I can be under the circumstances. How about you?"

S-Sam shrugged. "I-I'm good. I'm j-just worried about T-Trick and Cee." He paused, then burst out angrily, "I'm so s-sick of The D-Dome. I c-can't wait until it all comes c-crashing d-down!"

"I know." I hesitated, then said quietly, "Your father was killed in The Dome, wasn't he?"

S-Sam nodded solemnly. "I was n-nine."

My curiosity got the better of me. "What happened?" I asked. Then I felt guilty for making him think about it and added hastily, "You don't have to talk about it if you don't want to."

"N-No, it's all right. It was a l-long time ago. I d-don't really remember m-much about him, except that he was al-always running a s-scam of some kind or another. He and my m-mother were always f-fighting about it, h-how he would get c-caught one day. And he d-did, lost a l-lot of m-money. Then the C-Caseeno Boys came c-calling." S-Sam's eyes glowered in the gloomy half-light.

"And he had to figure out how to pay them back?" I asked.

"Y-Yeah," S-Sam sighed. "H-He tried to r-rob a couple of F-Fancies. There was a s-struggle — the w-woman got in the m-middle of things s-somehow, and she got knocked d-down, hit her h-head. He was g-grabbed by the B-Blues and t-taken to The D-Dome. The guy he was f-fighting snuck in a b-blade. I had to w-w-watch him d-d-d-die." S-Sam stopped walking for second, his round face haunted by the memory.

"I'm so sorry," I said quietly, touching him on the shoulder. "I want to see The Dome collapse too — although hopefully not with us *in* it!"

S-Sam laughed wryly, and so did I. Then he said, "All I c-care about n-now is saving T-Trick. I owe him. After m-my father died, he helped me, t-took care of m-my mother, p-protected us. He didn't n-need to, didn't even know me r-really, but he d-did. He's my b-best friend." He said this intensely, with pride, standing up taller. I might have had some doubts in the back of my mind before, but I knew in that moment that S-Sam could be counted on no matter what happened to us.

"Right," I said. "Let's keep moving. By the way, I couldn't help but notice that you're talking...well, better. I would have thought that a situation like this would make it worse."

"I know," S-Sam replied. "I'm s-surprised too. But I guess after s-surviving a night s-sleeping with a F-Frag army, I d-don't have much else to be a-afraid of!"

We continued on together in companionable silence, following the twists and turns of the Path until suddenly we could hear the faint murmur of whispering voices. Darv and Malachi stopped, Malachi cocking his head to one side and listening. He said something to Darv and they turned to face our group.

"It's just a little further now," Darv told us. "Everyone is almost in place. We'll meet with the Dominion and our allies first before we go above ground."

Rogan had come back to stand beside me and S-Sam. "Isn't there a way to get there without going up top? What if we're seen?"

"The closer we get to The Tower, the more dangerous it is — the only way to get there above ground from below is a public Skywalk. Better to come up to ground level well before then and avoid any guards. There's a back way to go, a causeway where the old train yard used to run out of Metro. If we keep close to the walls, we'll be almost impossible to see from higher up. We'll hit them from behind where they're not expecting an attack. Most of the Blues who still side with the Consortium will be inside The Dome, watching the spectacle, but we know there are patrols roaming around, guarding the Skywalk and its entrance."

Rogan nodded reluctantly, then looked at me. I shrugged. Darv, Malachi, and the Frags with them began moving again, and we followed. It was probably less than a minute until the Path led us to a wider corridor, long and low, with exits every few metres that disappeared into darkness. The sound of voices was getting louder. Then we took one of the exits and it opened onto a concourse full of hundreds of people. I gasped and looked over at Rogan — his eyes were wide. S-Sam was staring in awe. I'd never seen anything quite like it. There were Frags of course, but also Dominion fighters milling around, recognizable by the red leaf patches on their sleeves. Darv's other group, Les Coquins, were dressed the same, but had another symbol next to the leaf, a kind of three-petalled flower. Standing at one side of the great hall was a group of around fifty women all wearing military style gear, the backs of each of their shirts emblazoned with the emblem of a rising sun. Another larger group of men and women, all dark from the sun but light-haired, was hunkered down at the far end of the hall talking quietly. I assumed from the crown and wheat sheaf design roughly hand-stitched onto their jackets that they must be the rebel faction called the Wheat Kings.

In contrast, another group was laughing quietly, gathered around a man who looked like he was telling quite a story, making large gestures with his hands — they had nothing identifying them, but they were all tall, with the same blue eyes as Ceridwen, so I guessed they were from The Rock. The last group was comprised of rugged-looking men and women wearing heavy coats and boots, too heavy at least for the heat in the hall, but they didn't seem to be bothered by it. They were interspersed among the crowd, moving silently. Each of them was carrying what looked like a small, clear plastic tablet with images, words, and lights on it. I watched as one of the men approached some Wheat Kings. He tapped the tablet and it lit up; he pointed to something, moving his finger around its surface, speaking to them as he did it. They nodded in what seemed to be agreement, and he moved on to another group. With that kind of tech, he must be Inuksuk.

I was standing there with Rogan and S-Sam, watching from the periphery, when Darv caught my eye. He was with an older man; although he had his back to me, I could tell he was one of Les Coquins because of the symbols on his sleeve. Darv was holding him by the arm and speaking to him intensely. Then one of the Inuksuk approached them with her tablet; they both turned to face her and I could see him clearly. It was the man from my dream, the one with the scar on his face who had pulled the woman away from me! I gasped audibly, in shock — if *he* was real, then the woman in my dream must be too. Who was she?! Was she actually my mother?!

Rogan looked at me sharply. "What's wrong? What is it?" he demanded.

"I—" I didn't know what to say. I needed to know the truth and there was only one way to find out. I marched over to Darv and the man from my dream purposefully. He saw me coming and looked at me, his brow furrowing. As I got close, I called out, "I know you!"

He looked at Darv, who said, "Seguin, this is my... my daughter Dee."

The man, Seguin, stared at me. Angrily, I said, "You were with her that day, weren't you? Was it your idea to just leave us there?!"

Seguin looked at Darv and said something in the Kabac language. Darv sighed and nodded, and Seguin said simply, "It was to protect you. She cried for weeks. Don't blame her or your father for the past."

I clenched my fists in outrage. Who the hell was *he* to say something like that to me? I turned on my heel and stalked out of the hall without another word. My mind was in an uproar. I reached out for Cee with all my strength—he had to be close enough now for me to sense how he was feeling, to maybe get an impression of what our mother was like. In the dream, her tears had fallen onto my face—was that true too? I focused hard, trying to still my thoughts, and slowly, I began to get a glimmer of Cee's emotions. It was small sparks and flashes at first, but then they started coming faster and faster. Suddenly, it was as if someone had opened a floodgate, and my head was full of his fury and terror until I was reeling from it.

I knew I had to go to him; I didn't care what Darv said, what the plan was. He was my brother and he needed me; I could never forgive myself if he died before I had the chance to see him again. I looked up and saw a sign on the top of the archway ahead of me—it was a faded picture of The Tower, with an arrow pointing straight ahead. I took off, running blindly, down hallways and through archways, following the arrows on the signs. With every step closer to him, I could hear Cee more clearly in my head, his emotions flooding into my mind, building into a crescendo so loud that I couldn't hear anything else. I turned a last corner and came out suddenly into an open area. I stopped, looking for a sign to point me in the right direction. Then from behind me, cutting through the cacophony in my head, I heard another voice.

"What do we have here, boys?" the voice said. I whirled around to face a Blue, large and sneering. "Some Freeworld scum trying to sneak in the back door, eh?" he continued. He was joined by another Blue, who had appeared silently from behind a large pillar. He came towards me and I started to flee in the opposite direction towards an open archway, but two more guards materialized out of the shadows. I was surrounded.

I stood, breathing hard and looking around wildly for an escape route. They were starting to close in, the big one who spoke snickering as they got closer. I had no choice; I tried to make a break for it back the way I came, but the Blue was too quick. He lunged at me as I sprinted past him and grabbed me around the waist. We both went sprawling to the ground hard. "Ooh, you'll pay for that one!" he said in my ear as he pulled me upright. I screamed and struggled, trying to kick at him, but he motioned to one of the others who whipped a black hood out of his back pocket. The next thing, the hood was over my head — I couldn't see, but I kept lashing out and screaming incoherently. Then I was slapped across the side of my head and yanked roughly. The big Blue holding me said, "Stop now or I'll give you another one — only I won't be so gentle the next time!" I held still, knowing that the worst thing that could happen was if I was knocked out. Then there would be no chance of escape.

One of the other guards said, "Do you think this is the Freeworlder that old Cyclops has been looking for?"

My captor laughed loudly. "Could be. It wouldn't hurt to take her to the creepy little bastard. Even if she's not the one, he might like her anyway — maybe something in it for us too. Start walking!" he commanded, as he pushed me forward. "We've got someone to see."

30

Cee

"You're out of your mind!" I exclaimed to Varma. "I don't believe you. Durand? He beat Trick—broke his ribs!"

Varma shrugged. "Believe me or not. Durand plays his role well—all our lives depend on it, including his. Can you imagine what would happen if anyone found out that he was actually a member of Les Coquins? And trust me—a broken rib is a small price to pay for bringing down The Consortium." He took my arm and propelled me across the concrete courtyard where Durand was waiting. If the look of disdain on Durand's face wasn't real, then he was a better actor than Varma realized.

"Why didn't Trick say anything?!" I whispered. "I thought for sure that Durand would throw us both off The Tower, given half a chance! He could have told me!"

"And jeopardize everything? If you'd shown anything less than abject fear, Songe would have known it in a heartbeat. We needed to get both of you off the platform safely."

The sky was dark yellow with the impending thunderstorm; I could hear rumbling in the distance as we crossed the courtyard. When we reached Durand, he came forward, his face masked with contempt. Varma said, "We're ready."

"Wait a minute," I demanded. "Where's Trick?"

Durand glanced quickly from one side of the court-yard to the other, and then cuffed me hard across the head, knocking me backwards. "Don't you worry about your little friend, Freeworlder," he said loudly. "You'll see him soon enough." He grabbed my arm and pulled me along with him into the tunnel, Varma following closely behind.

As soon as we were inside the tunnel, away from anyone who could see or hear us, Durand let go of my arm and turned to face me. "Thaddeus is in the holding area," he said gruffly. "I'm taking you there now."

My head was still ringing from his blow, but I stood up straight. I knew I was risking another fist to my skull but I was burning with curiosity. "Are you really with the resistance? Do you know my...my father?" I asked quietly.

Durand looked me up and down, considering whether or not to respond. Finally, he said, "Yes."

"What's he like?" I couldn't help myself—if I was going to die soon, I needed to know that the man who was sending me to my death was worth it.

Durand sighed impatiently. "He's a hard man but a good man. We don't have time for this." He turned his back and started walking away briskly.

Varma gestured. "Come," he said firmly. "Someone might see us. We need to go."

We followed behind Durand, trying to keep up with his pace. "I have one last question," I whispered to Varma. "Why does Durand always call Trick 'Thaddeus'? I don't know anyone else who calls him by his real name."

Varma answered back in a low voice. "It's a sign of respect, the only one that Durand can afford him without giving the whole plot away."

I suddenly felt tremendous empathy for Durand, having to hurt someone he actually cared about, having to maintain a hateful outward appearance for a cause that he believed in so completely. We followed behind him for a few more minutes along the upward incline of the tunnel. As we got higher, I could hear the faint rumble of the crowd, muffled footsteps above our heads, voices talking and laughing excitedly. My stomach lurched again. I tried to control my fear but all I could think of was the crowd screaming for blood. We turned a corner and Durand halted in front of a set of double doors. "You'll wait in here," he said, unlocking them and pushing them open. Before I went in, he stopped me and said quietly, "There's a spycam inside, no audio, just visual. I don't know if anyone's actually watching but we can't be too careful. Mind how you act."

Inside, sitting on a bench, small and hunkered over, was Trick. I rushed over to him, and he looked up at me with a wan smile. He looked even worse than the last time I'd seen him. I sat down next to him and asked, "Are you okay?"

He straightened up, stifling a groan and replied, "I'll be fine. He packs quite a punch, that one." He gestured at Durand, who was standing in the doorway looking distressed. He said, "Thaddeus, I—"

"I know," Trick interrupted, waving him off. "It was necessary."

Inside the room, the thundering of footsteps and the hum of the crowd above us seemed to be amplified. I looked up towards the ceiling and when I looked back down, I realized that there was a large, black screen on the wall opposite us.

"Show's starting soon," said Varma, noticing my glance. "You'll be watching it from in here."

Durand stepped forward and picked up a small, clear plastic tablet from a shelf on the other side of the door. "Look straight ahead," he ordered, pointing it at each of us in turn. Then he pressed a button on the tablet and the screen on the wall sprang to life. "Time to choose your weapons.

I've linked the viewer to a virtual armoury," he said. "Whatever weapon you pick from the screen will be waiting for you inside The Dome."

An image appeared on the wall viewer—a dagger of some kind. "This is a dirk," Varma pointed at the screen. "Simple, yet deadly. Very effective for close combat. Nice little serrated edge near the hilt for drawing the maximum amount of blood."

The screen changed again to show a strange-looking glove fitted with spikes. "Ah," said Varma. "Now, this is a true classic. Known as a cestus. Used for centuries by the gladiators of old. Perfect for smashing your opponent's skull to a pulp." Trick looked uncomfortable, and I could feel the blood draining out of my face. "Come now, boys!" Varma laughed. "You've got to give the audience something to scream about!" He continued on as the next weapon appeared. It was a laser pruner. I felt my adrenaline spike.

"This one isn't something we typically offer, but it was added especially for you, Cee. Apparently you have some experience using this as a weapon, according to our dear Lieutenant-Guv. He was pretty insistent that we put it in the arsenal." I sat there, not saying a thing, my stomach roiling. The last time I'd used a laser pruner was the day I'd vowed I would never again use my hands for violence. Now, Songe was taunting me with it.

"Well, Cee, what do you say? Feel like lopping a couple of limbs off the little guy there?" He flourished his arm in an exaggerated way for the sake of the camera and I glared at him. "OK, up next—"

"Just give us each a blade," Trick interrupted. I nodded in silent assent.

"Suit yourself," Varma said. "A blade'll do the job just fine. Now, when the show starts, the wall screen will light up. You won't be able to hear any of the commentary without a propatainment implant, but the noise of the crowd will filter down to here. We'll be back to get you in a little while."

With that, he and Durand turned to leave. As they got to the doorway and out of the camera's sight, Durand hesitated. He looked back at us and mouthed the words "Je refuse". I gave him an almost imperceptible nod, and Durand vanished into the dark tunnel.

Trick looked at me sharply. "No—" he started to say, but I interrupted him.

"Enough," I said. "Neither of us is dying today. Now listen—I have so much to tell you!"

He looked at me with intense curiosity. "Is it true?" he asked. "Was it your mother?"

I launched into the story of the previous evening's events, talking quickly and quietly about what France had told me and what I needed to do. When I was finished, Trick looked thoughtful.

"Now things are starting to make sense," he pronounced. "It explains why no one ever spoke of her. If she truly is that deeply under cover, no one could know about it, least of all you and Dee."

"Elysia," I said. "Dee's birth name is Elysia. Mine's Niko."

Trick's eyebrows shot up. "It might take me a while to get used to that."

I was about to respond with "I feel the same way" when suddenly there was a roar from above us and the viewer on the wall came to life. Trick and I turned to stare at it. The screen was filled with a Fancy's head. Behind him, blurry in the background, were hundreds, maybe thousands of people. Through the open roof, the sky in the distance looked even darker and more sulphurous—I could imagine it rumbling ominously even if I couldn't hear it. The man was talking, but there was no audio. His head was shaved and covered with intricately tattooed hieroglyphics and he was wearing a pastel green diaphanous blouse. He was speaking very enthusiastically, gesturing at the crowd behind him and laughing in a jolly way that made his sim-mask crinkle. Then the screen switched to images of six people together in pairs: two men, one of whom looked very old, a couple of frightened-looking teenaged girls, and another two, a man and a woman, who looked like members of The Dead Kids gang. Each pair was lit up one at a time — the Fancy announcer appeared to be telling the audience about them, and each time we could hear the muffled cheering of the crowd. I wished I could hear what he was saying, get a sense of what possible crime had brought them here. Stealing, most likely; the TDK man was already one-handed — he'd obviously been down this road before. While I was speculating about who might win each match, a new couple appeared on the screen, and the crowd above went wild. It was Trick and me, the pictures that Durand had taken of us with the tablet staring back at us on the screen. It would almost have been worth having an implant to hear what the Fancy was saying now.

Then the pictures disappeared and the announcer was back, gesturing even more wildly than before as thousands of people above us began to stamp their feet. The screen switched to a shot of the floor of The Dome. The first set of opponents, the two men, were standing at either side. The cameras zoomed in and out, switching perspectives, and Trick and I were able to see the terror in the older man's face. Then the camera pulled back to a wider shot of the field, as the other man, a really large Russe judging by his genetic mods, began charging. The older man started running — we could hear the crowd laughing and booing — but the Russe was too quick. He caught him and threw him down to the ground, then sat on his chest. The camera switched back to the announcer, who was rolling his eyes and smirking. When the camera went back to the two fighters, the older man was flailing around. Then it zoomed in on his face — he was crying and looked like he was begging the Russe to let him up. The Russe just sat there, staring coldly straight ahead, his four arms crossed stubbornly across his massive chest, ignoring the other man's pleas. The crowd started to chant; it sounded from where Trick and I were sitting like "Choose, choose, choose, choose!" Finally, two Blue guards ran onto the field, hauled the Russe up and dragged him away, leaving the older man lying on the ground. He finally struggled to his feet, still crying. Suddenly he looked from one side to the other wildly—the camera panned over to a Blue guard carrying a small table with a thick, stained wooden top. Another Blue approached from the other side, carrying an object in each hand. They converged on the older man.

"What's he got?" I asked Trick, not sure if I wanted the answer.

"A bone saw and a cauterizing laser," he answered. "The saw is to satisfy the audience's lust for blood, and the laser is so that he survives to serve as a warning to others. These idiots still haven't figured out that The Dome is no deterrent," he continued with disdain. "They've made it a symbol of oppression that needs to be destroyed."

As Trick was speaking, the older man began to back away from the Blues, crying harder, his eyes wide with fear, but they put down what they were carrying and grabbed him, lifting him into the air, kicking, over to the table. They asked him something and he shook his head vigorously. One of the Blues shrugged, then forced the man's arm down onto the tabletop which I realized was stained with blood. The other Blue picked up the saw and began sawing the man's hand off. Blood sprayed everywhere and the crowd went wild with glee as the camera zoomed in close on the man's screaming face, then down to a close-up of the saw cutting through bone.

I thought I was going to be sick—my head was filled with hatred and horror until I thought it would explode. The ground started to rumble, and Trick put out a warning hand. "Stop!" he yelled over the booming noise of the crowd above us. "If you bring The Dome down now, we'll be crushed under it!"

I took a deep breath and tried to calm myself. Trick was right. There was no use in doing anything until we were safe in the middle of the field. I built up my mental wall as best I could, hoping that whatever minor vibrations might escape me would be disguised by the stomping feet of the crowd. We watched silently as the next pair, the two young girls, fought. The loser stood tall and brave, choosing a hand as well and gritting her teeth against the pain until she finally passed out. The crowd was a little more subdued that time, but then roared again when the next couple entered the ring, the pair that I thought were part of a TDK gang. They fought each other viciously, the woman finally overpowering the man after punching him in the face and disorienting him. But when the Blues tried to drag her away, she broke free and ran to him, throwing her arms around him and sobbing. He pressed his face into her hair and said something, then the Blues pulled her off him and the camera zoomed in. His face was full of fury as he made a rude hand gesture to the crowd with his remaining hand, then pointed at his own eye. The crowd practically swooned with excitement.

I had turned my face away, not willing to watch anymore, when the door opened. Varma and Durand were standing there, looking grim.

"It's time," Varma said softly. "Be strong."

They took us down the tunnel to a crossroads where we separated. "See you on the field," Trick said, tapping his head with his finger again. I nodded. My stomach was in knots and my mouth was dry with fear.

We walked on towards the end of the tunnel, the noise of the crowd increasing in intensity as we got closer to the exit. We stopped and Varma said, "You're on your own from this point on. I have to take my position with the others."

"Thanks," I said. "Thanks for everything." He gave me a small smile and took a shaky breath, then walked back the way we'd come, leaving me alone. I hesitated for a moment, then stepped out into the light. At the sight of me, the crowd went wild. I could see Fancies of all shapes and sizes, all screaming for death. Across the field, I could see Trick's slight figure, waiting. High above us was a giant screen projecting the same images of Trick and me that we'd seen on the wall viewer earlier. Suddenly a loud voice boomed across the field: "Fighters, take your weapons!" I looked around me, and saw a stand with my chosen blade on it. I picked it up, and across the field, Trick picked up his. We slowly began to approach each other and the crowd fell silent. The only noise was the rolling of thunder, getting closer. It wouldn't be long before the storm was here.

Trick and I finally met in the middle of the field. The crowd seemed to be holding its breath, waiting for a signal of some kind. Then the signal came as the voice boomed again: "Fighters! Begin!"

Trick and I looked at each other. "No matter what happens," he said. "It's been a pleasure. Are you sure?"

"Yes," I answered. "On the count of 3. One, two, three…"

We both threw down our weapons, turned to face the skybox, and at the same time, screamed out "Je Refuse!" It rang through The Dome, up to the highest seats. The crowd gasped and began to mutter.

The voice boomed again: "Fight or you *both* die!"

In unison, Trick and I screamed out again, "Je Refuse!" The first drops of rain started to come down, hot and heavy.

"It's time," said Trick. "Now. Do it now!" His face was creased with anxiety. The sound of the crowd grew and they began booing.

I let the wall in my mind fall, concentrating and trying to focus. Nothing happened except for a barely noticeable vibration.

"What's wrong?!" shouted Trick over the crowd.

"I don't know!" I shouted back. But I *did* know. I was frightened, more frightened than I'd ever been in my life. Not frightened of what he wanted me to do, frightened because if I did it, I would be breaking the vow I had made to myself. Only now I wasn't using my hands to commit violence, I was using my whole being. People were going to die, and it went against everything that I believed about myself, about the person that I had tried so hard to be for the last two years.

"You have to do it now!" he yelled. Then he stared at me hard, and walked closer. "Please," he whispered desperately, clutching his ribs and breathing hard. "Or else it's all been for nothing."

Trick was right. I thought about my mother, about Durand, and about all the other people who had made sacrifices, done the unthinkable to bring us to this moment, and I cast aside my fear and doubt once and for all. I redoubled my efforts, concentrating on my anger, the fury that I felt about the workhouse, about starving most of the time, about Dee having to thieve and getting hurt, of being used by parents who'd left us to fend for ourselves, and most of all, I thought of Songe, his sneering face, and what I had seen in Dee's mind so many years ago. The ground started to shake, softly at first, then more violently. I could see people in the crowd looking around with concern and then with panic as the shaking got worse. The whole Dome began to vibrate as the ground swelled up and buckled beneath my feet, heaving and breaking. Concrete started to fall from the decks above as the floors cracked and separated. The Fancies sitting up there were on their feet, looking around frantically and starting to climb over each other in order to get down to ground level. The upper decks were abandoned and people down below were being trampled. I saw a man hit by a flying piece of concrete—he crumpled to the ground but it barely registered. My head was filled with rage and pain—I couldn't have stopped ripping the world apart if I'd tried. Trick was standing in front of me, his face filled with awe as the overhang on the highest deck crumbled, large sections plummeting onto the field around us. He started laughing, a joyous sound that cut through the cacophony of shrieking and destruction, and threw his arms up to the sky with abandon. The hot rain came pouring down and lightning forked through the air, which was bristling with electricity. Suddenly, there was a flash of red and Trick fell to the ground, writhing in pain.

I looked towards the source of the red light and gasped—it was Songe, up in the skybox. Even from this distance, I could see France slumped over in a chair behind him. His face looked maniacal and he was gripping someone tightly around the neck. He had Dee! I started running towards the skybox as Songe leaned over a microphone and the voice—his voice—boomed again: "Stop breaking my Dome and I won't hurt your lovely sister. Or don't stop—I'll just kill you and keep her for myself. Either way, I win. Squadrons of Blues are already at The Tower—you've lost before you've even begun." He ran his fingers through Dee's long hair then gripped it tight, pulling her head back. I was right below the skybox now and our eyes locked. He grinned at me, then leaned over and kissed her on the forehead, his lips lingering on her skin. She struggled hard against him and spat at him. He released her hair, still keeping a tight grip around her neck with his other arm despite how hard she was trying to break free.

"No," I shouted back. "You have a simple choice. Let her go or I'll split *you* in half!" I didn't know if it would be possible but I envisioned him exploding from the inside out and refocused my energy. The glass window of the skybox shattered. Suddenly Songe's eyes went wide. I saw Dee break away from him, then red light burst from the skybox once more.

31

Dee

I was doing my best to stay calm, to not cause any trouble. The Blue who'd captured me was holding my arm, guiding me along, hauling me up if I stumbled. The feeling of his hand on my skin made me want to scream, and I was biting my lip inside the black hood, tense with the effort of holding myself together. But then, they started arguing.

"It's not fair," complained one. "I think we should get to 'sample the wares' first."

"No!" the Blue holding me barked at him. "We have our orders." His grip on my arm tightened and I bit down harder on my lip, drawing blood.

"Come on, Lafond," another implored. "Old Cyclops will never know." He and the other two Blues snickered.

The grip on my arm loosened slightly as "Lafond" seemed to consider it. "Well..." he started. I took advantage of his temporary distraction and broke free, yanking off the hood and making a run for it. I could see a tunnel up ahead and I made a beeline towards it, the Blues hot on my tail and yelling as they ran.

"You idiots!" Lafond roared at them. "If we lose her, I'm not taking the blame!"

I was almost at the tunnel when I heard the sound of something powering up. Then I was hit hard by a shocker blast from behind and felt everything go numb. I collapsed onto the floor.

I heard Lafond say, "Great. How are we supposed to explain this?!" from what seemed like very far away, and then the world went dark.

When I opened my eyes again, I wasn't sure how much time had passed. I was sitting on a cold metal chair in the middle of a dark room. There was a bright light shining in my face, making me squint. I tried to stand up and realized that my hands and feet were secured to the chair with Lobot cuffs. I tugged and pulled at the cuffs but they were on tight. Then I heard a voice.

"Well, isn't this a lovely surprise!" The voice sounded dangerously familiar, low and evil, but I couldn't see who it belonged to. The light shining in my eyes was too bright—I squinted harder but that did nothing. The voice continued, "I was wondering if I would see you again... hoping even. It's been so long since that day in the Shed. 'Sweets to the sweet'—remember?"

I realized with sudden horror who the voice belonged to—Songe. The room started to spin, and I cried out in my mind for Cee, but I couldn't feel him. I struggled harder against the Lobot cuffs, but Songe just laughed and said, "Don't bother. They're encrypted. I'm the only one who can release you and I have no intention of doing that. Yet."

I could hear his boots clicking across the floor. The bright light snapped off and we were left in shadow. Then he turned on a solar lamp and stepped into its glow. I gasped. One side of his face was a mass of faint scars, and in the dim light, there was a red flash as if there was some kind of device where his eye used to be. I knew that Cee had hurt him, but I'd never known all the details, hadn't wanted to know. By the time I was out of the infirmary, he'd been sent up North.

"What do you want?" My voice was reduced to a whisper by fear.

He leaned against the wall, folded his arms across his chest and looked up towards the ceiling as if pondering the question. "Hmm. Where do I begin?" he said. I stared at him, the dizziness getting worse, as he continued slowly, articulating each word with an edge of bitterness. "First, I know all about the plan you and your little friends have concocted. Unfortunately, *your* plan is interfering with *my* plan. It's terribly...annoying. Just as I'm on the verge of assassinating the Regional Commander and taking control of Trillium Province, along you and 'the Dominion' come to ruin everything. I would have been Dome Master, and my father would have finally accepted me, brought me home instead of leaving me to languish away in this obscene wasteland. But now..."

"It's too late," I said, quietly. "They're going to bring it all down."

"I KNOW!" he suddenly roared, pushing himself away from the wall. He stalked across the room and leaned down over me, his hands on the arms of the chair. I could feel the heat of his skin and I shuddered. He breathed in sharply, put his face close to mine and hissed, "They want your brother to lay waste to everything I've worked for and make me the Master of Dust. But I'd rather have The Dome. And I *will* have it! Even now, Blue squadrons are on their way to The Tower. Call it a welcoming party if you'd like." I closed my eyes and turned away from him. He must have sensed my fear and revulsion, because he straightened up and moved away, his back to me. "Your brother," he said bitterly. "He thinks he's so clever, but I'll tell you this—he can huff and he can puff, but if he tries to blow my house down, I will cut you into pretty little pieces right in front of him. My father—" His voice caught, an angry sob that seemed to rip through him. "My father will *know* who I am!!"

It occurred to me in that moment that he was mad, the kind of insanity that came from self-loathing and depravity, and it made me even more terrified. Ignoring what he'd just said, I whispered, "What are you going to do?"

He turned and said brightly, "I think it's time for a family reunion. When Cee sees you—ah, the look on his face when he realizes that his power means nothing!"

"You don't know what he's capable of," I shot back, my voice full of anger.

"Actually, I think I do," he said, sounding amused. "And I can't wait to stop him. Imagine how proud my father will be when I save The Dome and crush the rebellion!" He paused. "Do you know how I found out about your plan?" I stared at him blankly and he continued. "It was your friend Trick."

"I don't believe you!" I exclaimed in shock.

Songe shrugged. "Well, I already had a general outline, thanks to my spy. But it was Trick who painted in all the colourful details. It wasn't easy, you know. I had him beaten, ordered his ribs broken, all manner of things, and he wouldn't say a word. I even sent my spy out to the platform, and the boy killed him—threw him right off The Tower! After that, I took over and applied my own 'special' brand of torture and still, he refused to speak, no matter what I did to him. Do you know why he finally told me?"

I shook my head in disbelief. Songe laughed. "I said that if he didn't tell me what the Dominion was up to, he could watch me slowly dismember *your brother* an inch at a time. I would have done it, and he knew it. He confessed everything. It was the only time I've ever seen him cry." He paused and sighed. "Anyway, I would have killed him on the spot, but who am I to deprive the crowd of its bread and circuses?"

"You're sick!" I burst out.

"No," he smirked. "Just practical. As soon as I saw your brother being brought in, I arranged for the death match, knowing that you would come sneaking around. Call it karma, call it kismet—call it whatever you'd like but I always knew in my heart of hearts that we'd see each other again. Of course, I thought it would be a party for two. Now it turns out that I'm not only hosting you, but a veritable army of guests. And one of them is very, very special. Let's go and meet her. *Kai!*" The Lobot cuffs dropped off my wrists and ankles. I was free. I jumped out of the chair, but he held up his hand.

"Don't try anything silly," he ordered. His eye flashed, and a beam of red light shot out, hitting the chair and burning a sizzling hole through the metal. I stared at the chair with dread, realizing that if he could do that to metal, what might he do to skin? I had no choice but to play along, at least for now.

He opened the door and led me down a long open hallway. In the distance, I could hear what sounded like a crowd cheering. "Are we in The Dome?!" I asked, shocked.

"Where did you think we were?" he asked, sounding surprised. He gestured towards an archway in the distance. "Right this way to the best seats in the house!"

We walked through the archway, just as the crowd began to roar. My mind was in a panic—I looked down towards the field but Cee wasn't there. It was a man and a woman, fighting savagely. The man had the woman by the hair and was slamming her face into the ground. I looked away, disgusted and reached out for Cee. Still nothing. Why couldn't I sense him?! He had to be here somewhere!

The sky was dark with an impending storm, and I could hear the thunder rolling as it was getting closer. Songe propelled me through a group of Fancies, who were screaming and cheering at the fight going on down below. He pointed to a skybox. "That's where we're going," he said. The Fancies moved quickly out of our way when they saw Songe's Lieutenant-Governor's uniform. One of the men dipped his shaved and tattooed head deferentially as we went by, and another called out, "Excellent show!"

When we got to the skybox, he pushed me in and slammed the door behind us. There was a woman standing by the window — at the sound of the door, she spun to face us and her jaw dropped. I stared at her in shock. She was the woman in my dreams, brought to life. Songe laughed. "I believe introductions are in order." He gestured at the woman and said to me, "This is my dear Commander, France DuLac."

"What's going on, Lieutenant?!" she demanded, looking at me, her green eyes wide. "Why aren't you at The Tower?"

Songe pushed me towards a chair and said, "Sit." I did, swivelling so that I could see the woman. "Do you know this girl?" he asked her. "I met her several years ago, at the workhouse where she had been abandoned by her mother." He emphasized the word 'mother' and smiled at her dangerously.

The woman's eyes widened. "Elysia?" she whispered.

"So you *do* know her then?" Songe's voice was full of mock-horror. "For shame, Commander. Your lack of loyalty is truly astounding!" The woman, France, gave him a sharp glance and opened her mouth to rebuke him when he interrupted her. "Oh, don't bother. I know all about you and the Dominion plot. I would have been furious if I hadn't already planned to kill you."

She took a step back, trying to put as much distance between her and Songe as possible within the small skybox. Songe laughed harshly and said, "I'm not going to do it *now*, obviously. I might need you as a hostage, so stay where you are or I'll have to put a hole in you." He moved towards the window and said, "Let's see what's happening down below." France stared at me questioningly. Then I could hear her voice in my head as she said, "Don't say anything. If you can hear me, blink."

I shut my eyes quickly and opened them again, too astonished to say anything anyway. Songe hadn't noticed — he was preoccupied by what was being shown on a giant screen over the field. The fight was over, and the loser — the man, surprisingly, was having an eye removed as the crowd went wild. Songe clapped his hands together with glee and said, "Ooh, an eye. I certainly know how *that* feels thanks to your dear brother!" I blanched and looked back at the woman. France DuLac. My mother. Her voice filled my head again. "Can you answer back?"

I focused and thought, "I don't know," but she smiled and nodded once, so she must have heard me.

"Listen carefully," she projected. "Everything is going as planned. You weren't supposed to be here, but we can improvise—"

"Where's Cee?!" I hadn't meant to send the thought so forcefully and she flinched slightly.

"He's here. He's fine. He knows what to do." She glanced quickly at Songe, who was clapping along with the crowd as the Blues led the man away clutching his face and groaning. She grimaced in disgust. "I've never been this close to him before," she thought to me. "His mind — it's truly...evil."

Oblivious, Songe turned to us and smiled. "It's time," he said. He looked like he could barely contain his excitement.

"Time for what?" I demanded, but then I realized that two new opponents had taken the field. The giant screen lit up with their faces. It was Cee and Trick. Side by side, they presented a strong contrast — one tall, light-haired; the other small and dark. The only thing they had in common was that they both looked gaunt and worn-out. Trick's lip was split and bloody, and the side of Cee's face was swollen, the dark purple bruises a sharp contrast to his sunburned skin. I tried to reach out to him, but it was as if I was coming up against a brick wall—nothing! There was a small console in front of the skybox window. Songe leaned into a microphone mounted to it and his voice rang out: "Fighters, take your weapons!"

My heart began to race and I thought to France, "Can't you stop this?! Please!" but she shook her head slightly and thought back, "No. It's part of the plan, the most important part. The Dominion and their allies are outside, waiting to take The Tower and secure the city. And in order to do that, Cee has to create a distraction, bring The Dome down and create the chaos we need."

"But the Blues have been alerted! They have troops already on the way to meet Darv and the rest!" I exclaimed in my mind.

"We know," she answered silently. "Songe isn't the only one with spies. We're prepared for them, don't worry!"

It had started to rain now, hot droplets falling from a sky that was illuminated every few seconds by forks of lightning. Songe leaned over the microphone and his voice boomed out over the hush of the crowd: "Fighters begin!" He stood back smugly and then his face darkened. On the screen, Cee and Trick were standing immobile. Then, as if on cue, they both threw their weapons down in unison and yelled, "Je Refuse!" The crowd began to murmur in dissatisfaction. Lightning flashed again and I could feel my skin tingling from the electricity in the air, a sensation that I'd never noticed before.

I heard France take a sharp breath, as Songe said, more to himself than anything, "Oh no, you don't! None of that ridiculous rebel nonsense!" He leaned over the microphone again and called out, "Fight or you *both* die!" The crowd roared in anticipation.

Again, Cee and Trick yelled out, "Je Refuse!" The crowd began to boo angrily. Again, the lightning forked, and now my whole being was vibrating with energy. I was feeling strange, lightheaded, as if I was separating from my body. The Dome started to vibrate too, as Cee closed his eyes. Suddenly, the invisible wall dropped and I could feel him in my head, his violent fury overwhelming, and the vibrations grew until the ground was shaking. The skybox was heaving as The Dome itself started to split.

"Enough!" Songe yelled, and he turned to grab hold of me. France tried to intervene, but Songe's eye flashed and a burst of red energy hit her, knocking her back into the chair. Her mind called out to me, "The lightning!" then she slumped over, unconscious or dead I couldn't tell. I screamed in horror and ran towards the door of the sky-box, but Songe grabbed me by arm and pulled me back. I caught a glimpse of people fleeing in panic, pieces of The Dome tumbling down on them like the hot rain, then he put me in a headlock. His arm around my neck was so tight that I could barely breathe; red energy shot past me and I saw Trick hit the ground. Songe leaned over the microphone once more and said, "Stop breaking my Dome and I won't hurt your lovely sister. Or don't stop—I'll just kill you and keep her for myself. Either way, I win. Squadrons of Blues are already at The Tower—you've lost before you've even begun." Then he pulled my head back and put his lips to my forehead, letting them linger there. I twisted my head and spat at him, but he just laughed. I heard France moaning behind me—she wasn't dead. Her voice was in my head, crying out, "Elysia! Your brother controls the ground but the sky belongs to you! The lightning is your power!" At the same time, I could hear Cee yelling, giving Songe an ultimatum. I didn't know what France meant—again, she cried, "The lightning. Focus, Elysia!"

Suddenly, the skybox window imploded, and glass was flying everywhere. Songe let go of me and straightened up. He made a kind of choking sound, his eyes wide, and the terrible red beam flashed once more out onto the field.

I saw Cee fly backwards and then lie still. I couldn't hear him in my head anymore, and I shrieked. I burst out of the skybox, leaving Songe behind holding his head, and ran down the concrete steps into the storm, towards Cee lying on the field. The lightning was flashing every few seconds, tearing the air and filling it with an acrid smell — each time it sparked, I felt like I was being lifted off my feet. My skin was on fire with its energy as I finally reached Cee and fell onto my knees next to him. I shook him and he didn't respond — I couldn't tell if he was breathing or not. I started to sob and slammed my fist into the ground as another bolt hit the top of The Dome. As it did, I could feel myself pulsing with the electricity, and I heard France's voice in my head again, distant but compelling, calling, "This is your power. Concentrate on the lightning!"

I had no idea if I could do what she was asking, but I cleared my mind, pushing away Cee, Trick, Darv, the Dominion, Songe, until nothing was left but the storm. I pulled in its strength, feeling the electricity fill me until I couldn't contain it any longer and it burst out of me, hitting the walls of The Dome and blasting holes into the foundation. I gathered it up again, and this time, I deliberately directed the energy towards the giant screen. The force of the lightning shattered it, shards of glass raining down onto the field. Then I smiled grimly, knowing that I had the power to finish what Cee had started.

I looked up at the skybox where Songe was still standing, and I was overwhelmed with hatred. I could feel the energy building up again, and I concentrated until I was shaking with the effort. The electricity was running through me and flowing out of me into the field below as if we were one and the same. I could hear explosions in the distance around The Tower, and the ground in The Dome started to smoke. There was no one left inside, just bodies amid the rubble. I looked up at Songe and screamed, "Master of Dust — how do you like your kingdom now?!!" I threw a bolt of energy towards him, and the deck below the skybox exploded, pulverized pieces of concrete plummeting to the ground.

Songe just stared down at me, a disdainful look on his face. Then he came out of the skybox and descended the stairs. When he got to the field, he halted and gestured broadly. "I'll give you one choice. Stop, and I'll let you live."

"I'll never stop!" I called back, electricity sparking in the air around me, waiting for me to harness it.

"Defiant to the bitter end!" he sneered. He strode towards me forcefully through the pouring rain and then stopped a few metres away. "Why can't you, just for once, do what you're told?" he yelled, his voice filled with loathing. "It was always like that with you—always angry, always arguing, denying the truth of your existence. You fought against everything, as if you were better than all of us. No wonder I despised you! Do you know why I did what I did to you? Just to take you down a notch, to make you understand that you weren't special! That you were NOTHING! I was a GUARDIAN and you wouldn't give me the time of day—you wouldn't even *look* at me!"

"Be careful what you wish for!" I snarled back. "You thought you could destroy me, turn me into nothing, but how could someone like you possibly understand what I truly am? I'm the storm you could never fathom, and now you're the *only* thing I see!"

His face hardened. "Bring your storm! Your brother couldn't defeat me, and neither can you. I've waited so long for this moment, knowing that when it was over, you'd be mine again. And when you're down on your knees, begging me for mercy, no one will save you, not even the Dominion!"

My eyes blazed with the power of the electricity coursing through my body and the birthright running through my veins. "Saved by the Dominion?!" I laughed in the face of his arrogance. "I *am* the Dominion!"

I gathered in the lightning as Songe's eye flashed. I threw my arms out towards him, bright white light arcing from my fingertips to meet red. The two forms of energy collided, the lightning hitting the beam and launching it backwards, the force of the voltage turning it into a hot red and white spear that shot towards him. He put up his hands as if to ward off the inevitable, but it was no use—the spear hit its target. He fell to the ground holding his head and bellowing in pain as flames burst from his eye socket. "You ruined everything!" he screamed. He struggled to his feet and staggered towards me. I gave one last awful push with my mind, and enveloped him in a cloud of white dancing heat. He fell back down to the ground, writhing in agony as his body began to hiss and burn. "Sweets to the sweet," I whispered. He looked up at me one last time in horror, then the fire consumed him, leaving nothing behind but ash.

The storm still raged around me, but I couldn't control it anymore. The air was metallic-tasting, charged and dense with sparking light that mingled with the surging, hot rain. Through the tempest, I could see a figure running onto the field towards me. It was Rogan. I called his name but my voice was carried away by the wind. I was spent, exhausted by the storm, and I fell to the ground next to Cee. I tried to reach out to him, desperate to know if he was still alive, but the world started to blur. Just before I lost consciousness, I felt the sensation of someone squeezing my hand. I sent back the sensation of home, and then there was nothing else.

32

Cee

I woke up, disoriented, my skull feeling like it was about to split open. I moved my head and winced with the effort. There was a gasp and what sounded like a sob. I tried to focus on the source and turned slightly again. Lights exploded in front of my eyes, and I groaned in pain. Then I felt something in my head—an intense feeling of worry. I sent back reassurance, and a pair of arms wrapped themselves around me, the worry changing to a crescendo of joy.

"You're back!" Dee's voice was choked with tears. "It's been days!"

"Take it easy!" I said, feeling the joy too, trying to laugh, but my voice came out weak and hoarse. Dee loosened her grip and sat on the edge of the bed I was lying on. Her face came into view. She looked tired, but her green eyes were dancing with excitement as she held a cup to my mouth. I sipped from it gladly, the cool water soothing my dry throat. The room was drenched with sunlight that poured in through the large windows, and the sky outside was clear, a pristine blue. "Where are we?" I asked her, once I'd finished drinking.

"In The Tower. I'm so happy you're—"

"The Tower!" I interrupted, struggling to sit up. "Why are we in The Tower?! Are we prisoners?" The joy turned to dread—after everything we'd gone through, nothing had changed. She sent a wave of calm, and I lay back again, closing my eyes against the pounding in my head.

"It's all right," she said. "The Tower's ours now. And I'm so, so happy that you're awake. Ahnah—that's the name of the Inuksuk doctor who's been taking care of you—didn't know how long you'd be unconscious. Your brain took quite a beating."

"The rest of me too, from what it feels like. Even my fingertips are aching."

Dee took my hand and said, in mock-sympathy, "Would you like some TastiRum and Lullybies?"

"Ugh, no! Wait, did you say 'Inuksuk' doctor?"

Dee laughed, a relaxed, lighthearted sound that filled the room. "Oh," she said. "I have so much to tell you!"

We were just about to start filling in the gaps in each other's stories when the doctor, Ahnah, came into the room. Her eyebrows shot up when she saw that I was awake, then she quietly checked a tablet that took readings from a bracelet around my wrist. She nodded to herself and gave us both a small smile, then left again.

"The Inuksuk have amazing technology, but they don't talk much," Dee told me. "You'd most likely be dead without Ahnah. When Rogan and S-Sam found us, you were barely breathing."

"Rogan and S-Sam are all right? I'm glad," I said.

"You're not still angry with Rogan, are you?" Dee asked tentatively.

I shook my head, and then grimaced as the pain redoubled. "Maybe a little TastiRum wouldn't be so bad," I laughed weakly. "No, I'm not angry with Rogan. The second I found out that he'd gotten you the medicine you needed, I could have forgiven him anything. And Trick?

I'd almost forgotten about him. Where is he? The last time I saw him, he'd been hit by some kind of energy blast—is he okay?"

Dee's face fell. "He—he didn't make it."

My eyes widened in shock. "What?!" I asked in disbelief.

"I'm so sorry," Dee said, taking my hand. "The Inuksuk doctors did everything they could to save him, but apparently he was already suffering from some pretty serious internal injuries when the blast hit him, thanks to Songe. Ahnah said it was incredible that he could still stand upright let alone walk across the floor of The Dome."

I turned away from her and closed my eyes. I remembered him going down on the field, and a wave of guilt washed over me. I should have done something more to protect him—after everything he'd already been through, it seemed outrageously unfair that his life should be cut so short. If it wasn't for Trick, I would never have made it to The Dome, never found the strength to bring it down. He didn't deserve to die. I had a sudden vision of him, a young boy with bruises on his face and a swollen lip cheerfully holding out a piece of chocolate cake to me and I couldn't help but cry.

"I'm sorry," Dee said again after a few moments, her eyes brimming too. "He was so brave, standing there. You both were."

I wiped the tears roughly from my cheeks. "How's S-Sam taking it?"

"Not good," she said. "He can barely speak. When we were with the Skeleton Army, he told me about everything that Trick had done for him and his mother after his father died in The Dome. He's just devastated—he really loved Trick."

We stayed in silence for a moment longer, but then my curiosity was piqued. "Skeleton Army? That sounds ominous," I said. "Who are they?"

"It's a long story," she said. "Maybe we should both start at the beginning."

We began at the point where I had left her to go to Liberty with Rogan, and we talked until the sun was low in the sky. I told her about The Tower, and Songe, and Trick pushing Little Jimmy off the platform, meeting France and finding out about my power. She told me all about Darv, Malachi Thorn, the Frags, and about her own power.

"Lightning, huh?" I raised my eyebrows. "Why am I not surprised? But I've been making the ground quake all my life, even if it was unknowingly. Why not you? Why haven't you been able to do this before?"

"France says that yours is an implant, but my power — well, it just *is*. It's all part of..." she gestured with her finger between my head and hers. "She says she always knew I had some kind of ability, but neither she nor Darv knew how it would eventually manifest until the storm. Darv was as surprised as she was! You'll meet him soon," Dee added. "He's been very...anxious about you. I think you'll like him."

The way she spoke of him made me wonder. "Do *you* like him?" I asked.

"He's...all right," she said, then laughed. "I think he and I are a little too much alike. He doesn't like to listen to anyone either. And when his mind's made up—"

"You can't change it," I finished. "Definitely reminds me of someone I know. But how did they take The Tower? Songe knew about the plan—he'd sent out squadrons of Blues to intercept the Dominion, he said."

Dee laughed bitterly. "Songe." She said it as if the name itself left a bad taste in her mouth. "The smug bastard didn't realize that the Blues hated him too. Most of them had long since shifted their loyalties. As soon as the first charges blew and it became obvious that they were going to lose the battle, the ones who hadn't joined Darv just fled."

At the mention of Songe, I felt a darkness in her mind that could only be explained one way. "You killed him," I stated, not needing to ask the question.

She nodded and said simply, "He's gone."

"How do you feel?"

She sent me a sensation of satisfaction mingled with anger. Suddenly, the sensation crystallized into an image of Songe at the end, head on fire, screaming and then disintegrating into ash. I looked at her in surprise. "Visual images? When did you learn to do that?!"

"I've been practicing with France—our mother," she answered, smiling. She sent another image, this time of a tiny, white dog, its tail wagging fiercely.

"You kept it?!" I was thrilled. "Where is it?"

"It's your 'get well' present. He's not here but don't worry— he's in good hands right now. You'll be seeing him soon enough." She sent another mind picture, this one of Sarah holding the dog. It filled me with a sense of longing and I sighed.

"I can't wait to get back to Divinity," I said wistfully. "I've really missed it." I'd forgotten how much the idea of home and the simple life meant to me, and I was dying to get back to the tent, do some carving, go to the Tap, and most of all, see Sarah.

Dee took my hand and said solemnly, "You need to prepare yourself though. Divinity isn't the same as we left it. When the Blues still loyal to The Consortium turned tail and ran, they wreaked as much havoc as they could. Divinity suffered a lot of damage. We can rebuild—in fact, it's already started. But there's one thing you need to know." She hesitated. "Auntie May...she's dead."

"Auntie May?!" I exclaimed. "How? Why would anyone kill *her*?"

Dee shook her head sadly. "You know what she was like, never taking kindly to threats from anyone, not even the Blues. They tried to tear down her stall and she wasn't having it. She went at them with her billy club and they shot her."

"That's awful," I said. "I can't believe even the Blues would kill an old woman in cold blood like that."

"Well, they didn't get far," Dee replied angrily. "A group of Freeworlders saw the Blues running away from the Hidden Market and overpowered them. They didn't last long."

I sighed and nodded. My head was actually feeling better, although I was exhausted, completely bone-weary. Dee could sense it right away and said, "I should let you get some sleep. We're going to be here for a few days yet. The last thing I'll tell you tonight is good news. When The Dome started to quake, all the Fancies came running out, and Malachi's Skeleton Army was able to capture a lot of them, including the relatives of some highly-placed Consortium members. The Frags have successfully negotiated an exchange, and the first group of their children has already landed in Fujian."

"Seriously?" I asked in shock. "Why would The Consortium cave in so easily?"

"They didn't have much choice. The unrest back in the Consortium countries had already reached its boiling point. When the Dominion captured The Tower, they sent a message out across Adanac and discovered that the situation was the same everywhere—very few Blues, most of the Fancies easily captured. Rebel groups and Freeworlders across the country rallied and took the Towers, all eight of them, leaving The Consortium with virtually no power in Adanac. They're too busy fighting their own battles to bother with us anymore. The last transports pulled out yesterday—we let them go with a stern warning to never come back."

"But how do we know they won't?" I asked skeptically. "It's not like we can actually trust The Consortium!"

Dee laughed. "We don't have to trust *them*," she reassured me. "Whatever you were doing to bring down The Dome was felt around the world. We started getting messages from The Old Kingdom and Marseilles demanding to know what was happening. When Darv responded, they offered their support. The Consortium's propaganda machine had been hiding the truth from us for years, that most of the other countries across the water had formed their own alliance against The Consortium. Now we're under the protection of The Coalition. I don't think even The Consortium would risk all-out war with *them*—they're not stupid."

"No, I suppose not," I replied, and then yawned widely.

"Sleep now," Dee ordered, stroking my forehead affectionately. She leaned over and kissed me on the cheek, then got up and went to the door, giving me one last happy glance before she left.

For the first time in ages, I closed my eyes without fear and slept peacefully, dreaming of a little white dog and a girl with brown hair.

33

Dee

Heart singing, feet flying.

It was Band Night and the Tap was packed, people spilling out of the doors and dancing in the streets.

It had been a few weeks now since The Dome had fallen and The Tower was taken. Once Cee had recovered to the point where we could travel, we quickly made our way back to Divinity. As we emerged out of Old K and could see the edge of the tent city, my heart leapt. I could sense Cee's excitement too as his pace quickened. I knew how anxious he was to get back—he kept insisting it was little Titus that he couldn't wait to see, but he couldn't hide the truth from me. His head was full of Sarah whether he was willing to admit it to me or not.

He'd met Darv the day after he woke up, and it was like the two of them had known each other all Cee's life. Darv had gotten some carving tools from somewhere, and while Cee was getting better, the two of them would sit on the platform of The Tower, Cee carving and Darv telling stories about growing up in Terrebonne, about his mother—our grandmother—and how she was an artist too with her loom. I'd join them sometimes, just watching and listening, amazed at how well they seemed to understand each other, and how easily Cee had forgiven both Darv and France for leaving us the way they did. I understood now that it was truly for our own protection, but I still resented the loss in my own way. France sensed it and made a real effort to forge a bond between her and me. We had daily 'lessons' where she helped me strengthen my abilities — we must have been a curious sight, the two of us walking along, an almost identical pair, neither of us ever speaking, but every once in a while bursting out in laughter or looking at each other in surprise.

S-Sam had finally started to come back out of his shell a little. He'd stayed locked in his room for the first couple of weeks, emerging only to get something to eat, speaking to nobody, his eyes red and swollen. Finally, I got him to open the door and let me in. We talked for a while — at least, I talked and he listened. We agreed to have a remembrance ceremony for Trick, and helping me organize it seemed to give him some relief. One night, we all gathered in what was left of The Dome where Trick's body had been laid to rest along with all the others who had died that day, Fancies, Blues, or Dominion, and we celebrated the life of our friend. Someone had found an abandoned Farm store and had made chocolate cake. We all took turns talking about Trick and what he meant to us. When it was S-Sam's time to speak, no one knew what to expect, but he stood tall and proud, giving an almost stutter-free tribute to Trick and his friendship and loyalty that made everyone in the crowd weep, especially Durand. I never told anyone what Songe had said about Trick, that he had betrayed the Dominion in the end. I knew he'd only done it to save Cee, and it hadn't mattered anyway.

I'd been spending a lot of time with Rogan these past few weeks too. Being with him gave me a sense of calm that truly helped me heal from the wounds of the past. He was scared to death when I ran off, but by the time he realized I was gone and tried to follow me, I'd already been taken by the Blues. He had become almost indispensable to Darv lately—Seguin, Darv's second-in-command, had been severely injured during the attack, and he was still recovering. Darv recognized Rogan's resourcefulness and had started relying on him heavily as a sounding board for his ideas to rebuild Adanac, even taking Rogan's advice on occasion, which shocked me, knowing how strong-headed Darv could be. Rogan had gone ahead to Divinity last week with a plan to utilize the glassed-in gardens in Liberty for edible crops, while I had stayed behind with Cee. I had to admit to myself how much I'd been missing Rogan, which explained the quickening of my heart as we got closer to home.

It had been over a week now that we'd been back, and there had been a rising sense of anticipation in the air, people taking time out of the work of the day to discuss a celebration until finally word had rung out across Divinity: "Band Night at the Tap!"

I made my way through the crowd, looking for Malachi. He and a lot of the Frags had joined in the rebuilding while they were waiting for the arrival of their children. The first group had driven up in a solar transport the day before yesterday, and the reunion was a joy to behold. Malachi was stalking around, tears streaming down his rugged face, grabbing people and lifting them off their feet. Other people were sobbing in disbelief and hugging the newcomers, who ranged in age from about six years old to young adults, all looking thin and exhausted, but ecstatic at the same time. Most of them were here in the Tap now, enjoying the music but standing close to their parents as if terrified that someone might take them away again.

I found Malachi by the fountains next to a beautiful girl about twenty years old with a corona of dark, curly hair loose around her face. I walked over and he introduced me, his gravelly voice filled with pride and wonder. "Elysia! This

is my granddaughter, Aurora!" She smiled shyly but she had a haunted look about her. I wondered how long it would take for the Frag children to feel safe, to feel part of a family again, especially the ones who'd been gone so long. We all spoke for a minute then I moved on, weaving in between the dancing couples, looking for Cee.

I was slowly getting used to people calling us "Elysia" and "Niko", but I still couldn't do it myself. In my head, we would always be Cee and Dee, the twins, one calm and steadfast, the other stubborn and charged with energy. Just then, Darv and France flew by, doing some kind of fast-paced waltz with the rest of the dancers. Darv, usually so serious, was laughing at something France had said, his good eye fixed on her with adoration. He saw me and called out, "Join in, chère!" as they spun away exuberantly. My parents — it still seemed unreal. I smiled and continued on, until I found Cee. He was tucked into a dimly lit corner with Sarah, the two of them using the noise of the music as an excuse to lean in close and speak into each other's ears. Little Titus was lying at Cee's feet, content despite the crowds and the din. Cee put his arm on Sarah's shoulder and whispered something to her that made her laugh and lightly touch the polished wooden bead that she was wearing around her neck. She casually brushed back a lock of Cee's hair and I could almost see him blush from where I was standing. After everything that he'd been through, it made my heart soar to see him so happy. Then I felt someone punch me lightly on the arm.

"I still think we should have sold him to the butcher," Rogan teased. "We would have gotten some good coin for that little ball of fluff."

I laughed and punched him back. "Cee would never have forgiven you. You know, he lets that dog sleep on his bed with him?"

Rogan snickered, then his face grew serious. "How are you? Is this too much for you? Let's go somewhere a little more quiet for a minute." He took my arm gently and steered me over to an alcove by the doorway.

"Oh, stop mothering me!" I protested, half-humorously, half-seriously. "I'm perfectly fine. And this is good for me, seeing everyone enjoying themselves."

"Some more than most," he said, pointing at a group of Rock faction members, who'd obviously been into the TastiRum and who were singing loudly to the music as they strode around outside the Tap. Ceridwen was part of the group, hood down, her face delightfully bewildered and beaming as they swept her along with them. Darv said that when she had first seen them, she walked up to them without hesitation and asked, "Of charity, what kin are you to me? What countryman? What name? What parentage?" and their leader, a bold man named Brennan replied, "Most wonderful! The Rock lives in you as it does in us!" They had taken her in as one of their own immediately, without hesitation, seeming to understand everything she said, no matter how cryptic.

Rogan turned to me then, with a strange look on his face. "You know," he said. "After I found you, when you were still unconscious, Ceridwen came to me and said, 'It is not in the stars to hold our destiny but in ourselves.' I think I know what she meant."

"And what's that?" I asked. He came closer and I felt myself start to tremble.

"That I should take things into my own hands and not wait. I've wanted to say this for a while, but everything has been so…complicated." He cleared his throat nervously. "I—you…Look. You are the most wonderful, infuriating, brave person I've ever known. I couldn't imagine a day without seeing your face. When I lost you in Un-Station, I thought I'd go mad, and when I found you in The Dome, I knew I could never be without you. You are everything to me. Everything." He paused. "So there it is—"

Before he had a chance to say anything else, I threw my arms around him and held him tight. "For someone so hard to understand," I whispered to him, "Ceridwen gives really good advice." I grabbed his hand and pulled him out of the alcove and onto the dance floor. I could feel Cee in my head, curious, and I sent back a sensation of elation as Rogan spun me around to the music. Cee sent back the same feeling, along with another, more familiar one. There was still a lot of work ahead, and who could say what the future would bring, but we both knew one thing. We were home.

Also by Suzanne Craig-Whytock

ISBN: 9781772310658

Cassandra Wilson's life isn't easy. She's spent most of her teenage years taking care of her much younger brother, working to support her widowed mother, coping with high school and its pressures, and still grieving over the death of her beloved father. The smile on her face has become an easy way of disguising her true feelings and the fact that she really isn't sure who she is anymore. Her life suddenly begins to change when she learns that her mother has been secretly dating a co-worker for months and plans to introduce him to the family. Feeling betrayed, and fearing that her mother's new boyfriend will try to take the place of her father, Cassandra decides it's time to start living a little herself. That impulsive decision marks the beginning of a series of suspenseful twists, turns, and revelations involving a strange cast of characters who may just help her find what she's looking for — a real reason to smile.